P9-API-319

SHARP-SHOOTER

The 50-millimeter gun with telescopic sights was a deadly little weapon, accurate as a star gauge rifle used by snipers, and fitted with IR ranging and aiming gear. Garvin flipped a high explosive shell into the chamber. In the telescopic sight he got the cross hairs fixed on the prop, which was churning white foam. She was riding high in the water

Range finder adjustment and the fifteen hundred meters per second velocity of the projectile made for pinpoint accuracy. He set off a correction for target velocity and found that uniform tracking kept the cross hair on the phosphorescence stirred up by the propeller.

He fired.

The engine raced crazily as the launch lost way. "She's adrift!"

Also by E. Hoffmann Price
Published by Ballantine Books:

THE DEVIL WIVES OF LI FONG

THE JADE ENCHANTRESS

OPERATION LONGLIFE

OPERATION MISFIT

OPERATION EXILE

E. Hoffmann Price

A Del Rey Book

BALLANTINE BOOKS • NEW YORK

A Del Rey Book
Published by Ballantine Books

Copyright © 1986 by E. Hoffmann Price

All rights reserved under International and Pan-American
Copyright Conventions. Published in the United States of
America by Ballantine Books, a division of Random House,
Inc., New York, and simultaneously in Canada by Random
House of Canada, Limited, Toronto, Canada.

Library of Congress Catalog Card Number: 82-90835

ISBN 0-345-32599-0

Manufactured in the United States of America

First Edition: January 1986

Cover Art by David B. Mattingly

TO ELLEN AND OTIS ADELBERT KLINE:
their hospitality and his advice
helped an amateur become a professional.
1926–1933

Chapter 1

SHORTLY AFTER THAT chronic troublemaker Roderick David Garvin resigned himself to exile as a war criminal and began to enjoy his job as General Superintendent of Martian Ecology & Agriculture, Alexander Heflin, styled Alexander I, Imperator of the Democratic North American Imperium, bitched things up by phoning to call him back to Terra as a special consultant.

Sun squint and space squint contributed to Garvin's paradoxical expression. His public could never decide from the look of him whether the keynote was lurking ferocity or bawdy laughter. Garvin had been tanned by sun bouncing from sand dunes and snow-capped peaks in Chinese Turkistan during the critical fighting around Kashgar and the Dzungarian Gap. In the course of that war he had become a hero and, soon thereafter, an exiled war criminal with three wives: marriages lawfully contracted in a Moslem jurisdiction.

"Alex, what the hell do you want to consult me about?"

"I'll tell you when you see me," the Imperator answered.

Garvin's wry grimace seconded the derisive expression in his hazel-flecked, grayish eyes. "Meaning no one knows what he is doing, and everyone is busy doing it."

"You sound like a graduate victim of bureaucracy!" Alexander sighed. On the video screen he looked much older than he should have, considering how little time had elapsed since the onetime enemies, now close friends, had parted. "I did my damnedest to get you a parliamentary pardon," the Imperator continued, "but the best I could manage was parole."

"Wait a goddamn minute! When we said our good-byes in that palace in Tun-huang, you were the Imperator who rated a nine-yak-tail standard, like Genghis Khan, and Lani the Imperatrix rated a nine-deck golden parasol. Now you tell me you had to kiss bureaucratic arses to get me a parole?"

The aquiline, aristocratic features blossomed into a magnificent and persuasive glow that would have convinced anyone but Rod Garvin, who had known him when. "This assignment is fascinating. It's a challenge." The dark eyes were intense, and for a moment the Imperator's mouth became as thin as a sword's edge and twice as hard. "Rod, this is not fun and games. This is not whores and liquor. If I commanded you to set out at once, I could not enforce it. Since you and I are cousins-in-law, I ask you not to let me down."

That Flora, Garvin's Number One Wife, was Alexander Heflin's fifth cousin was not what decided the issue. That the chairman of the Consortium, which for twenty years had kept the former republic from self-destruction, was in desperate need of one he could trust was what made Garvin agree. "Alex, I'll have them hold the *Martian Queen* long enough for me to brief my office staff. I'll not go home to pack up. The purser can fix me up with gear and cash."

Once the passenger hatch was secured behind Garvin, the *Martian Queen*'s jets fired up. She had been waiting forty-seven minutes for him to brief his office lady, put her in charge of Eck & Ag, and record a message to Flora:

"Darling, just got a call from the head of the Holy Family. He wants me at headquarters immediately. The

situation must be supertough or he'd have told me to bring you and Camille and Azadeh and Aljai. Tell them I am awfully sorry about not being with them for our wedding anniversary party."

Twenty-odd years before, when homeward bound after circling Saturn, Garvin had landed on an asteroid for routine repair of minor damage caused by the whirling junk-yard of the solar system. Mutiny and the destruction of his cruiser, the *Saturnienne*, had left him marooned from A.D. 2080, Terrestrian chronology, to about A.D. 2086.

The *Saturnienne* written off as lost in space, Garvin's wife, Flora, had every reason to consider herself the widow of a space hero. As a teenage brat, Flora had a burning passion for her considerably older and already distinguished fifth cousin, Alexander Heflin. Since the onetime brat was now old enough as well as big enough, and also supposedly a widow, Flora and Alex finally settled down to find out what they had missed years previously. Learning how much each had missed, the two had decided to marry.

Because of intensive premarital honeymooning and confusion in getting the X's on the wrong page of her calendar, they did not know that Flora was pregnant. And neither expected Rod Garvin to return from an uncharted asteroid, piloting a space cruiser built a quarter of a million years ago by a prehistoric spacefaring race far ahead of Terrestrian A.D. 2086 models. The planetoid, thus far unknown, had been inhabited.

All that Flora and Alex had expected was war, and this they got in full measure. Garvin returned, joined the fight, and became a hero until the Marxist-loving liberal majority that ruled the Parliamentary Republic declared him a war criminal for brutality in destroying an armored force invading Chinese Turkistan; the Slivovitz Empire's troops had been harmed!

Alexander declared martial law after a striking victory,

and in a neat coup he became Imperator. His bride-to-be, Flora Garvin, could not and would not marry her lover. To dump a war hero to become Alexander's Imperatrix would have made her an unspeakable bitch, and the Imperator her male equivalent.

Instead of getting a divorce because of Garvin's two concubines collected during his six adventurous years, the reunited spouses resumed their marriage. Garvin knew that Flora was pregnant. Alexander did not; happily, she had not told him. However, at Camille's birth, Garvin and Flora had sent the Imperator a scrambled-frequency message, giving him the facts of the infant's ancestry.

Camille, accordingly, was Alexander's daughter. And Toghrul Bek was the son of Azadeh and Rod Garvin. Flora and Garvin did not debate as to which had had the busiest six years while apart from the other. And for good measure, Flora was included in the contract under which Garvin had married Azadeh and Aljai. The Moslem imam, a scrupulous gentleman, had balked at marrying Garvin to a pair of concubines until and unless the Number One Wife signed the contract and accepted the girls as co-wives.

Clearly, Azadeh and Aljai had married Garvin at the signing of the contract, but whether he now was walking out on the anniversary of two brides or three was a question he left for Islamic doctors of law.

A few minutes after Alexander's call, another came from Megapolis Alpha, the capital of North America. The woman who spoke from the visiphone wore an apple-green jade crepe de chine blouse that by contrast exaggerated the tawny copper of her hair. Lani's eyes, large, dark, and almond-shaped like those in Egyptian temple paintings, suggested that she was Isis wearing a human body. The ultimate incredibilities were chin line and skin texture, as fine as they had been the first time Garvin had undressed Lani in her apartment overlooking the Mall late one afternoon of September, A.D. 2080. Then she had been operating a gourmet restaurant by day and enjoying her nights as a licensed Rest & Recreation Girl.

Now, October 9, 2102, Lani, Imperatrix of North America, had a problem to throw at Garvin, the unwitting cause of each advance from happy hooker to worried empress.

Lani spoke the language of the Asteroidal folk among whom they had been marooned for six years, a language from which modern Uighur had been derived. This warned Garvin that she had reached another crisis. He cut her short.

"I'm switching you to audio-video recorder. Once I'm aboard the *Martian Queen*, I'll play it back and call you."

He flipped the switch to "record," killing sound and visual projection. Even though the girl who was to run the shop until Garvin's return was loyal and could not understand the alien language, she might recognize the unveiled empress and identify her as the woman who had vanished the night Inspector Morgan had faded forever from Maritania. Lani's disappearance that same night had led to the broadcasting of her image.

Now the *Martian Queen* was well above the interlocking domes, the bubbles that confined the artificial atmosphere of Maritania. Garvin had not yet shaken free from the impact of Lani's calling to reveal things top secret. Although the altitude was too great for him to distinguish details, the green of agricultural domes and the glint of lakes that covered several thousand hectares of what once had been red and barren desert baited his mind from old memories.

There were fish in the lakes. Crane and heron, ducks and geese, were engrossed in the serious business of being aquatic birds with, thus far, no hunters to harass them. Poultry and sheep, pheasants, grouse, and polo ponies populated Animal Husbandry, a department in which was cultivated a small experimental vineyard.

Much of this was the result of Garvin's effort to turn Mars from a sterile triumph of science into a livable planet. But the polo ponies were reminders of his provisional promise when taking leave of Alub Arslan, the paramount prince of that cozy asteroid: "You folks have kept war a gentleman's game! And if I live long enough, I'll send you horses for cavalry and polo."

As Mars receded, Garvin's thoughts closed in on the immediate present. Terra had always been an insane planet, with North America the vortex of madness, infested by idealists whose slogans kept a hysterical and childish population of TV addicts bent not only on reforming their own country but also meddling in the doings of every other land where human rights were not duly respected. As Garvin saw things, North America's passion for "rights" infringed on, and deprived, as many as or more than it benefited. However, seeking to export those doctrines was what had flung dung into the fan of international well-being.

But what made Garvin frown was the prospect of his stepdaughter's plunge into the Terrestian educational madhouse, which Flora considered essential for Camille's cultural development.

Despite her congenital hatred of space and spacing, Flora had been the most congenial Number One Wife Garvin could imagine. She never blamed him for dragging her from wonderful Earth to horrible Mars, never knifed him for returning from the Asteroid just in time to keep her from becoming Imperatrix of North America, never suggested that he was a shade too fond of Azadeh.

And Flora never forgot to let him know how everlastingly grateful she remained because of his accepting Camille as *their* daughter. There was nothing—absolutely nothing—wrong with Flora except her counting the days until she could send Camille to a fashionable school for young ladies of good North American families.

Despite crew and fellow passengers, spacefaring was inherently solitary. It made for cogitating on the past and on what the future threatened or promised. Accordingly, since his next glimpse of verdure was presently fifty-six million kilometers ahead of him, Garvin set out for his stateroom, where the audio-video recorder waited. Getting Lani's message, spoken in prehistoric Proto-Uighur, was far more urgent than pondering Flora's idiosyncrasies.

For hell's sweet sake, he summed up, *she and Alex produced Camille. It is none of my business. Azadeh and I, we had a six-year head start on them, and Flora never dips her beak into how we ought to make a North American gentleman of Toghrul Bek.*

Garvin grinned sourly. Azadeh would sooner be the mother of a porcupine than of a fifty-percent American gentleman. When he was exiled, Azadeh's affection had reverted to premarital burning passion. That North America had rejected him demonstrated that her first judgment of him had been perfect.

Passing the casino, Garvin barely glanced in. During his almost thirty-five years he had gambled much, but never with money. Where life or career was the stakes, only the ignorant or the born loser dealt with Garvin. When circumstance permitted, he paid the funeral expenses. Except in war, killing should never prevent man-to-man courtesy.

The crowded bar, however, beckoned. Seeing that there was less congestion in the cocktail lounge, he considered making a brief stop. But he had his own store of alcohol—and Lani's message waited.

Chapter 2

IN HIS STATEROOM, Garvin poured a dollop of single-malt Scotch and plugged in the audio-video recorder and playback. When he was alone with Lani's voice and image, her words set his memories and his consciousness working on two levels at once. Neither interfered with the other; there was no confusion.

"Alex could not risk giving you details in English," Lani was saying. "He might have gambled on code, cipher, or scrambled frequency, though there is no real security left. So he relied on voice, face to face, eye to eye, over a gap of sixty more or less million kilometers to get you to a consultation in a spot that was not bugged. With the Imperial Department of Education specializing in Socialistic Studies, nobody would understand archaic Proto-Uighur.

"Whether there is going to be a Marxist takeover by invitation of the Liberal Parliament or a forthright invasion to 'liberate' North America from imperialism, there is going to be civil war, and a nasty one..."

Six years on the Asteroid, with Aljai, the long-haired dictionary who spoke nothing but the most archaic Proto-Uighur, made it easy for Garvin to understand Lani, ex-wife of Alub Arslan who, like his other three wives, spoke

8

only Proto-Uighur. And his two-tracking consciousness was remembering, at the same time:

...Flora bitched up my space job...then balked at our getting out of that goddamn megapolitan life and moving to Katmandu...Lani and I figured on eloping to a high and thinly populated country with no thought control...computer foul-up shanghaied us to Martian Development Observation Stations, twenty kay-ems apart, but we made out...luck got me command of the Saturnienne *...circumnavigate Saturn...by a space hero, or a hero lost in space, during shakedown and final inspection at Mars, figured on liberating Lani...*

The Imperial Voice was saying, "Most of the Army is loyal...Simianoids and rural people hate Marxists and intellectual phonies of all kinds...the generals are all for Alex..."

Parallel consciousness followed Garvin's memories: *...got there in time to see Lani whack Inspector Morgan with her geologist's hammer...sexual harassment by Morgan, gone forever...dumped car and body into a crevasse...stowed Lani aboard the* Saturnienne...

Lani, the Imperatrix: "The here and now problem where you come in is that major scientists are going crazy. This is not a science fiction cliché of two centuries ago! It's a synthetic narcotic. Hallucinogen. They are as convincing as if they had good sense. They've done tremendous damage. Morale is devastated, don't you see, nobody knows what big name is going to qualify for a padded cell..."

...Lani, the Happy Hooker, and my technical adviser, Space Admiral Josiah Ambrose Courtney, Retired, decided that the beautiful stowaway should marry him and get his pension when his heart condition finished him...which it did, on the Asteroid, when I blew the Saturnienne *to stop a mutiny...any mutineers who think they can win when Garvin is in command are fruit and nuts...So the*

Admiral's widow married Alub Arslan and became a princess.

Garvin cut the player, phoned the Four Seasons Palace, and got Lani in the apartment from which she had called.

"Got you first buzz," he said. "You must have been sitting on the phone."

"I was. I called Maritania to tell you not to come."

"Not to?"

He could not tell himself that women were crazy. He had been crazy about quite too many of them. Lani, however, seemed a near miss.

"Rod, there's no use." She was about to spill tears all over the boudoir. "When you land, head for Mona's Nameless Island. Or for the Gulf Coast. And right before you take off for Mars, phone and tell him you can't make it."

This was the first time he had ever seen Lani irrational. A good record over the years. "All *right*," she continued, as if reading his thought. "I *am* irrational."

Hearing her speak his thought made Lani seem level-headed as ever. "Far as I can figure, you did not invent mad scientists. If Alex had been able to speak Proto-Uighur, he'd have briefed me so that I could figure answers on the way."

"Rod, seriously, I am not rational. I was not when I phoned you. Yes, the Army is all for Alex, but in a civil war, with one side backed by a dangerous foreign power, the Imperium is bound to fall apart. Because it is not yet established, not well enough to stand the stress. Alex has not had time to weed out—all right, kill off!—the home-grown troublemakers. The entire bureaucracy is an inside enemy, all the way to the highest levels! They have blocked his every move to make the Imperium solid. If they do not succeed soon, it will be too late—too late for them!"

"Me savvy plenty," he admitted, forgetting his Uighur. "And so, if they don't get their war going soon, they'll be buggered through their oilskins?"

"As usual, Rod, terse and elegant. That's the way they worked to upset the Parliamentary Republic, but Alex beat them."

"So far, you are totally rational. And, I'll admit, he needs a lot more than a consultant. Even one like me. I mean, the kind who blunders in with more luck than good sense and makes it."

"But this time you can't. Wait till I tell you. Alex is working on a secret weapon. So he tells me. That's what's got me worried crazy. The soundproofed room in the palace is not quite as well insulated as he thinks.

"What he is actually doing is practicing playing bagpipes."

"Sweet Jesus on a life raft!" Then Garvin regained control. "Think nothing of it, darling! Wait till I tell you what I've been thinking ever since the *Queen* blasted off. Especially while I was playing back the record of your phone call."

Lani cut in. "I'd been thinking, which is why I called you. You and I met for fun and games. The only thing you ever *tried* to do for me was get me out of that awful Martian observation station."

"After I'd bungled you into it, I had to, didn't I?"

"You picked exactly the minute that made you stow me away in the *Saturnienne* instead of putting me on an Earthbound cruiser to send me home to running my gourmet restaurant and having fun being a happy hooker.

"If you hadn't loaded Morgan's body into his car and nudged it over the edge into a ravine two thousand meters deep, I'd have ended in jail instead of being promoted to admiral's wife, admiral's widow, then princess by marriage. And when three jealous wives were planning murder, you got us back to Earth in time to win a battle, become a space hero, and keep Flora from marrying Alex and becoming Imperatrix.

"Here we go again, you paroled from exile and me teetering on the brink of being ex-Empress of North America. Our fates are linked together, but this time I can't go any higher."

This left Garvin groping. Adding it up, she had urged him to get out while he could instead of rising from war criminal up to the level of those who count.

"Remember," Lani resumed, "once you were telling me about the *I Ching* and the Taoist maxim: 'When Sun is at zenith, midnight begins.' Imperatrix is my peak; I've touched the meridian."

"Not downgrading North America," he countered, "but there have been bigger empires, and they lasted longer. Because they never forbade their armies to win, and that way offend world opinion, and make the enemy say nasty things about them. Which is a history we'll have a hard time living down.

"And this egalitarian crap, the 'democracy' of Thomas Jefferson, was fatal idiocy. Back in the early 1700s, an English scholar and historian said that a democracy can't last long once the electorate finds out how easy it is to vote into office the candidate who will dish out the juiciest social programs and richest benefits dug out of the sucker taxpayer's jeans.

"The Britisher I'm citing was Alexander Tyler. And in 1830, a Frenchman, Alexis de Tocqueville, after spending six months in the new republic, said about the same thing and a lot of other things that have come dangerously true.

"Alex wanted a consultant. Whatever he's got in mind, you have a preview of what he's going to hear. Get back to what the founders of the republic figured and short-circuit the notion that democracy is a magic word, when it has almost always caused a disaster. Like beginning with Athens.

"Goddammit, madame, I'll talk Alex into building the biggest empire that ever existed, bigger than Genghis Khan's and a couple of others thrown in for a bonus."

"Never mind that girl at Nameless Island." Lani laughed softly and looked renewed. "So far, whenever you've sounded off like one of those Marines, you've made good."

"If I reverse the charges, it might cause gossip. See you at the Four Seasons Palace."

Garvin cut the connection. Now that he faced a stateroom with only one occupant in addition to sobering silence, he realized that whatever scientific logic dictated, his own hunch-setup, his lifelong insight, had declared that Lani's rhetoric was sound. He and she clearly were destiny-linked. Even though he might be crazier than the mad ones who troubled Alex, he still felt that it required something by him, in the course of furthering his own interests, to boost Lani to a status significantly higher than a creaky empire offered. He did not know whether to find out if the purser had bagpipes for sale or for rent, or join the club just as he was.

Chapter 3

FROM THE SPACEPORT, Garvin's helicopter taxi gave
him a grand view of rebuilt Megapolis Alpha and his first
sight of the enlarged campus and new university buildings.
The Education Lobby had finally rammed the nine hundred
billion pazor budget through Parliament. But instead of
being upgraded by schooling, the moderately bright and
potentially competent were bogging down in egalitarianism. Democracy in education resulted in mediocracy for
all but a handful of a privately sponsored elite but for
which the Magnificent Society could not have outlived its
founders. As the chopper carried him westward past
Megapolis Alpha's limits and toward the car rental station,
Garvin read the latest in a news magazine he had picked
up in the spaceport snack bar.

> But for skimping on education, there would not have been
> funds for the recent imperialistic war ... with today's edu-
> cators specializing in the instruction of the handicapped and
> eliminating the rigorous scientific and mathematical disci-
> plines that serve only warmongers, the scope of learning is
> vastly expanded. Since morons are now qualifying for doc-
> toral degrees, it is undemocratic to exclude imbeciles, who
> are only a step below morons. Today's tremendous advances
> in the science of pedagogy can and must eliminate the dis-
> crimination which has thus far excluded them ...

"This," Garvin told himself aloud, "will update Flora on Terran education for Camille. Or will it?"

Following the freeway a hundred kilometers, Garvin bypassed Selfridge, a nondescript town in an agricultural area, and turned off on a road that led into densely wooded country. Instead of turning on his headlights when he entered the forest's premature darkness, he relied on an invisible infrared beam and reflection sensor to warn him of outcropping rocks, stumps, and vehicles such as his own. His ID card got him past the first and second checkpoints. The third was at trail's end, where an orderly took charge of his car and luggage.

Handing Garvin a key, the orderly indicated the elevator entrance. "Six floors down. We'll take the car to rental parking. You'll be in six-fourteen and ahead of your things, but the refrigerator is stocked. The boss will phone when he has a breather."

Garvin had time for two snorts of Trinidad rum, cold cuts, goat's milk cheese, sourdough rye, and a couple of bottles of porter, and then an hour of siesta before Alexander Heflin called him to a conference room on the same level.

Lean, stately, impressive as ever, the Imperator was not as straight-up as he had been in the days before war had terminated the Parliamentary Republic of North America. Although the Slivovitz Socialist Empire had been soundly clobbered and sadly crippled by the revolt and secession of the Georgian, the Armenian, and the Moslem slave-republics, the Imperator was weary from wondering who had won the war.

"Alex," Garvin said. "If you're too tired to deal with a consultant, fit me into next week's agenda. There are people I'd like to see at Nameless Island."

"I'd like to play it that way—no, goddammit, I wouldn't! With more enemies in my own country than we ever had abroad, it's good to see a friend instead of another bureaucrat or elected slob!

"Ostensibly you are here to tell the Consortium what they want to know about the Martian mining, manufacturing, and agricultural projects. The potential, the projection for the next five years, for instance."

"The silly sons of bitches could have gotten all that in writing instead of dished off the cuff."

Alexander smiled sourly. "They fit your specs precisely, which is why they bought the idea of giving you a temporary parole."

"The Consortium! They used to be tough, but gentlemen, and smart enough to tell shit from wild honey. What's gone wrong?"

"This is not the old Consortium that used to run the country. These are elected, and they are experts in nothing but the charisma that gets votes. Sit down!" He gestured to lounging chairs, examples of the Chinese-designed "drunken lord," the prototype of the chaise lounge. Parallel to the cocktail table that separated them, the chairs were oriented so that the occupants faced each other. "How's Flora?"

"Taking to Martian exile a lot better than I expected. With that blessing, I am not inclined to borrow trouble."

The Imperator chuckled. "I'll lend you some of mine! Don't tell me you have none."

"Your daughter is busy learning English, Gook, and Proto-Uighur from Azadeh and Aljai, respectively. They're spoiling her, and Flora is outnumbered. Yakking about sending her away from horrible Mars and getting her some exposure to North American culture. Likes the idea of a Switzerland kindergarten and leans toward private schools, the kind she got, only those are un-Democratic."

"So you have troubles?" Without waiting for an answer, the Imperator gestured to the table. "Brandy? Scotch? And I got a couple of cases of Avery's dark sherry. And some Palomino y Vergara, very pale, very dry."

"You off spirits?"

Alexander sighed. "Well, no, but I'm getting too god-damn old."

"Seeing what these Liberal assholes have done for *you*, I feel that way myself. I'll take dark; that Avery must be the tenth generation in the wine business."

"Well, speaking of troubles, remember? You are actually here to help me cope with an epidemic of insanity among leading scientists."

The way Alexander said it made the problem real in a way that Lani's extravagant recital had not.

Garvin choked, sputtered, and wiped dark sherry from his chin. "Goddammit, Alex, a century and a half ago every punk who could spell C-A-T and knew nothing about P-U-S-S-Y had to write about mad scientists. Largely because he couldn't write about real people, not until even the fans got puking sick of it. The chief astronomer at the Martian Observatory, prime meridian north, has a collection going all the way back to H. G. Wells."

"I'd be a lot happier if they'd stayed back in the 1890s! This is no gag. Top scientists are going crazy. One developed a flu antitoxin, government-sponsored, and all that. It touched off an epidemic of Asiatic cholera. Another discovered a new approach in the design of high-rise buildings. Really revolutionary. Architects bought the idea. Half a dozen were completed before they all fell apart.

"For starters, we figured it was the usual swindle: pay off the right people and skimp on material. What blew things was when the biggest nuclear reactor plant in the world did the wrong things. The breakthrough was spectacular, but not in the way we figured the scientist intended. The biggest names in the country cooked up those nightmares. There was a lot of controversy before each project. But each innovator was crazy-smart enough to fool highly rated rivals doing their best to cut a rival down.

"We did not wake up to what was going on until one of the Old Masters had a lucid interval and realized what he had done. He took an overdose of something. There was an autopsy. He had been addicted to a new narcotic, a synthetic, maybe a derivative of hashish."

"Like morphine and heroin are opium derivatives, and a lot more serious?"

"Right. We found some of the stuff."

"Those Slivovitz bastards! Serves us right in making so much information sharing and fraternizing mandatory."

"Correct in principle," Alexander conceded. "But wrong in fact. Our intelligence people working over there tell us that there are swarms of mad Marxists hooked on the same narcotic."

Garvin pulled a long face. "Science is our Great Green God, and ditto for the Slivovitz people. They can no more trust their scientists than we can ours. We're like kids who got caramel-coated soap from Santa Claus." Scowling, he paused. "Tough titty. But where do I come in?"

"The Society of Assassins made hashish famous a thousand years ago," Alexander replied. "Murdered a prime minister of Iran. Had plans for Richard the Lion-Hearted but settled for small-fry Crusaders."

"Could be Ismailians or some other fanatic sect of the Shi'ah Moslems, like in Egypt, or Syria or Iran or Turkistan," Garvin agreed. "With history barred from our schools as irrelevant—'nothing but memorizing dates and names of battles, aw, Jesus, it's dull stuff, let's demonstrate'—Ismailians would not expect to be suspected. They catch you eating ham on rye or guzzling liquor?"

Alexander shook his head. "When I converted to Islam to get an alliance with the Moslem world against the Slivovitz Empire, I knew they checked up on converts. That we have a couple million bona fide Moslems in North America wasn't—isn't—enough. Our official front has been strictly orthodox. Outside our private apartments,

Lani has never been seen without a veil.

"It simply has been Moslem suspicion and distrust, ever since the atrocities committed by the Crusaders. Their memories go back for centuries. Damn few Americans ever heard of Lincoln or World War One or the Hitler war."

"Does sound like Islam is getting back at the infidels," Garvin commented. "Despising us as much as they hate Marxists. But where do I come in?"

"Well, some Moslems have noses like yours. Others have grayish-greenish hazel eyes like yours. Those people come in all sizes and shapes and colors. You've had a lot of experience in Turkistan, and you fought in Syria in one of those wars our troops were forbidden to win.

"You have a knack for languages and a handy trick for hiding it—like the time you were raping the Arabic language and claimed you were from Afghanistan, and someone said, 'Even for an Afghan, that is the lousiest Arabic I ever heard!'"

Garvin chuckled. "Well, it worked. And when I was in Egypt, I screwed up the Arabic, leaving out all the vowels, speaking nothing but consonants, like in el Moghreb. So the Egyptians who bitch up the language in a way that'd give people in Syria the blind staggers—well, the goddamn Egyptians figured, '*Y'allahi!* Those clowns from the far west, you never know whether they are talking or coughing.' But I still haven't heard what I am supposed to do."

"A cloak-and-dagger assignment in Lebanon, Syria, Egypt, Yemen. Pick up gossip—you understand more than you can speak."

Garvin sighed. "That'd be more fun. Well, for a little while. But you've got the approach arse-backward. Ever tell you the story about the two yogis meditating and prowling around in desert country with cactus and sharp rocks cropping out?"

"Your yarns are always entertaining, but why not keep this one for the happy hour?"

"Hear me out and that hour's going to be happier. Now, those yogis had a cave in a rocky hill, and the water supply was quite a piece away, and so was the village where they made their begging rounds, scrounging chow.

"They did a lot of meditating, and finally Number One Yogi said, 'Brother, if we can beg enough coin and eat less food, we can finally save up and buy sheepskins to carpet the path to the spring and to the village.'

"So they went into a trance and, when they woke up, agreed that it was a brilliant thought. But to be sure, they meditated some more, and Number Two Yogi came up with a better answer. It was simple: 'Let us ask the villagers for the skin of one sheep, and when we have tanned it, we'll tie pieces of it to our feet, and then we can walk all over and scrounge better food and more handouts.'"

"Smart fellows, those Orientals," Alexander admitted. "But it leaves me groping."

"That's to puzzle the bastards that have bugged your conference room," Garvin countered. "It is this way: I'd spend the rest of my life playing a dervish who spoke lousy Arabic.

"The simple approach is to cook up some kind of imitation Nobel Prize thing, with an award and a diploma and stuff. That'll draw the scientists from all over North America. Award each one a certificate of merit, send them all to Mars to explore the great possibilities of low g processes and techniques. We have good laboratories. Great facilities.

"We'll pick out the fruitcakes from the sane ones, providing there are no psychologists or psychiatrists screwing things up. I'll go to Nameless Island—getting Mona to release all Doc Brandon's technical and personnel files to your personal custody will be no trouble.

"That'll give you a directory of everyone who was

really first class in Doc's estimation. There you have the answer the Number Two Yogi doped out. And I'll guarantee you that no one is going to smuggle narcotics to Maritania, much less get the handful of sane scientists hooked on drugs.

"Make me Governor-General or the like and there'll be no bill of rights, no due process of law, or any other constitutional *demokratikrap* to bollix things up."

"Beginning with the time you bugged the thought-control computer system and loused up an election that the old Consortium had carefully planned," Alexander said, "you've done nicely, and human rights and the constitution never broke your stride. But—"

"Alex," Garvin cut in. "Pardon my rudeness. But just in case their addiction to autoerotic practices has not made the Consortium lose its collective memory, so they'll forget that I'm supposed to render a report to them, I'll give you a good answer, one that they'll believe, no questions whatever."

Alexander reached for brandy. "Tell me, and happy hour begins."

"Tell those assholes that you found me and the *Martian Queen*'s new space concubine dead drunk in her apartment, and when we are conscious, I'll render my report."

Alexander chuckled. "They would never believe the actual facts. Straight or with a splash of Red Rock?"

Chapter 4

NAMELESS ISLAND WAS created when the severe earthquake of August 17, 2031, pushed a chain of puny obstructions to navigation high above sea level, forming the rocky spine of a body of land not far south of Savannah, Georgia, about twenty kilometers offshore. It was well into the Gulf Stream's change of direction and had a tropical climate.

Avery Jarvis, "Doc," Brandon, then a spry youngster whose one hundred twenty-ninth birthday was only a week behind him, induced the Secretary of the Interior to give him title to those menaces to navigation, visible only at low tide, *as of thirty days before the great quake*. Doc imported teak seedlings, the inhabitants of a Burmese village, several elephants, and a Hindu elephant-master named Habeeb. These arrived not long after Doc had built a helicopter landing field, guest house, and the office building and laboratories of the Brandon Foundation. This was Doc's refuge from the idiot world that he and his fellow scientists had in their childish and utopian ignorance created, a thought-controlled collection of Megapolises crowded by intellectuals, as they fondly termed themselves, and idealists complaining about the occupational therapy that demanded a four-hour week of hard labor. A rural class of so-called serfs, a.k.a. coolies, plus Simianoids, a product of genetic engineering, furnished victuals to feed and paid taxes to support the Magnificent Parliamentary Democracy which, by A.D. 2112, had become a dictatorship.

Brandon anecdotes, some of them relatively true, raced through Garvin's mind as the jet whisked him southeastward. Although he had met Doc only once, Garvin and his wives had been guests of Mona, the deceased scientist's heiress.

Mona was a sixth-generation Simianoid. When she was an infant, Doc gave her out for adoption by one of a colony of Alleluia Stompers, fundamental religionists of the hinterland. When full grown, she had returned to Nameless Island, where she and Doc learned that despite the teachings of Democracy and Marxism, heredity prevailed over environment. The pioneer of genetic engineering, Doc's late father, had created the first generation of Simianoids, a race with human bodies—six different physical types—and modified human minds, combining the common sense of the chimpanzee and the orangutan with the human capacity for abstract thinking yet devoid of the human horror of doing a day's work or doing anything even mildly unpleasant. The Simianoid had none of that conceit whereby each thought that he or she was the first to suspect that the world fell short of paradise and that he or she was the first to devise remedies.

To offset the human passion for reproduction of the species, the Simianoids were polyandrous. The emotional wiring diagram was just right: A female with four husbands never found life dull.

Soaring over field and forest, Garvin found verdure universal except for insignificant towns and industrial areas. His congenital aversion to cities took charge.

Destroying the cities would help, he cogitated.

Nothing but science feeds the Megapolises and their parasites. Don't even have to nuke the megapolitan madhouses. Ship the key scientists to Mars, and how long could those mechanical-electronic-technological nightmares carry on?

The nearest field at which a jet could land was a hundred thirty kilometers from the coast. Garvin phoned Mona, then rented a car to drive to the fishing village where the Nameless Island launch would be waiting. The mistress of the island would be at the wheel. Isaiah, the black steward, had died.

Driving along a fine stretch of highway, Garvin knew that he was near Mona's childhood home. Alternating right and left, a kilometer apart, were enormous billboards lettered by one who knew his work: "ARE YOU BURDENED WITH SIN & GUILT"... "REPENT AND BE SAVED"... "ARE YOU PREPARED TO FACE YOUR MAKER"... This was Alleluia Stomper land. And soon after "MAKE YOUR PEACE WITH GOD" was behind him, he was handing car keys to the harbor master, saying that he did not know when he would return.

The waiting launch flew the North American Imperium's colors, alongside the smaller flag of the Republic of Burma. Behind the tawny-haired girl at the wheel, two elders of the Burmese village stood in the cockpit. U Po Mya, the older, carried a double-barrel .600 Jefferies elephant gun. Maung Gauk had a 5.45-millimeter assault carbine. Each smoked a cheroot about fifteen millimeters in diameter, and long enough to reach from the tip of the middle finger to a bit beyond the wrist. Their red caps and green jackets were gilt-embroidered, and instead of the Burmese *longyi*, which wrapped around the waist something like a kilt, they wore jodhpurs.

But Mona monopolized the scene. Low sun brought ruddy golden glints to her hair. Her fragile piña cloth blouse, pulled snug in the crisp breeze, dramatized curves that reminded Garvin of Gussie, the office lady who would supervise Martian Eck & Ag until his return.

"Dive aboard, Rod!"

He plopped himself into an angle of the cockpit. Mona goosed the throttle, swung clear of the pier, and in a moment had the setting sun astern.

"Naturally, I didn't ask what brought you back to Earth. Awfully glad to see you."

"When I don't have problems, Alexander supplies them."

"Which is why you're traveling solo?" Her gray-greenish eyes, with their slightly feline expression, held a twinkle that made it clear that the mountain trails and deserts and combat wounds she and Doc had shared in Turkistan had not quenched her eagerness to enjoy life to the limit before she was too old—which would be never plus a day.

"Sorry about Isaiah." Garvin paused to repeat his appreciative scrutiny. "Running the plantation yourself, and looking good as new."

Her smile accented fine lines that suggested that Mona had laughed before she had learned to talk. "Doc was so busy with worthwhile things, he never taught me how to worry."

"The international situation seems to be as bad as what's going on in this country, and Alexander has plenty of worries. Which is why I'm here. To ask you whether Doc's files have information that would help with Imperial defense. Things are critical, and Doc never more than hinted at what he could do if he—mmm, wanted to."

The smile became cryptic. "You almost said '*had to*.'"

He nodded. "Neville Ingerman and Harry Offendorf, those grade-A sons of bitches, thought they had Doc where he would have to talk and tell all. Doc killed two men— not the two he should have, but the meeting adjourned, and he walked, I say *walked*, out. Did not have to run.

Took a moment for me to remember."

"They knew him a lot better than you did, but they did not understand. You're doing all right, Rod."

It was near sunset when Garvin went with Mona to the guest house, which perched on a headland reaching abruptly from the sea. The armed escort followed with Garvin's luggage.

"Now that you're in your home away from home, I'll bring you the drippingest absinthe drip in the western hemisphere."

Garvin had scarcely reshaped the upholstery of his lounging chair in the billiard room when Mona returned with two goblets of shaved ice in each of which sat a glass saucer whose center was needlepoint-perforated. The top dishes contained only a fraction of their original ninety cubic centimeters of Nameless Island illegal genuine laboratory-distilled absinthe.

The goblets were frosty from exposure to the humid air. Greenish absinthe turned milky-cloudy as it dripped into the ice. Mona removed the empty drippers. "I chilled everything in the coldest corner of the freezer, so it took a long time for the syrupy liqueur to dribble through."

Garvin tasted. He tasted a second time. He was young and happy again. "Madame Broadtail," he said, using Doc Brandon's pet name for Mona. "You told me that Captain Isaiah Winthrop, Litt D, PhD, died. Don't crap me! This is exactly how he used to make them."

Mona sighed. "Isaiah always intended to give Doc the recipe. Once he knew Doc would never come back from the war, Isaiah lost no time telling me the recipe. And when he briefed me on the basics of being steward of the island, I knew he didn't have long to live."

"Then he didn't have much time to enjoy his PhD. Too bad."

"You'd be surprised," Mona countered. "A brand-new

PhD proudly handed Isaiah the thesis the university press had just gotten from the printer and said, 'This might help you with your graduate work.' And when Isaiah learned that the new scholar was going to teach philosophy at that very university, he bought a copy of the thesis.

"The bottom quarter of just about every page was footnotes and bibliographical references. So when he took this brand-new Dr. Kyle's courses, he paroted sixty percent of that scholar, and the rest was a rehash of footnote stuff the new prof cited as sustaining authority."

Garvin frowned. "All a degree does is save a stupid would-be boss or personnel manager the trouble of sizing up a candidate for a job, and Isaiah wasn't about to hunt work on the mainland."

"Rod, you haven't been to school enough! Isaiah had already quit being a believer. Getting his PhD proved beyond any doubt that he had seen through the entire racket. Seeing through academe—the supreme illumination. Really satori!"

"Keno! Now I get it! He was liberated, so he briefed you on how to be steward, and being tired, he died. First drink today. Let's dedicate it to Isaiah Winthrop, Doctor of Literature and Doctor of Philosophy."

They did so.

"Before I forget," Garvin said then, "my office lady, Gussie, wanted me to find out if there are any Trappick nunneries or monasteries that are coed."

"How'd anyone handling your office ever get around to poverty, chastity, and the rest?"

"Being a standard Simianoid, she's not interested in either. The thing started with one of Gussie's schoolmates, a standard human girl. They met at a cultural exchange project. Psychologists making another million-pazor study."

Mona laughed softly. "When Doc told me about a charade like that, I told him it'd make more sense if they had Simianoids and chimpanzees make a study of social scientists. He nearly laughed himself silly and said I rated a broadtail jacket—sorry. Carry on about Gussie's friend; I always interrupt."

"That girl heard about a Trappick outfit the bureaucrats cracked down on because it wouldn't admit female monks or nuns. Violating civil rights. Discrimination."

"Fun is fun, but you're going too far."

"You and your culturally deprived Burmese teak loggers haven't met enough bureaucrats. Maybe you could tell me a thing or two about Alleluia Stompers and the Testifiers."

"No problem. They have been sending me leaflets trying to convert me back into the fold. I could tell them I repented drinking and sinning with Doc, and that I want a list of all the monasteries and nunneries—I mean, the Trappick kind that the Harlot of Rome is running.

"And no smarty-ass quips out of you. I know very well that the Harlot of Rome is not a girl in an Eyetalian cathouse. I'll contribute a thousand pazors for them to make a survey and find out if there are any coed outfits."

"You mean the Stompers would do a serious job for one thousand North American skivvy paper pazors?"

She frowned. "What's skivvy paper?"

"Sweet Jesus! I shouldn't have said that to a nice girl."

"I'm not a nice girl."

"All *right*, snoopy! But you might meet one someday, and other nice people, and blat it out like I did, and be embarrassed."

"If they were as nice as all that, they'd not know it wasn't nice. Anyway, their curiosity would needle them into tracking down every coed spot as a den of iniquity, with a higher pregnancy percentage than the Amazon Companies had before, during, and after the war."

"Pick up the chips, Madame Broadtail. Bank's busted."
He glanced at his watch. "Alexander has a scientist problem, and Doc having been the World Series Dean of Scientists, he'd have correspondence and records about the real and the phonies."

"I have the same apartment I had during Doc's days, right next to the Foundation office. Dinner will be a gourmet quickie. When the chef learned I was not going to have hospitality the way Doc always did, he went to New Orleans, about the only city left where they know how to eat and how to cook for people who know food. Opened a marvelous restaurant, they tell me.

"We'll have Alexander's problems for dessert and coffee and liqueurs according to whim and impulse."

Mona got a second round of drips from the freezer. Purely as a guess, based on the solids precipitated by dilution when the ice melted and the mix turned milky, Garvin estimated that the absinthe liqueur must be at least one hundred thirty proof, perhaps higher.

When they drank their way well into the third preprepared drip, Garvin wondered whether he was getting a high compliment or, as a newcomer, was being tested for worthiness to be an associate of the Mona-Doc Brandon Society. Her speech was unslurred, her hand steady, her vocal pitch low and smooth.

The only change that he could perceive was in Mona's eyes, which were animation-sharpened and a shade nearer absinthe color. She was burning alcohol and botanicals as fast as they hit bottom, thanks to the metabolism of all Simianoids, and an occasional nonstandard human, such as Doc Brandon.

If Doc Brandon's honorary widow and sole heiress brings out a fourth one of these goddamn drips, Roderick David Garvin is resigning, and without apology.

"Rod," Mona said abruptly, cutting short their discussion. "None of your wives is jealous of the other two, so I don't see how the three of them could object if you moved in with me for the duration."

"Don't you dare hide in the teak jungle while I'm getting my luggage."

Chapter 5

BLACK-EYED PEAS. Ham hocks. Turnip greens. Hominy grits. McEwan's stout, blacker even than what Guinness had been making since 1759.

"Not gourmet," Mona admitted, "but it's your fault. You shouldn't have got me all nostalgic quoting those 'REPENT AND BE SAVED' markers along the highway."

"This is something I bet you couldn't get even at Antoine's," Garvin countered. "Fact is, this is a combination Eck & Ag ought to develop. The ingredients, I mean. But the dessert—"

"Alexander's problems will keep, and we started with a fair cargo of liqueur well dripped."

"First thing I know, you'll be telling me that absinthe makes people feel dissolute and immoral."

"If they're wired up properly, they don't need absinthe." Mona stretched and sighed contentedly. There was a long, comfortable pause. Then she abruptly ended the meditative silence. "Awfully awkward, two perfect strangers plopping into bed. Let's take a shower together and get acquainted first."

"Desserts are fattening," Garvin conceded, and followed his hostess from the dining nook.

He was not surprised to find that the stall was big

enough for two. They had no problem getting the spray
and temperature just right.

"Doc used to mock me for my thirty-minute showers,"
she remarked in the course of reciprocal back-washings.
"I was always too tactful to tell that lecherous old devil
that I didn't want to interrupt him when he was watching
Flora Garvin's famous Sudzo TV show while you were
marooned on the asteroid."

Since Garvin would scarcely be addicted to watching
old reruns of Flora rinsing pink panties with forget-me-
nots as she sang the Sudzo theme song, the shower was
not prolonged. Mona took an enormous towel from the
rack and tossed its mate to her guest. "Last one in bed's
a dirty name!"

It was a tie; neither was a dirty name.

Whether it was the full moon's intrusion and the
chanting of Burmese villagers as they burned joss
sticks, whanged gongs, and kept hardwood "fish-heads"
*tick-tock-tick-tock*ing, all against the ever-changing, never-
changing voice of the mellow *gamelan* that kept him awake,
Garvin did not know, and he cared not at all. Maybe Mona
was overstimulating, as some were, when a lover finally
broke a long dry spell. And Garvin relished the Burmese
music, as probably did the seven hundred million forest
devils, *nats*, whom the ceremony was intended to pacify.
In any event, the happy Burmese were not morbidly concerned about repenting or being saved. Everyone, including the seven hundred million *nats*, would evolve, after
a billion eternities, to become *devas*, or *boddhisattvas*,
or at least fully human. Meanwhile, it was good to chant
and whang gongs.

Mona, breathing softly, was sound asleep. At times,
during peaks of ecstasy, she had been almost unintelligible. Once at least, she had seemed to fancy that her
lover was Doc.

No doubt Mona had found lovers, old friends and new, but those had been on the mainland. This was not a matter of racism or of finding Asiatics unattractive. "For me to do things with a local man would be bad business," she had told Garvin during a breathing spell. "I am in command here, trustor and trustee, looking out for Doc's people. Going ashore and taking care of my polyandrous makeup . . . mmm . . . better than nothing . . . Oh, there are exceptions, but North American males are either manly clods and clowns or they are creepy bastards, a lot of them so sweet and gentle, modeled after the sociologist's prescription, tender and diaper-changing stuffed shirts, so female that going to bed with one makes me feel like a lesbian."

The moon sank. Skyglow tapered off. It was time for seven hundred million *nats* to go to sleep and for each teak forester to snuggle up to a Burmese girl. Whether it was the termination of the music, or the intercom's jangle that awakened Garvin, there came an excursion into that no-man's-land between waking and sleep. He did not know whether he was busy with Girl-Watcher's Braille or obeying "general quarters" piped by an idiot bosun. And when he was finally sure, it turned out to be quite simple:

He and Mona were on their feet, each keeping the other from tumbling to the deck or back to bed. She twisted loose and bounded to the fiendish phone. She singsonged something in Burmese, slapped the instrument to its cradle, and with one hand flipped her sleeping gown into a corner while the other hand snatched up practical underwear and horrible jeans.

"For hell's sweet sake, skip the girl watching—there's nothing you've not seen. Get dressed, take your thumb out, grab your gun; we're going to the ridge to see what's going on."

Scrambling into his clothes, Garvin saw the carbines in the rack in a far corner.

"How about one of those five-forty-fives?"

"Okay. I just thought you'd feel more at home with your eleven-millimeter cannon."

Moments later, Garvin was following Mona up the path that led to the spine of the island. At the summit, Mona paused.

"Couple of the older men noticed night operations offshore. Someone approaching from the southeast. When the moon was pretty low."

"Hell of a note, trying to see by this no-light."

"Infrared viewing always fascinated Doc." Mona caught his hand. "I'll show you."

Thanks to her guidance, Garvin did not slash himself to pieces on outcropping rocks, thorns, or the knife-edged tropical grass. The going was better when they entered a stand of teak.

"We're at the middle one of the five peaks," Mona said. "The village isn't alerted, not so far."

"They understand infrared?"

"Nothing to understand. Simply use it. Like nobody understands daylight, but we all see by it."

U Po Mya was at the entrance of a concrete dome with a slot like that of a machine gun emplacement. After addressing Mona in Burmese, he spoke in English to Garvin: "Plenty fun tonight. You look-see?"

"Yes. I think with you."

A deep green bulb illuminated the interior of the dome. The viewing slot was at ground level. Garvin followed down the steps to the floor. The infrared beam projector was a tube very much like a rifleman's spotting scope. The invisible IR beam bounced off whatever it reached and was focused on a sensor screen whose composition responded to variations of heat wavelengths so that it emitted a visible image in a way analogous to a TV's response to waves not visible to the eye. Garvin saw why U Po Mya had phoned.

A launch of seagoing size was about a thousand meters offshore, keeping a fixed distance from the coastline, which it was skirting very slowly.

"Making or taking soundings," Garvin muttered. "Funny thing, don't see anyone heaving the lead or working a machine."

Mona spoke to old U Po Mya. She converted his answer into dry-cleaned and colorless English. In effect, aside from the crew members' mothers letting pigs take improper liberties with them whenever their sons were not at it, the mayor of this village noted something odd.

"Please clarify."

"Sometimes a bill rang; he heard it clearly when the wind was right. Something bounced up out of the water. A crewman fooled around with line and hooked rod and dumped the thing back into the water, and the launch moved on. Funny business, I'd say."

"So do I. Once I was researching soundings and read about the *submarine sentry*."

"All right, visiting scientist, but where does the submarine come in?"

"Can't say where, but it probably won't be until after the survey is made. Or maybe someone is planning a surface landing party to take possession of this lovely little offshore island after giving the simple natives red calico and beads. Whatever the pitch is, someone wants to know how deep the water is close to shore, to avoid running aground and maybe getting blown out of the water.

"The sentry thing is a float with a rod hooked to it. When the end of the rod scrapes mud or rock, it unlocks the float, which rises and rings a bell. They'd be logging each spot where the bell rings."

"I begin to get it. Doc always did have fun with infrared, and he never trusted these piddling rum and banana democracies in the West Indies."

"Apparently that boatload of people out there figures

your island is easy pickings and doesn't suspect there
might be small-bore, extra-high-velocity, extra-nasty artillery along this ridge. While I watch and study, you ask
the old man about weapons. And I do not mean a .600
Jefferies elephant gun."

"Got a plan?"

"I'll know better when I hear more and see more."

Garvin tuned out the exchange of Burmese and read
areas of the sensor screen, using a magnifier. The vessel
was not blacked out perfectly. The submarine sentry was
forward. The phosphorescence stirred up by its cable was
distinct from that of the boat's prow. The Leeward, Wind-
ward, Lesser Antilles area being dotted with tiny "nations"
as changeable as a dog's fleas, each bankrupt president
could get his democracy refinanced by altruistic nations
and at the same time be taken over by Marxist powers:
Many an island had great value as a submarine base, or
a landing area for bombers, or a base for troublemaking
in more important places.

Nameless Island might well be on someone's list of
goodies.

Now accustomed to blackout illumination, Garvin got
a good look at a 50-millimeter gun with telescopic sights.
It was a deadly little weapon, accurate as the star gauge
rifles used by snipers. It was fitted with IR ranging and
aiming gear. Garvin turned to Mona. "Tell U Po Mya that
nobody aboard that offshore prowler must know that there
are white people on this island. If they don't know already,
then keep it so.

"It may be dangerous for a canoe or the island launch
to approach the strangers. Again, it may be quite safe,
and the strangers may be happy to have friendly natives,
nonwhite natives, to help them.

"Get a fast-paddling boat, pirogue, canoe, anything
except the launch. Must not have noise. Daub the boat,
or two or three boats, with black paint. Hide close to

shore, in dark coves, until the strangers are in trouble and want help. Brown natives are always friendly, stupid, helpful to strangers. Play it up.

"I want to find out who those sons of bitches are, where they are from, what they are trying to do. Once they are on this island, they must not leave. Not until I get word to Alexander."

Chapter 6

"YOU STAY HERE," Garvin said to Mona, "just in case we see something that U Po Mya couldn't see from water level. Have him keep someone on the phone. And there ought to be a runner who knows where the canoes will hide out."

This instruction was all that the mayor needed. He took a shortcut, apparently bouncing from tree to tree as he made for the gilded *hti* of the pagoda, the center of the sea-level village.

Garvin turned to the sensor and studied the moving image of the spy boat. "Phone the message center," he said after some minutes. "I begin to think I know what I'm doing."

Presently, Mona turned from the phone and reported. "They are in a couple of canoes in the cove between first hilltop north and the one south of it. Ready and waiting."

Going to the 50-millimeter gun, Garvin flipped a high-explosive shell into the chamber and handed Mona another for a follow-up if needed. He closed the switch of the circuit that activated the infrared projector. In the telescopic sight he got the cross hairs fixed on the prop, which was churning white foam. She was riding high in the water.

Range finder adjustment automatically corrected for

increasing distance and accordingly compensated for the
increased lead; this and the fifteen-hundred-meters-per-
second velocity of the projectile made for pinpoint accuracy. He set off a correction for target velocity and found
that uniform tracking kept the cross hair on the phosphorescence stirred up by the propeller.

He fired.

Nitrous fumes billowed when the breechblock swung
out. He saw the flash as the high-explosive projectile let
go. They heard the blast as Mona flipped the reload home.
The launch lost way.

"She's adrift!"

The engine raced crazily. Two crewmen came on deck.
Moments elapsed before another man cut off the engine.

"Probably think they hit a floating mine and are lucky
to get off with so little damage. A second shot would set
them thinking they were in real trouble."

Several moments elapsed before a signal pistol spewed
distress flares skyward. Garvin opened the breech and
withdrew the shell.

"They must figure that signaling is going to get them
a good reception. Mustn't risk spoiling their happy hopes."

Time dragged, minute after lead-footed minute.

"I feel as if I had red ants crawling all over me," Mona
said. "What's U Po Mya waiting for?"

"He's allowing the time it would take a rescue boat to
come from the pier. If he came into view right away,
they'd figure it odd that someone just happened to be so
near. I forgot to tell him, but he had sense enough to
figure it out—God*damm*it!"

"What's wrong?"

Garvin slammed a shell home and resumed tracking.
"Those fellows may be foxy. Ready to blind anyone with
a searchlight if he comes to answer the signal. And gun
him out."

She was drifting with the tide and current.

"Turn your scope and see if you can spot anything in the cove."

Mona searched the darkness.

"Still there and waiting," she finally reported. And later, when Garvin was sweating carpet tacks, she added, "Two boats, moving out into open water."

A spotlight blazed from the forward deck and winked out. A lantern glowed; someone waggled it as if signaling. Garvin was getting these details through his gun scope. They still might start trouble, but in that case he would finish it.

At last two fishing boats, paddle-driven, came alongside the spy boat. Aboard each were two islanders with assault carbines. There were other firearms, not identifiable. Flashlights winked. The rescue party cast lines, which the spy's crew made fast.

Tide and current favored the men from the island; slowly, they got the disabled spy boat under way. After phoning, Mona took the carbine and went down the steep slope to the village, where the message center man came from his phone station to meet them, holding a battered but serviceable ten-gauge shotgun.

Mona translated. "After putting his head beneath my golden feet, he said, 'Divinity, the shit-eaters are well in tow, and no trouble.'"

Not to be outpointed in Burmese elegance, Garvin answered, "Please tell the Builder of Pagodas that after thanking him, I'm heading for the waterfront."

"So am I," Mona added, and translated the decision.

She went through the long stretch of teak that clothed the flatland between village and western shore and presently swung past the menagerie cages whose inhabitants she had donated to the Brandon Foundation Zoo in Savannah. Among those examples of Doc's genetic engineering were creatures extinct as long ago as the Jurassic period, and ichthyornises, the last of whose kind had left their bones in Cretaceous rocks, until Brandon had gene-spliced modern replicas. There were also a few relatively commonplace beasts, such as an Australian kiwi whose only peculiarity was the wings that could carry it twenty meters or more in fine flight.

But for the ignorance of her Stomper foster parents, staunch antievolutionists, both Simianoid Mona and Doc Brandon would have been burned at the stake. Garvin, following her through darkness and rustling bamboo, relished the jest, until the sound of voices alerted them to back into deeper shadow.

Five men, escorted with all Burmese courtesy, were coming toward the village. Torchlight revealed the quintet as foreigners and of diverse complexions: black, pale yellow, East Indian swarthy, and two bullet-headed, square-faced whites. Two rear-guard villagers, for reasons of their own, dallied well behind the happily chattering main party and visitors from the spy boat.

Mona stepped from darkness to halt the rear guard. Question and elaborate answer ensued. Garvin recognized *payaaaa*: divinity. He had not yet learned the words for placing one's head beneath anyone's golden feet. In due course, Mona translated.

"The strangers are happy. They are going to talk to U Po Mya about how much salvage they owe him for saving their boat. Very nice people. They want to buy all the teak trees on the low, flat side of the island. Maybe root out all the stumps to make a long wide road, a nice level stretch for hauling other teak from the high ridge."

"This begins to sound interesting," Garvin conceded. "I wonder, now, whether a tug to tow a raft of logs to wherever they'd be going would draw enough water to make soundings necessary on the eastern side of the island."

"Anything else you'd like to know? Give it in one

package and I'll save a lot of time."

"Our visitors are dealing with the head man, a brown little native fellow. Anyone mention you or any other white boss?"

"Rod, you seem to be developing nasty suspicions."

They could no longer hear the visitors' escort, much less see the torchlight. He could not read Mona's expression, but her voice had changed to that whimsical note she used when, in amiable mockery, she wanted to suggest that he was a simpleton, or that she was not such.

"Madame Broadtail, why the hell do you suppose I shot the prop off that boat instead of sinking her? Quit horsing around! I want to know whether our visitors plan to save the natives from being exploited by Imperialists."

"You're either psychic or you understand more Burmese than you let on. We don't need to waste any more time with this interpreter routine. There are no visitors in the boat. They searched her from stem to stern."

"I think I'd like a look. Mind if I frisk her while the crew is busy crapping the quaint natives? Will you be in your apartment mixing something good for our nerves?"

"Our nerves will keep." She hefted the assault carbine. "Go ahead and give her a pelvic examination, but I'm going along."

Dismissing the rear guard, Mona headed for the pier. The way was clear until Habeeb, the elephant man, stepped from the shadow of the guest house verandah. Even without moonlight, he was readily recognized: two meters high, plus altitude added by an enormous turban, Habeeb was conspicuous. He had a sawed-off ten-gauge shotgun cradled in the crook of his elbow.

Habeeb salaamed. "Madame," he said in English, "the chief elder of the village made it clear that no visitor must leave this island without your permission."

"Quite right," Mona answered. "You searched her?"

"Yes. None of that human garbage is hiding there."

"Carry on, Habeeb."

They boarded the boat. With a flashlight they picked their way to the master's cabin. There they found charts and a large book, solidly bound, that was apparently the log. But the script was strange, and all Garvin could read was the dates—the numerals, that is.

"Not German but just as bad as that Gothic nightmare stuff. Only thing I'm sure of, it's not civilized Latin-Italic writing."

He took a long look at the charts.

The records made it clear that the boat had set out to make soundings. That was no great blaze of revelation.

"Make anything of it?" Mona asked.

"I don't have to. You and Doc have a crew of quaint Asiatics who are perfectly trained. I'd bet that Habeeb has exactly five shells for his sawed-off shotgun."

"Five?"

"Naturally. Only five visitors who are not supposed to leave. Doc Brandon's bones are buried in Turkistan, not far from Kashgar, but he is still running Nameless Island, along with you and general principles."

"Right, but never mind sentimentality! What the hell do *you* propose doing with this package we do not want leaving the island?"

"I'm going to phone Alexander and tell him to get this boat on a trailer and haul it from Savannah, which is where I am towing her, if your Burmese slaves allow such a caper." He paused as he followed her from forward deck to dock. "Better pick up the visitors. Helicopter, and by night."

Habeeb blocked their way. One of the Burmese rear guard was with him. "Madame," the elephant master said. "It would be most untactful to go to the village. There is a native ceremony. What you call it, a negotiation, I mean, preliminary blessing sort of thing."

The newly arrived villager had a fresh torch. The wa-

vering flame, whipped by sea breeze, played tricks with
Mona's facial expressions. Garvin could no more read her
features than she could guess what he was making of
things. Unhappily, Mona did not understand Proto-Uighur,
and to question her in English would be detrimental to
discipline.

Noncommittally, or so he hoped he sounded, Garvin
said, "Goddamn funny, no gongs, no chanting. Whether
it's a wedding, a funeral, keeping the *nats* happy, or just
for the fun of it, the way they were sounding off when
they brought the visitors to town. Odd business."

"Madame Esmitt, please assure the Old Master's friend
that it would be nondelicate to intrude on folk ritual."

Mona sighed. "Rod, maybe he's right."

The first hints of daybreak were beginning to offset the
tricks played by the breeze flirting with torch flame. Garvin saw that, like himself, the mistress of Nameless Island
was worn to shreds. Thought flashed from one to the
other.

"Habeeb," Mona said. "This man fought in battle beside
the Old Master. Each knew the other's mind, in life and
in death."

Habeeb bowed at least ninety degrees. He made a
sweeping gesture and then pantomimed scooping dust and
putting it on face and beard. He said something in Hindi
or some other of India's several hundred languages. Since
his suggestion had been courteously considered rather
than brusquely rejected, Habeeb knew that he was
respected by mistress, and by her guest, as well as by all
elephants.

Mona gestured for Garvin to take the lead, and she
followed.

"Somehow," he said after a few strides, "I got the idea
that Habeeb isn't too worried about how things turned
out. And the old man, what's his name—he said something."

"Well, you and I got permission to carry on. What he said was, 'Builder of Pagodas, those swine-buggered sons of immoral mothers, it's too late now to do anything.'"

"I've got to learn that poetic Burmese language!"

"If you want to sleep with one of the unmarried girls, you'd better learn some useful basic phrases."

"That language has six or nine tones, and every time I ever try to say anything in Mandarin, I get all four tones screwed up."

"You can talk yourself out of anything and never skip a beat!"

"Isn't that, not at all. It'd take two or three of those dainty dolls to fill one broadtail jacket."

Daybreak augmented by torches lighted the plaza in which five men were the focal point of interest. Women and children peeped from bamboo shacks perched on stilts a meter and a half high. The adult male population lined the village square. Two of the strangers from the sea were kneeling; the remaining three were lying on their sides.

Deftly hitched and evenly spaced by a single long rope, the visitors were arranged in a straight line, each with his wrists behind him. The two still kneeling made no sound: they had turban cloth wrapped about mouth and throat. An agile Burmese elder, stripped to waistcloth, was loping down the line. He carried what some called a *parang*. Others might have called it a Chinese beheading blade. Steel twinkled—one-two-three-slash!

A head dropped to the ground.

The old man moved as if dancing in a *pwé*: one-two-three, slash and pirouette. The final head fell, and the old man bowed to the mayor, His Honor, U Po Mya. The latter addressed Mona.

She translated: "He said, 'Divinity, I sent Habeeb to detain you. You were pleased to say that none of these visitors were to leave the island. You arrived before your command was obeyed. I grovel in the dust.'"

"While the mayor is busy groveling, I'm going to your office to phone Alexander. We won't need a helicopter to get our visitors to Imperial Intelligence. Their finger-prints, or some of them at least, are on the boat's papers.

"Trying to make a deal for a nice wide long road through the teak stand on the west coast of the island sounds too much like a landing strip for heap big bombers. I can't read the Kirilli-krap script or print except for the latitude and longitude of the pipsqueak island these characters took off from, but that'll give Intelligence something to work on till the no-name boat gets from Savannah to Megapolis Alpha or wherever Alexander wants it."

"Sounds good, but I'll have to show you how to work Doc's hot line to Alexander." She saw that U Po Mya was giving orders to bury the visitors well out at sea. She turned back to Garvin. "Last one in bed is a dirty name."

Chapter 7

BY MIDAFTERNOON, the fishing village was a good many kilometers behind them. "You look tense and worn out, though I don't wonder," Mona said.

"This crate steers like a truck with the power assist blown. Road's crazy, too. Car skates all over on loose gravel. The natives zigzag from berm to berm, and I've been waiting for the one who can't dodge me."

"Maybe we ought to find a motel and rest up."

"Mmm ... well, the fuel is low, and a pit stop would give me a chance to unkink."

Five kilometers farther, a happy local pumped fuel until it bubbled over the collar. "They done been flinging gravel at yo win-shield, suh."

"Everyone's been overtaking us. How the hell do they do it?"

"Well, suh, you hadn't ought to drive slow. Iffen you flo-board it, you dig in and get pulling powah. You flings rocks at theah win-shields."

"My arms are half dead fighting the wheel."

The amiable man chuckled. "Everyone is taking both lanes of a one-and-a-half-lane road. You been driving through the fringe of Mamie-Belle."

"I heard of Jump Off, and Fiery Gizzard, but Mamie-Belle—"

"Ain't a town, she's a dang hurricane. No wonder yo arm is plumb wore out. We got the warning couple hours ago. This here is the quiet edge of things. It's raising ructions all along the coast. You-all got out in time."

There was a motel maybe four or five miles off. "We don't talk that kilo*meeter* stuff. Yonder, thattaway to Kirby town, then you turns right and in half a mile you gets to the Old Still. It's a sure-enough copper still, but the bottom's cut out and it don't cook off whiskey no more."

The twisting wind and driving rain made for nasty going. By the time Garvin saw the big commercial-size pot still, he was happy to get a roof over passengers and camper. Mona snatched up a big handbag and the food and drink hamper. "I knew it took more than a hysterical female, gunning a powerboat to a halt and supervising head choppings, to leave you worn out," she said. "I saw a place back there offering Brunswick stew, but let's settle for liquor and canned stuff."

Garvin followed her into the motel apartment and plopped himself into a chair. "It was not the hysterical female. It was not the head choppings. What I was strained by was aiming and tracking by infrared and wondering if I could hit her prop with the first fifty-millimeter HE shell so they'd blame it on a floating mine. A second shot would have warned them, and there'd have been a nasty shootout. Doc invent the gun and accessories?"

"In his spare time, he did."

"Warlike old devil!"

She shook her head. "He simply liked privacy, and he figured if anything ever happened to him, people would start picking on the villagers. Being neither white nor Christian, they'd be fair game. He posted beaches and anchorages. He warned people on the mainland. He knew some of the bad ones would be back, so he gave the villagers some drill on repelling boarders."

"They didn't learn head chopping, not with dry runs." He regarded Madame Broadtail's greenish eyes and the odd little twitch at the corners of her mouth.

"Well," she said, "maybe they did rescue a few trespassers purely for experimental purposes. Like they use animals in the interests of science."

"Mona, darling, you thought of that and made a point of seeing that they knew their business."

"Oh, all right, snoopy! I always hated to think of a beginner taking two or three awkward whacks. Even when I was a kid and read Grimm's Fairy Tales and Arabian Nights stuff, I shuddered at the thought of some poor guy getting his head haggled off instead of being taken off with one neat swish."

Her green eyes were dark now, and compassionate, humane in a most non-Simianoidish way.

"Just like my Azadeh! Sweetest, kindest woman I ever met, but if heads needed taking off, you haggled them off until practice made perfect."

"Lover, you *do* understand!"

The storm screamed. The old motel shuddered, but being the work of nonunion craftsmen not too arrogant to cut miters through which you could not fling a cat and who drove nails straight and true, frame and siding and shingles stayed put. The sturdy heap drummed, quivered, and resonated. Gusts of rain played symphonies, and a flurry of hail offered percussion.

Mona snapped on the archaic talkie-squawkie, two-dimensional and with poor color: ". . . losses of small shipping along the coast . . . warnings ignored . . ."

By the time the electric heater had canned crayfish bisque, crab and shrimp custard, and crepes suzettes ready to eat, the storm news ended. "Whoever it was is likely to figure that the weather finished their nameless boat," Madame Broadtail said. Garvin's expression changed.

"Relax!" she added. "In the first place, my people have been towing teak rafts so long that they are weather wise, and their fishing makes them even more so. And they pay attention to news reports."

Garvin relaxed. "I might have known. And a lot more of them understand English than admit they do. The way all this turned out, it's lucky you'd been pawing through Doc's files for quite some time before Alex called me. Or we couldn't have grabbed the important stuff and bailed out the way we did."

"Fortunate," she agreed, "but not coincidence. I'd been thinking about Lani's career, the way she came up from nowhere. When Doc and I were in the hospital—that monastery, you know—recuperating from wounds and heard about Lani's becoming Imperatrix, Doc told me about her background."

Garvin's eyes narrowed. "Was that after he learned that he and I were on the Human Rights blacklist?"

"Come to think of it, it was. Is that important?"

"You didn't have to be a soothsayer to predict Liberal reaction when anyone hurt a Marxist enemy. Meaning Doc figured he and I were in trouble with a lot of governmental high-ups, real Fat Boys, and he figured his next move."

"Time for him to walk out of his body for keeps?"

"Keno! Probably told you where to look her up? Her record, I mean, in the files."

Mona nodded.

"Then her history is important, and you took his hint?"

"I lost no time, soon as I came back here, alone and feeling low. If it were simply interesting stuff about genetic engineering or about an unusual life story, I'd figure we have plenty of problems for here and now. But with your being called from exile, and the fix the Imperium is in— well, I'll give you the sketch.

"Lani is one of a few special variations of the Simianoids. There were experimental strains developed by Doc's father—"

"The hell you say!"

"I do say. Lani has genes for extremely long life, not like Doc but far beyond today's standard, and not showing her age. Old man Brandon started, and Doc carried on, modifying and cloning. None of the Simianoid women are pregnancy-prone, but some of the substrains are practically immune. It'd take an act of Parliament to get one of them—you and your low mind!"

"I wasn't laughing."

"You were busting yourself not to!"

Garvin's laughter, an unusual phenomenon, overwhelmed the voice of the storm. "I just pictured the whole goddamn Parliament, those lardass bastards—an act of Parlia—" He broke off in bawdy laughter, in which Mona joined.

"Anyway," she chipped in when she could speak coherently, "you didn't mention an act of God!"

"You blasphemous bitch!" he said in mock horror. "Of course I didn't."

"You weren't raised in a Stomper family."

"Those ignorant fundamentalists to this day don't know that around four or five thousand B.C. the Egyptians had a virgin mother. Isis, you know," Garvin said. "And Sri Krishna had two virgin mothers."

"Not even the Imperial bureaucracy would undertake that trick. But I was telling you about Lani. Doc was surprised when she came back with her son by Alub Arslan. He figured there must have been something in the air, water, diet, or something, that turned up hormones that seldom show up on Earth.

"Anyway, Lani was raised by a conventional family, not Cracker-Stomper, not Testifiers, just stuffy but really good people. Doc made his point. Environment had nothing to do except hinder the critter's real nature. She made her own environment. And the Stompers were happy to turn me over to Doc: I was getting to be a bit lacking in feelings of guilt and penitence."

"So you and Lani go against North American Democracy's religion, and the fundamental creed of Marxism, and of all psychologists, that you're born a tabla rasa, and the first one who starts writing on your blank pages sets your course for life! Only Democracy, Egalitarianism, and Marxism could buy that crap, and they *have* to buy it, or fold up their tents and have their mouths stuffed with dust, as Omar Khayyam put it.

"And you and Lani have real basics in common."

"Oh, you're demented!" Having slipped into something comfortable, her unwitting response by way of seconding her idea that Garvin was three levels below cretin was an effective pantomime: She smoothed out the filmy, see-through fabric, the downward sweep of her palm drawing the garment quite snug.

The Imperatrix was princess-shaped from chin to knee and all the way downward; no one would ever tag her as Madame Broadtail. Mona, elegantly shaped, fitted with exquisite legs, rated a queen-size bra.

"I wasn't referring to architectural specs, and not even to the eyes. Hers are dark and like Isis in temple frescoes. I was referring to emotional quirks."

"Oh. Being Simianoids, wired up for polyandry with at least four husbands, we're alike?"

"In a most unusual way. It was after the beheadings. In the plaza, remember? I had barely completed my remarks on phoning Alex, when you grabbed my hand and said something about last one in bed's a dirty name. If it hadn't been so public, you'd not have waited to get away from the plaza. And we didn't phone Alex for quite a while."

"Mmm...well, yes, I did go rather wild, but—"

"Only once in a busy lifetime." Garvin grinned. "Any other hour should be even half as busy. Except—"

"Except what?"

"I never mention a lady's name, but with Inspector Morgan dead from a hammer whack, Dome Number Five was plenty private, and it was too long a walk from garden to bedroom. Now what were you going to tell me about Lani?"

"It seems sometimes that a female Simianoid is born with a pillow book in her head. If she weren't, she might get too tired, like the standard North American doll. Anyway, in his spare time, Doc practiced astrology."

"For Christ's sweet sake! He believe in it?"

"You ought to know Doc never in his life *believed* in anything. A thing either worked or it did not work. Being a scientist, he experimented.

"He set up a horoscope, and he logged the critical phases of that infant's future. He did not predict details. But he did give the dates of dark and dangerous periods and the times she would rise in the world. He was never so crazy as to predict she would be an empress, but according to the books, that happened when she'd hit a predicted peak.

"Knowing her history, he looked you up, because your lives were interlocked. He did not have your birth data. He could not use the *I Ching* simply because he didn't shape the questions right or because the future had not solidified enough for prediction. His notes are not decisive, not after she became Imperatrix.

"But he was sure that you and Lani were tied together. He simply did not know for how long or what would happen when one or the other died and snapped the chain of destiny, or whatever you want to call it."

"It looks," Garvin said after a long pause, "as if Lani and I are linked. You two young ladies are sort of different—or maybe not. She got knocked up on an asteroid, and you've not been on an asteroid, so maybe you are not so different."

"I've never had four husbands at once, though that's not to belittle Doc."

"Naturally not. Whenever you were too tired, there was one of those Burmese girls."

"Oh, you nasty bastard! I'd've brought one or two along if you'd reminded me."

"Madame Broadtail, we are getting along nicely. I did not bring my three wives. That storm is letting up, and maybe there is some new news."

He glanced at his watch. "Time for a drink before it'll be on."

She mixed her Amer Picon with grenadine and a brandy float.

"Doc used to tell me about the Basque Hotel & Restaurant in Winnemucca, Nevada. They had an annual Amer Picon derby. The man who drank the most of those drinks any time during a calendar year got a prize and a certificate of merit. Doc never competed. It would've been unethical. But he liked those Basques. They were the goddamnedest liars, and they made the best sourdough bread. Using the starter that Queen Isabella gave Christopher Columbus, who gave it to Ponce de Leon, who gave it to Hernando de Soto—"

The broadcast came on. After a rehash of the weather, the news got down to new news: "S.S. *Poindexter*, Greek registry, steaming from Trinidad to Jacksonville, Florida, and for unspecified reasons taking an inappropriate course, noted unusual activity on Calabasas Cay, seventy-eight degrees eighteen minutes west and twenty-seven degrees thirty-one minutes north. Either heavy bombing from the air or massive shelling by a battleship's forty-two-centimeter or heavier guns apparently rendered useless a very long landing strip alleged to have been noted by other passing ships."

Ignoring the drivel that followed, Mona and Garvin eyed each other. "Phoning Alex," he said, "seems to have got quick action."

Chapter 8

FACING THE LIBERAL imitation of the old-time Consortium, Garvin felt as if he were looking back at a former incarnation and wondering what evils he had done to deserve such a nightmarish present. There were sufficient old-timers here to accentuate the mockery. During better days the group had stayed behind the scene to keep the former Parliamentary Democracy and its thought-controlled citizens from self-destruction. Now the Consortium, like the nation it served, was diluted by the sewerage of ideologies, of social doctrines that benefited a realistic minority and befuddled the naive ideologues.

Those surviving from the earlier years looked weary and worn.

No goddamn wonder was Garvin's thought as he approached the conference room and paused in the vestibule for a moment of orientation. He caught the eye of Ambridge with the beetling brows and the swarthy squarish face on which skepticism was deeply engraved in every line. Long ago, Ambridge had doubted everything and everyone but himself. The new order had quenched invincible assurance.

Irvin, slick as ever, was outwardly unchanged except for white hair that prevailed over a feeble black minority.

The smooth face, as amiable as the dark eyes, always seconded the ever-ready smile, expressing unfailing agreement with whatever was proposed, when all the while the indomitable inner man was devising a way of doing as he had planned from the beginning. But Irvin had succumbed.

Then Garvin saw an acceptable newcomer, a man new to the Consortium but bitterly against the times. His presence was the result of one of those political compromises that even an outnumbered Imperator could at times exact. That man was Benjamin "Hardrock" Pike, so nicknamed because of his mining experience—drilling and blasting his way to follow ore veins in quartz and other cantankerous stuff—before he had enlisted in the Marine Corps. Of that honorable body of men he became commandant. Despite the civilian blue pinstripe jacket, bare of all combat ribbons, he did not have to put into words the belief that the object of war was to destroy the sons of bitches before they could outrun you and find someone with whom to negotiate. His face spoke for him.

Garvin stepped from the vestibule. He halted, assumed the exaggerated position of attention taught in boot camp, and snapped an equally exaggerated hand salute. "General Pike, what did you do to get retired? Big enough but not old enough."

"When a screwing is official, you are never too young. After you creamed those Slivovitz bastards, there was nothing left for me to do, so I applauded too loudly."

"Hence the pyramids?"

"Hence the pyramids!"

Although guffaws and belly laughter roared and thundered along the crescent-shaped conference table, there was a marked majority of nonparticipants. Garvin began to suspect that he and Hardrock Pike had committed a social error.

Alexander's entrance checked the buzz and rumble of voices.

He had never been able to enter ballroom, drawing room, or locker room, however casually, however comfortably, without being stately. Any other way would have been artificial. His being his natural self was what brought the group to its collective feet. The most remorseless, most avaricious of Liberals, bleeding the taxpayer dry to buy the votes of the underprivileged, would be thinking, *If I had that bastard's presence, I'd be worth a billion!*

"Gentlemen of the Consortium," the Imperator began, "and you members of the Imperial Parliament who have been so kind as to join us, after bidding you good morning I should present our questionee of the day, a war criminal you have so generously paroled, temporarily, to inform you on Martian affairs, not only on Eck & Ag, but on matters not so handily categorized.

"I take pleasure in presenting Roderick David Garvin, remembered by some as a war hero and condemned by the majority for victory in battle. Others remember him as the first and thus far only space captain to circumnavigate Saturn. Homeward bound, he discovered the first inhabited asteroid.

"I recommend him for advancement to the rank of Brevet Admiral, Space Fleet, with no increase in retirement pay."

In the ensuing silence General Pike's Marine whisper rumbled like the sound of distant bombardment: "Balls! Those tight-assed slobs wouldn't give a carton of issue hardtack to a criminal who won't vote for them."

Grim old Ambridge's brows beetled more than ever as he whispered his reply. "Too busy paroling or pardoning the rapists, murderers, and arsonists who do vote for them."

Garvin followed Alexander to chairs at the center of the crescent-shaped table. A refreshment cart came into view. A member of the Carters Union, seconded by a helper who pushed the cart, followed. The featherbedder, at twenty-seven pazors an hour, was necessary: In the event of emergency, such as the Master Pusher's having a stroke or heart attack, there would be no one to take over.

When the cart halted, the Bartenders Union took charge. A file of white-jacketed servers, one for each member or visitor, set to work.

"Who's that sitting over yonder with his feet on a chair?" Garvin asked.

Alexander chuckled. "That is the Emergency Road Servicer Technician to put on a spare if a tire goes flat. Usually, there is an Electrician to replace a blown fuse, but I heard he has taken the day off, with pay. It is his birthday."

"Electrician? What for?"

"In case the battery-powered mixer for making a Ramos Fizz blows a fuse. Jurisdictional flare-up if anyone else replaced one."

General Pike's ears were sharper than the expression on his leathery face. "Rod," he whispered. "If you joined the union, your brevet rank would get you good pay. They are busting their tails to get the armed forces into the International Brotherhood of Meat Cutters. You can't lose. You pay your dues, you kick back, under the table, twice as much to the shop steward or business manager. And you vote the way you are goddamn well told to vote."

"You seem to know all about unions."

"Ought to. Belonged to one. Talked out of turn, didn't vote right. Two tough guys had orders to take care of me. That was their mistake. When they were at the dead-on-arrival stage, I joined an outfit whose business it was to kill armed forces of the enemy, not unarmed working stiffs. Silly bastards didn't know I was armed, so they didn't make the same mistake a second time."

"Jesus, Alex," Garvin muttered. "I bitched things up, hailing General Pike. Sorry about that."

"Think nothing of it. This is not the Consortium you used to meet. The crescent table is old stuff, but the symbolism is new. As chairman, I've always been in the middle, well, of the table. Still am in the middle, and take that any way you please. Maybe now it means that there is neither head nor foot."

"Now I get it. Can't tell their eyebrows from their ankles.

With basics established, Alexander called the meeting to order. A clerk collected question slips for Garvin to survey while another read the agenda and the minutes of the previous meeting.

"Rod," the egalitarian clerk present said. "The visiting members of Parliament have numbered the slips in the order in which they'd like to have questions answered."

"Number one is from the Honorable Neville Ingerman, Minister of Defense," Garvin began. "His question concerns the Asteroidal nuclear-powered cruisers with directional jets permitting hovering horizontal flight at levels so low that tank gunnery is ineffective against them. I refer to the cruisers whose exhaust blast destroyed a couple of Slivovitz tank divisions in the battles of Kashgar and the Dzungarian Gap.

"The Honorable Mr. Ingerman wants to know how many such cruisers there are, how many are in service, and where they are stationed." Standing, Garvin turned to confront the bland, pleasant man.

Ever courteous, the Minister of Defense got to his feet. He looked boyish, younger than his age. The hand brushing back wavy blond hair enhanced the Boy Scout effect. His slacks of hard-finished gray worsted and his navy-blue jacket of cashmere would never get a second glance from any but those who had bought—or wished they could afford—the like. His genuine leather shoes were correspondingly costly and equally simple.

Not a phony cell among the million billions that made his well-formed body from toenails to hair not too well trimmed or perfectly styled. Having never known other than the quiet simplicity of gracious living, Ingerman's ideal was to be expressed by "transferring" the earnings of others so that the underprivileged, regardless of merit, could enjoy gracious living.

The true idealist would sell his grandmother to the glue factory for hide and tallow if such would further the Cause of Humanity. This man was the Idealist's idealist to the core.

"The cruisers that saved our hides in what was going to be just another border incident are in the hands of the owners. The number is not definite, but my guess is, sufficient to succeed in any mission they undertake. Their speed is sixty percent higher than the best Terrestrian cruisers now in operation. Their home station is classified information.

"Sir, any questions?"

"By whose authority," the Minister asked, "were they sent to the Asteroid? What authority classified the directional coordinates of that asteroid?"

Garvin's voice became smooth, his words as gentle as those of the enemy. "The owner, Prince Alub Arslan, recalled them after their mission was accomplished. The pilots I had trained took them home. The Khan—the prince, if you prefer—has requested reimbursement of operational expenses in the war that his cruisers shortened. Thus far, his inquiries have been heeded as if he were a madman shouting down a deep well. I forwarded those requests."

The Minister looked disturbed. "I must look into this. But the classifying?"

"Alub Arslan, the Khan, classified the information," Garvin improvised, rather than taking credit for his own foresight in having destroyed the log sheets that could serve to trace the Asteroid. "Studying carefully celestial ephemerides and the planetoids listed, noting the ones which have an extremely low albedo and exceptional mass with correspondingly high g, the inquirer has only to explore the whirling junkyard between Mars and Jupiter.

"If the primitive natives were to repel invaders of their spatial domain by vaporizing an entire exploratory flotilla, I fear that the visitors would have no recourse. If the Coalition of Nations risks sending out an exploration party or a punitive expedition, there might not be survivors to confirm my prediction.

"Further questions, sir?"

Ingerman was undisturbed by what might have been deemed sarcasm. "I dislike anything savoring of coercion, but I must remind you that while you are temporarily paroled from exile to discuss other matters, the question of Asteroidal battle cruisers was not contemplated when you were summoned.

"What I wish to convey is that my question relates to a new issue, quite recently called to the attention of an Imperial Parliamentary Commission." He sighed. "It is my duty to let you know that failure to cooperate could be penalized."

I can be as bland as he is and twice as sweet, Garvin thought. "Mr. Minister of Defense, anyone who is about to face an Imperial Commission is inclined to beg that body's indulgence. I came prepared only for questions germane to Martian Ecology and Agriculture.

"With your permission, I'll answer the question posed by the Honorable Harry Offendorf. Although I have not had time for more than a glance at his query, it seems possibly to be relevant to yours."

Garvin's guess had been correct. Harry Offendorf, hearing his name mentioned, snapped to his feet to hear what the questionee had to offer in reply to his penciled addendum. The subject was hot; getting up to fight on foot indicated eagerness rather than courtesy. His status exempted him from niceties of politesse.

Formerly Chairman of the Parliamentary Committee on Public Welfare and Education, Harry Offendorf had risen in the hierarchy. The tall, broad, ruddy, black-haired man was now Chairman of International and Spatial Relations. However, he retained the stigmata of his original office: sincere goodwill made him a dangerous opponent. He truly wished all the world to share his illumination, the satori of all who live in the invisible world of *one world, one language, one government.*

Harry Offendorf had spearheaded the plot to kidnap Doc Brandon and sequester him under guard, to wheedle, persuade, or amiably wear him into surrendering the supposed secret of everlasting life. Before the mission was fairly under way, Doc Brandon, armed with a double-barrel derringer hidden from his captors, had killed the guard and another and walked out.

Doc killed the wrong two men, but in a pinch, it's tough trying to be perfect, Garvin thought. He wondered which two men he would eventually have to liquidate and when.

Aware of the treason at work at every level of the Imperium short of the Imperator himself, Garvin was curious about the boat that had made soundings near Nameless Island. A leak in intelligence? Or had a very high minister secretly commissioned that "submarine sentry" whose crew had lost their heads?

"I take the liberty of first responding to your postscript," Garvin said, "the addendum relating to who destroyed a newly constructed landing stretch on Calabasas Cay. My opinion is that whoever leveled that runway was preparing to take a whack at the Imperium of North America. A broadcast described it as long enough for the largest freighter or troop carrier for an airborne landing.

"For commercial purposes that strip is as useless as teats on a sherry cask. It has only military value. Without ever having seen Calabasas Cay, I assure you that neither Alub Khan nor I had a thing to do with the destruction.

"The broadcaster quoted an official opinion: one or more of the world's few battleships mounting rifles forty-two centimeters bore, or a bomber dropping explosives, could have made those tremendous craters.

"If those prehistoric cruisers from the Asteroid had come near enough to make any individually recognizable craters, the entire Cay would have melted, and the Caribbean Sea would still be boiling."

"Admiral Garvin," the Honorable Neville Ingerman cut in. "You are not being as cooperative as I had hoped. I repeat, your parole is only with respect to questions regarding what you call 'Eck & Ag.' I trust that your attitude will not cause your presence with us to constitute a violation of parole."

Garvin smiled amiably. "Gentlemen, an admiral without pay is not impressive in this socially minded democracy. But if my parole evaporates and the Imperial Government restrains me, His Highness, Alub Arslan, the Extravagant Lion of the Asteroid, a man devoid of any ideals, will send a flotilla of archaic cruisers, and they will fly as low as those which vaporized several Slivovitz divisions of armor, tanks, and troop carriers.

"The exhaust jets are so many thousand degrees centigrade that not one of us, I or my guards, will feel pain. I'll evaporate with you, wherever I am or you are.

"If Alub Arslan, the Gur Khan, is not certain he has vaporized the correct locale, the proper persons, his extravagance will be lavish. Not mentioning names, but there would be a lot of vapor, no matter how wrong the guess. The Marxist tank divisions that vanished were only a sample."

His pause was purely a matter of rhetoric.

"That's buggering them through their oilskins!" General Pike whispered to Ambridge.

"Gentlemen," Garvin resumed. "I should have time to prepare my brief, don't you think?"

The Honorables wasted no time exchanging glances. "Time extended as required," Neville Ingerman answered. "Thank you."

Chapter 9

MONA WAS HAPPY to share Garvin's austere rooms six levels below the surface. Being in Imperial headquarters enabled her to keep in close touch with Nameless Island and her people there. When Alexander invited her to sit with him and Garvin to discuss the spy boat, which had been towed by the Burmese teak loggers to Savannah and then brought by trailer to Imperial Intelligence, she would gladly have settled for a cot twelve levels below ground.

Mona's six years or more with Doc Brandon had given her a broad and at times detailed knowledge of his work, his associates, and his contacts with the micronations that swarmed in the Caribbean waters. Often, in whimsy, he had spoken of his plan to secede from the Parliamentary Republic and declare Nameless Island an independent nation.

"Rod," Alexander was saying, "how far could you rely on Alub Arslan's flying from his Asteroid to get you out of trouble if Ingerman and Offendorf considered you a menace and I could not protect you?"

Garvin eyed the Imperator. "If you *could* not?"

"Rod, there seem to be facts that you are unable to grasp! My so-called awesome power comes to a smooth and silent halt when the Bureaucracy wants it that way.

Each key Bureaucrat rules a subempire, which from each head down to Willie the office boy is Liberal, because that's where the pay and the perks are. If I played being sultan and said, 'Off with his head!' there would not be one goddamn ax available in North America.

"I am a stuffed shirt. Stuffed with what? Get rid of the R and you have the answer. Most of the Army is loyal, being Simianoid, and the same goes for most of the other armed forces. But martial law has its limits. The thought-controlled electorate has become a lot more plastic than it was before the war."

Garvin pulled a long face and then brightened. "It is this way: When the humanitarians and idealists saw molten metal, molten rock, and sand paving the Silk Road where an enemy division thought it was rolling to victory, the Board of Visitors got a case of puking horrors. Seeing the Golden Road to Samarkand surfaced with an alloy of men and metals did something to them. I am not important enough even for sincere idealists like Ingerman and Offendorf to risk their hides to see whether Alub Arslan Khan would back me up.

"I've seen that exhaust blast working. The target is calcined, evaporated before the nerves can transmit sensation. It is the most humane of weapons—hell, you've seen conventional weaponry at work in your package of battle experience. *They* don't know. They've lived sheltered lives, sitting and theorizing, developing pratcallouses instead of battle wounds.

"Those fellows are sincere. They'd face small arms, artillery, machine guns, they'd be first-class martyrs, but I gave them puking horrors!"

Alexander chuckled. "I hope you are right. You're the most insidious son of a bitch since Dr. Fu Manchu."

Mona took over. "Alex, *we* talked a lot. You owe me and us some inside stuff."

"Such as?"

"The first broadcast about Calabasas Cay mentioned superbig naval guns or heavy bombing from the air. Later broadcasts played up the heap-big many-centimeter bores, no mention of air bombing. Now Rod tells us that Harry Offendorf was in a sweat, a last-minute breaking out with a severe itch from wondering whether Calabasas was blasted by cruisers from the Asteroid. Someone seems awfully anxious about Alub Arslan's flotilla. Or anxious to hang something on Rod."

"Or me," Alex added, filling her pause.

Garvin frowned. "When the media focused on battleships, that was to get the Imperium on the hook. It took a lot of work to level off so much of Calabasas. That island is valued by an enemy who has plenty of friends in our country."

"Cause for war?"

"Could be. That note penciled on his prepared question list was a last-minute inspiration. The submarine sentry folks talked landing strip with the villagers. Other people, supposed poachers, had talked landing strip to Mona's loggers. Whether they'd come to fish or to highjack teak logs, nobody'll ever know. Nameless Island is lots nearer the mainland than Calabasas Cay. What island is roughly that distance south of the Cay?"

"Imperial Intelligence could read the Cyrillic script," Mona cut in. "We couldn't."

"For amateurs, you two are doing nicely," Alexander admitted. "But the boat's papers did not help. They traced the engine of that boat. You nabbed the fourth owners. It had been overhauled. The work had been done for people in Bellegarde, Sainte Véronique Island. Used to belong to the United Kingdom, but like our country, the Liberals of the United Kingdom began giving things away and being sweet instead of looking out for their own interests.

"Hence another independent nation, fourteen degrees north, sixty-one degrees west. Go back into your so-called irrelevant historical studies protesting students used to riot about. Not much more than a century ago, the then United States learned that a foreign enemy had been 'improving' Grenada, about twelve north, sixty-two west. A nice pattern of landing fields, and potential supply depots, marshaling bases. Like stepping stones in an old-fashioned garden.

"Mona, your home was going to be the final stepping-stone."

"You're as good as saying that some high officials of the Imperium and their foreign enemy friends were disturbed because your Intelligence got you some embarrassing facts. And wondering whether foreign friends should declare war before the heavy battleships that went to the cay are likely to obliterate Sainte Véronique and picturesque Grenada."

"Fair summary," Alexander replied.

"Looks like we ought to take our thumbs out and hurry up with the unmad scientists," Garvin said.

"Right!" Alexander agreed. "In Doc Brandon's records we found pedigrees of outstanding scientists way back to Nikola Tesla, the man nobody ever heard of. The man who showed the world how to use alternating current.

"He worked for Edison, saw he was only a plodding improver, bailed out, and settled down to inspirational work that goes way beyond mere so-called inventing.

"There are some living today who are in that category, the real operators. Intelligence had never heard of them. Thanks to our freedom of information laws, enemies know more about us than we know about ourselves. But there is an innermost elite, the kind that keep their own counsel and never get Nobel Prizes and stuff."

"Glad that somebody has sense," Garvin grumbled. "I've always been suspicious of the chumps who scream

for academic freedom and exchange of scientific knowledge. Sharing with your enemies."

Alexander nodded. "Like Alan Nunn May, when he
gave our Noble Red Allies every scrap of information on
a really hot subject. That was soon after the now forgotten
Hitler war. Hot subject then—*the inside answers on producing Uranium 235.*

"It was not greed on May's part, and it was not a
glamour girl spy who worked on him. He was not a homo-
sexual blackmailed into treason—the way things used to
be arranged. And unlike so many intellectuals then and
now, he was not a communist stooge.

"May was an idealist who believed that Dr. Ruther-
ford's having done all the essential work in Uranium 235
did not give Britain the right to monopolize the secret. It
was the U.K.'s moral obligation to share knowledge with
a wartime ally. And since his country was not acting honorably, he felt obliged to live up to a higher code of ethics.

"So instead of being hanged as a spy or a traitor, he
was let off with a sentence of forty-two years in prison.
And around that same time, another upper-class English
gentleman, serving in the embassy in Washington and acting as one of an allied commission on atomic energy,
pulled a similar trick."

"I'll be a son of a bitch! Then I've not been far off the
beam about idealists and intellectuals!"

"If anything, you have been guilty of massive under-
statement. I wasted martial law on rapists, looters, and
muggers. It is too late for me to go back to school for a
course in Elementary Dictatorship, 1 and 2." He paused
and sighed. Then a glow of transfiguration suffused his
features. "I'll make up for my errors! Still a chance."

That flash of illumination troubled Garvin; he recalled
Lani's remarks on the skirl of bagpipes outwitting the
soundproof study in the Four Seasons Palace. A desperate

Nero, piping instead of fiddling? "Screw the idealists and let's get back to nonmad scientists."

Alexander smiled. "That is pretty well settled. Nothing for you to do but convoy them to Mars, and guard them against Ismailian agents pushing disguised narcotics.

"You two rate a good rest, and Lani and I would like to see you in private. Come over for dinner, and during cocktails your gear will be moved in with us."

Chapter 10

IN WHIMSICAL SELF-MOCKERY, Alexander called their year-round residence the Four Seasons Palace, since this was a democratic imperium, as Britain once had been. The real article, he often pointed out to his consort, Byzantine or Manchu, would have had one for each season. The Imperial Couple, however, was not doing badly.

The only palace they had was perched on some three hundred hectares of headland that overlooked a moderately historic river's junction with another not quite as historic. The plateau's climate was artificial, with cloud and mist patterns and ultraviolet projection to give foreign and domestic satellites a tough time.

In addition to being restricted, the area presented other problems for planes or space cruisers, whether Terrestrian, Martian, or trans-Martian. The heat radiation from any such soaring menaces had wavelengths between 0.00129 and 0.00173 centimeter, which would be picked up and transmitted to computers that directed the defensive artillery. Knocked out and in flames, the flier's debris—scrap metal, blazing oil, and molten alloy droplets—would by inertia be carried well away from the headland.

Several days after Mona and Garvin were installed comfortably in adjoining apartments in the Four Seasons

Palace, all but a handful of the Imperium's elite scientists, plus those from Canada and from the United States of Mexico, had been moved into guest houses nestled among the oaks and conifers of the headland.

Eileen, the Number One Lady-in-Waiting, had wheeled in the cocktail-hour cart and withdrawn. This was essential because of her close resemblance to the Imperatrix. With such a lovely look-alike, a weary Imperator might inadvertently pat the nonimperial derriere of his unconsort and all the more so if Eileen were standing by the cart, mixing one of the Doc Brandon absinthe drips.

Mona had brought a case of champagne bottles, Rehoboams, each equal to two Jeroboams, each of which contained as much as a pair of magnums. However illegally, she had refilled the empties with Doc Brandon's genuine, no-nonsense absinthe.

"Rod is still halfway between sulking and going mutinous, threatening to burn the city hall, hang the mayor, shoot the clergy, and rape the nuns," a long-faced Imperator was saying. "Meaning in simple language that anyone who imagines he is going back to Mars to Eck & Ag when there is a war cooking around the corner is seriously demented."

"He's in exile—he couldn't stay. Have they blocked his promotion?" Lani asked.

"They've okayed it, and he suggests they shove it! I told him you were going to Maritania as a symbol of legitimate government. That you'd need him as local adviser. Also, as a matter of policy, you should be in Maritania to avoid even a remote chance of being taken as a prisoner of war or being held as a hostage."

Lani wondered what Garvin had said to that.

"Darling, most if it bordered on lèse majesté until he finally became coherent," Alexander told her. "Every important move he's made where you were even indi-

rectly involved, you ended zooming in status. And from
where you now are, how can you go higher? And all the
less so if he went offstage and you did likewise."

"Why not convince him that I am not complaining?"

"He threw the *I Ching* at me!"

Lani was able to smile. "Welcome to the club. I mean
that fine fraternity of people who tried to argue with Garvin.
Don't worry about getting the *Book of Changes* heaved
at you. He's just slept with too many Chinese girls, but
before I forget it, what do the *I Ching* and Taoist philosophy have to do with all this?"

Alexander was happy to discuss anything as rational
as Taoist viewpoints. "When you are flipping the coins
or doing things with yarrow stalks, you can come up with
only two odd numbers, either nine or seven. Or only two
even numbers, either six or eight. The even ones are yin,
but let's not get too complicated—forget them and take
a look at the odd ones, which are yang: power, might,
solar, positive, conquering, and so forth.

"Seven is young yang, an unbroken line of the hexa-
gram, and at rest.

"Nine is old yang, and changing."

"I'm still getting nowhere," Lani said, "though it is not
as incomprehensible as Garvinization!"

"Old yang is as yangish as possible: for the person
inquiring of the *I Ching*, it means that for him, he cannot
be more important, more conquering. When a person or
group or nation gets the utmost possible of a quality, that
excess becomes the opposite of that quality."

Lani frowned. "You mean that for the past century or
so, everybody and his brother was getting more and more
rights, more freedom, until finally no one had any rights
and nobody had freedom? Like when everyone was free
to rape, no woman could poke her nose out of doors
without being raped, and she not only was not free to
promenade unmolested, she wasn't free to take a derrin-

ger in her handbag to defend herself?"

"Now you've got it! And people going to a university were not free to study, because there were so many who were free to smash every window on the campus. Freedom to boo and heave garbage at a speaker whose remarks were not applauded played hell with that one's freedom of speech."

Lani smiled and looked happy. "Now I understand how the excess of a quality leads to the very opposite of that quality. But Rod still has me puzzled. He cannot get out of here any more than anyone can get in. Not even paratroopers—they'd be shot down in flames before their plane got into position."

Alexander shook his head. "All that is true, but he'd not stop short of mutiny. If I ever put him under guard and bundled him back to Mars, he'd lose face, and he'd be useless as Viceroy or Governor-General or whatever.

"Goddamn him, Rod is uncanny! It's his cumulative record. He'd still be on that Asteroid if Alub Arslan's other wives had not been planning to poison you. He got you back to Terra, split-second timed, and became a war hero, making it impossible for Flora to divorce him for having two concubines. And making it impossible for me to marry Flora.

"And here you arrived, the fairy princess, ex-wife of the prince who ruled an Asteroid! I didn't know she was pregnant when she called off the arrangement we had."

"But for him," Lani admitted, "I'd rate Eileen's job. Rod does seem to have you stopped in your tracks."

"He does! Look at his Nameless Island caper! Blundered and did a grand job. I was giving him credit, trying to butter him up a bit, get him into a cooperative mood. The way he handled that spy boat situation—and now he's using that against me!"

At that one, the Imperatrix sat up very straight. "That I've got to hear!"

"The way Neville Ingerman and Harry Offendorf reacted to the Nameless Island project's results, and our navy's shelling Calabasas Cay practically below mean sea level, has convinced Rod that he practically touched off a war that we are by no means ready to fight. And he spoke words to this effect: "When I start a war, I goddamn well stay and finish it. Is that clear?"

"Just restore the profane cursing and swearing, the scatalogical embellishments, and other trimmings, and it is perfect Garvin," Lani said. "And it has you stopped in your tracks." It was a level assertion, not a quiet query.

"It has. And martial law would not be worth a damn."

A long silence followed. The absinthe drips were milky; not a shred of ice remained. The frost that once had coated the glasses was gone.

Finally Lani spoke. "I'll try to talk sense into him. I've done a lot of thinking. It began before you sent for him."

"See what you can do."

Lani drew a deep breath. "It is a gamble. I need a free hand, no questions and no suggestions."

"His wife is the mother of my only daughter. He knew this before I did. And before he married her. No questions."

Chapter 11

THE FOUR SEASONS PALACE had been built well over two centuries before, back in the days of the Republic to which citizens had pledged allegiance and mobbed those who refused to do so. A massive three-story heap of granite, it once had been the residence of a family whose wealth, plowed back, had helped develop the industrial era. That family, like others, facing threats of confiscation by government and redistribution to buy the votes of the congenital have-nots, avoided further penalties by dedicating their properties to the public as showplaces of historic interest.

From their adjoining suites on the second floor, whose center was in a hectare or so of space that served as a library, trophy room, and cocktail assembly area, Rod and Mona could look out through leaded-glass panes and see the guest quarters connected by canopied walks with the guest clubhouse. And there was a polo field.

"Cavalry-style golf is in again," Garvin observed without wondering at Mona's long silence. "So many horse turds elected to Parliament."

Having for some while been engrossed in thoughts all her own, Mona had no urge to comment. Sensing his dark mood, she had mixed Amer Picon with grenadine, charged water, and a brandy float; but aside from kicking off her high heels, Mona was fully dressed.

They had come in from the personal and Imperial garden. With the grounds infested by visiting scientists, neither Garvin nor Mona went beyond the personal precincts. He had not decided whether his notoriety as a war criminal, his fame as a war hero, or his taking the rap Doc Brandon had escaped by walking out of his body and not returning had made the visitors eager for interviews. As far as Garvin was concerned, the first cocktail party constituted life membership, fully paid up.

"Goddamn nearly like being under arrest in quarters."

Her mood becoming ever more pensive, Mona said nothing.

Aside from the family dinner on the evening of their moving into the Four Seasons Palace, they had seen little of Lani and Alexander.

Eventually, Garvin broke the silence. "Madame Broadtail—"

His glance shifted to the gilt snake-reptile-alligator-or-something high heels. That woman was uncanny. Those dainty three and a half things and ankles to match and comparable elegance all the way upward and onward...

"Madame Broadtail, pay no attention to me. If you were not here, I'd be locked up in the booby hatch for talking to myself. Son of a bitch! I'd not be Imperial, not even if you paid me."

"No matter how things go, you and I are not going to be together much longer. First thing I know, you'll be spacing to Mars."

"Like hell I will!"

"Now that I've made up for the long dry spell," Mona said, ignoring the interruption and sighing contentedly, "I can talk about Doc and not feel so deadly sad." There was silence. "I know you don't mind my reminiscences about him."

"If Eck & Ag ever produces broadtail sheep, I'll see that you get the first jacket."

"I'd settle for the fourth one. After all, fun is fun, and you do have three wives."

"They are stacked up as beautifully as you are, but the way you have it all arranged, it's your own special pattern. So you still rate the first one."

"You *do* mean most of the sweet things you say." Mona sighed. "But save a few for your farewell night with the Imperatrix. Before you take off for Maritania."

"*She* is going. I am not."

"That's just what I meant."

"Oh, for hell's sweet sake!"

"I know you're not trying to fool me, but you're fooling yourself."

"Goddammit, woman! How many times do I have to tell you that she and I were playmates before she married the admiral, and that's history. And when the Gur Khan gave me a junior-grade palace, with Lani and her luggage sitting there, a brand-new widow with nowhere to go and waiting for me to take over, we had a cozy talk. She said she'd never shack up with or marry anyone as woman-crazy as I was, and let's not ruin our beautiful past. Now that *that* is settled, you go ahead with Doc Brandon reminiscences and memoirs, and I'd love it. If he had dodged more bullets, it wouldn't have been such a short get-acquainted. He was in bad shape. But the few words we did have, they were—they meant a lot to me. It is as if I had known him a long time. As if he and I had soldiered in the same outfit."

"That's not at all strange. I never truly knew Doc until that last night, the night he, well, died, though it wasn't like other people's dying."

"During your six years with him, more happened to you than you realize," he countered. "It's become a part of you, and you've digested it—well, it's become female substance, and when you dish it out, it rubs off on me."

Mona pondered that one. "Which is as good as saying that you've absorbed my borrowings from Doc and become a sort of clone. Not looking or sounding like him but being practically him, different but of the same substance."

"Sweet Jesus! This is beginning to sound like a Byzantine Christian convention getting ready to settle a debate by burning each other at the stake."

"So I'm silly now! You told me back at the island that when a lover and his girl are really mated, it's as if she'd given birth to him, that he was all new, reborn again. Sometimes I've thought you were talking about us in a left-handed way."

"How weird can we get?"

"Not as weird as you think!" she retorted. "Remember when I began using awful language like yours, only in my own way, and singing that song about 'Three Whores Came Down from Canada,' I wasn't imitating you, I was being myself, as modified by you."

"Next move, you'll step out of the shower singing 'The Bastard King of England' and claim you got it by osmosis! Biologists or genetic engineers hearing your doctrines would end up perching in trees, screaming like eagles."

Then she put her arms around Garvin and got busy soaking his shirt with tears. From the hips upward, every bit of Mona cooperated in weeping.

"For Christ's sweet sake!" Garvin was dismayed. "What'd I say wrong that time?"

The massive sobbings continued. Nails like tiger claws dug through his polo shirt.

"It's not you—darling, you didn't say anything wrong. It—it—it's those goddamn scientists. Those—those—" She groped for higher pejoratives.

Garvin's pause to fumble for an appropriate expression gave her a chance.

"Don't you *dare* ask me whether I was raised in a

whorehouse! I'm just talking the only language you understand!"

Coherent, perfect articulation, marvelous enunciation, but trying to fit scientists into the context was becoming difficult. She was a lot like Flora except that in lieu of improper language, his Number One Wife began hurling Haviland china.

Then came the great illumination: "Don't tell me you're knocked up."

"Of course I'm not! The way I went wild after that head-chopping scenario, I knew I'd be, with the mood I was in. But I'm not, and I'll never be. That's where those scientists come in!

"Whichever of them designed genes for Simianoids wired us up so we don't get that way too often, not even with four husbands. How Lani made it with the Gur Khan—maybe the Asteroid has wild hormones or the right climate.

"And I was hoping I'd have a son to remember Doc Brandon by—or, well, to remember you, you're so much like him, in spirit."

"Now I begin to get it. You are so sure we won't be seeing each other again. But with the Doc Brandon influence becoming part of your makeup and that rubbing off on me, my being so simpatico with Doc, if the scientists had designed you Simianoids properly, you'd be giving birth to a sort of Rod Garvin-Doc Brandon monster."

Mona sat up, bright, glowing, beautiful. "You do understand! My makeup must be a bleary mess."

He followed her to the dressing alcove, and as she repaired the tear damage, he heard the rest of her thoughts.

"Well, I guess I shouldn't complain. This is the only time I ever had any regrets. Doc and I hadn't gotten to the serious stage; it was all fun and games. And there is only one of you, and there ought to be four for anything to work."

"Instead of four of me or four of Doc—Jesus, woman! The entire solar system is not big enough for four of any of us. Be realistic!" She was about to shout him down, but he maintained his right of way. "I'll put the nonmad scientists to work the minute I get them to Mars. They had better cook up a hormone for you so one genius can start you producing a sort of Brandon with the brains beaten out."

"Last one in bed is a dirty name!"

"Wait a minute! That hormone won't be till after the war—"

"This is just because I'm in a happy mood!"

Chapter 12

THE INTERCOM BUZZER sounded. The visitor couldn't be Mona. When he had taken leave of her after a couple of days of farewells in succession, she had declared most convincingly that she would need at least as long to catch up on her sleep.

"Garvin speaking. What's on your mind?" he demanded.

"Admiral Garvin, Her Imperial Highness asks me to inquire whether you are engaged."

"My respects to Her Imperial Highness, and please say that I am not engaged. What's on the agenda?"

"A private audience with Her Imperial Highness."

"Before you publish the orders, would you mind clearing up this admiral business? Didn't know I was promoted. So, no uniform, no cocked hat, no orders and decorations, no sword."

The secretary's voice suggested that keeping a straight face was presenting problems. "Admiral Garvin, it would be reckless to suggest that you come as you are. Would thirty minutes suffice for you to appear informally?"

"Fifteen would be plenty. By the way, isn't she an Imperial Majesty?"

"Admiral Garvin, you may consult the Protocol Department and then let me know. One of the ladies-in-waiting will be at your door to guide you."

Garvin took a second shower to make sure he was wholly rid of Mona's perfume. Fourteen minutes from start, he was pacing the floor. At the even quarter, he opened the door. A redheaded girl about Lani's build was at the jamb. She wore an informal, turquoise, ankle-length gown, white gloves, pearl ear pendants, and a flirtation veil through which he could see that the neck yoke of her gown was high and that a lapis lazuli "Hand of Fatima" depended from her pearl necklace.

Like the mistress, she wore the Moslem talisman to scare devils and repel the evils of human envy.

"Her Imperial Highness's secretary told me that you were concerned about protocol. Please be informal."

Garvin followed his guide to a door that he had assumed to be that of a service closet, but that opened on a short passageway, leading to stairs and a narrow hallway. A second door, opening into a hallway even more narrow and slightly upgrade, evidently was getting close to headquarters: the Lady-in-Waiting locked that door behind them.

The final door responded to touch. Garvin stepped into an irregular pentagonal room whose ceiling was off level.

Lani, wearing a turquoise gown, long skirt, and veil, extended her ungloved hand. "So good seeing you, Rod. Eileen, before you leave, please stand by me."

The lady did so.

"Rod," Lani said. "You've seen me only once at dinner and a couple of times at cocktails, and, of course, that time at Tun-Huang. Are Eileen and I convincing as look-alikes?"

"Imperial Highness—"

"Let's have none of *that*! This is private, and when I speak of look-alikes, you can be sure this is top secret. Take your time and do speak your mind. Never mind how *you* think it may sound. I want snap judgments, impressions, and no matter if you imagine your notions are silly, or offensive, or—well, whatever pops up, sound off. It'll help. This is not for fun."

Garvin backed off three meters. He cocked his head, squinted, shifted, and viewed the women from different angles.

"This is putting me in a nasty spot! It is this way: If Eileen is not perfectly convincing, she'd not be shot at, and you would. If she is a perfect look-alike and you appear to be seen at two distant places at the same time, you're each in danger."

"Rod, give us credit for having figured that out already."

"I asked for that! The only Imperatrix in this country is always veiled in public. If you've checked each other's voices by comparing recordings—I don't think you'd need to compare color photos, though makeup that looks identical in person often films very different."

"So far, so good, and we'll have to compare pictures or tapes."

"Security keeps people from getting too close," Garvin resumed. "Even if your body chemistries are different, there'd hardly be a point in comparing your responses to the same perfume.

"Eileen, you ought to ease up a bit. You're a bit too Imperial. The real article is more matter-of-fact and less majestic looking or moving."

He paused. The women exchanged glances.

"I don't know how long you ladies have worked at this act," he went on. "The only way to make it closer to perfect is to watch newsreels and compare those showing the real article with those showing the stand-in on camera.

"That's the tough test, Eileen. When you're facing cameras in public, don't be too tense, don't be too relaxed. No matter how you feel, you have to appear as though you feel like your prototype."

She grimaced wryly. "And now I'll be watching lookie-squawkie, getting tense every time, wondering if I loused things up."

Lani nodded. "Eileen, you've heard it. Thank you. That will be all."

The door closed behind the look-alike. Lani flipped the deadlock.

Done with professional girl watching, Garvin glanced about the room. "The geometry of this place is cockeyed," he said.

Lani lowered her veil. "Don't try to figure it out. When this old heap was remodeled, things did not come out even."

Garvin noted the bookcases, the bits of bronze, the ceramics; a three-panel Ming screen; a desk, a few watercolors, a lounge, two chairs. The deep-blue, apricot, and persimmon tones of the Khotan rug suggested that the library at Tun-Huang had been looted.

"...so I did things with the odd space," Lani was saying. "My escape from a twenty-four-hour-a-day job. Like Alexander, except his refuge is hot-lined to headquarters and—well, unspecified spots. And almost perfectly soundproofed. So is mine, but I do not practice bagpiping."

Garvin gestured. "That cupboard reminds me of Tun-Huang. Couldn't figure whether it was a bookcase with room for liquor or a minibar with a few books for when you're weary of drinking."

"That's the very one you saw there." She sighed. "Seems years ago! And now all this hocus-pocus! You have it figured out you are not going back to Mars?"

"There was war in the air, has been quite some time, but after that caper at Nameless Island and 'somebody' bombing Calabasas Cay, I'm damn near pushed into the position of having started a war."

"And you are famous for sticking around, finishing any

war you are supposed to have started, when you actually didn't?"

"Goddammit, you begin to sound like those student punks! My view is, first you win the war, and when that is done, you have fun debating with the surviving enemies."

"Standard Garvin, but I thought I'd ask."

He grinned amiably. "Immutable, insoluble, inscrutable—"

"Well, I am stuck with going to Mars. For civilian morale. If there ever was such a thing. But I am leaving a stand-in."

Garvin frowned. "This is getting a bit cryptic!"

"It really is not, not if you understand the plan. Some of it is mine, of course. It's like this:

"Alexander is worried silly about my getting assassinated or taken as a prisoner of war and held as a hostage. So to humor him, I'll go to Mars. Meanwhile, I'll keep strictly under cover while I am there, and Eileen will be here, keeping up the civilian morale. They cannot say the Imperatrix ran out and hid. Alexander can relax—"

"Playing the bagpipe!"

"And winning the war. And if anything does happen to Eileen, she knows the risk, and being a tinplate Imperatrix could be fun, even if dangerous. Well, anyone liquidating her and thinking he has accomplished something—"

"I get it! You'll get on the air from Maritania and shout into the mike, 'Fooled you bastards, don't you wish you were dead?'"

"I'd revise the rhetoric, but in effect, yes, exactly. A phony Imperatrix for a phony brainwashed public."

"So you didn't need my advice."

"Of course I didn't. I am not asking what your plans are. If anything fouls up, you'll know I did not spill anything. This is Götterdämmerung, the twilight of the gods.

Alex realizes the fact—he may have an answer. Whatever it is, I'd rather not know. It might—it *might*—be too horrible to think of, but if my getting out of North America is going to make it easier for him, I want to do that for him."

Garvin pondered. "Doc Brandon made up his mind to stage a banzai charge. Goddammit, draft dodgers *followed* him and Mona. He blew the trap that would have rolled up the main line.

"The enemy tank division got there too late. I polished them off, but they were dead ducks when I hit them. Alex may have an answer all his own. But I am not running out on him. And neither are you!

"You and Alex tackled a losing game. I didn't know it at the time, and neither did he. The country is rotten to the core. A swarm of parasites living off the producers of groceries. The criminal is the hero of the courts because the lunatic fringe gets the brainwashed public sentimentality worked up so that rape, torture of children, and mugging the elderly get parole instead of 'killed while resisting arrest.' When there is a death sentence, a million slobs cry and shriek, 'Two wrongs do not make a right.' Third and fourth offenders are favorites of the gods. Exterminate cockroaches and mosquitos but coddle dangerous human vermin.

"But what can you expect of a nation that kisses the ass of every banana republic dictator, provided he is Marxist! Götterdämmerung, hell! It's the twilight of the slobs!

"I am right in staying. You are right in leaving."

For a long moment, they eyed each other.

"Rod, we've never been in love with each other, but saying good-bye is—" She choked. "But we've shared—so much—it's as if—we had been—"

When they finally let go of each other, Lani spoke first.

"Neither ever realized until right now how we have been linked." She pulled herself together and sparkled through her tears. "No one can get into this refuge, not without a slab of plastic explosive.

"There's an exit to the outside. We have all the time we need." She gestured. "In the room beyond—"

"I've heard those words at old-fashioned funeral doings."

He followed her into a room whose geometry was as weird as that of the boudoir. Lani indicated the keys on the vanity. "In case of earthquake, bombing, or my heart failure, open the little door in that corner next to the shower. In an emergency, get out. Yes, I have a reputation to protect. The happy hooker's thought for Alex and the Imperium."

She seated herself in a dainty chair with frilly, upholstered sides, and legs and back tailored to the final millimeter for height, arm's reach, and the length of the legs she extended.

"Remember how we met in the plaza in prewar Megapolis Alpha?"

"Low sun behind you, cutting through your skirt."

"We stopped at the electronic astrologer's booth before we went to my apartment."

"On the ninety-seventh floor," Garvin interpolated.

"You do remember! And you wondered where the furniture was."

"All the automation did bug me! You just pushed buttons, and things came up out of the floor. And from the bulkheads. Now I'm left wondering which was real, then or now."

"Next morning, I found the horoscope printout. Mine said, 'New friend will lead you in a strange way of living.'"

Garvin sighed. "That was getting acquainted. Parting is something else."

"Who could have predicted our good-byes would be in the Four Seasons Palace, leaving it ankle deep in tears!" Lani twisted about in her frilly chair and stretched her legs. "This time you're going to undress me."

Chapter 13

A LONG TIME PASSED before Garvin stirred. He had been neither awake nor asleep; he was emerging from distress such as neither life nor death could offer. This was a blend of each, so proportioned that each despaired of prevailing, with Garvin hoping against survival.

At last he knew that he was in space, the space of the solar system, not the polydimensional superspace of unreality. His awareness was cued by the harmonics of vibration, the dampings and the augmentations, which he felt rather than heard. The voice of alloy shells, of girders whose compositions were of different alloys, of inner tissues, of other ingredients—all vibrated from the tremendous blast of propellant jets, braking jets, and directional jets as someone guided her to Mars or to the Moon.

Garvin had been out of circulation so long that he could not guess which cruiser was carrying him, although each had her own voice. But presently destination became a matter of total indifference. He realized that he was alive, which he regretted. Head splitting, miserably nauseated, he was dismayed by the horror of survival.

Another blackout was no relief; that damnable drumming came through.

There was a shower in this stateroom, a luxury not offered on the hop skip and jump to the Moon or the space laboratories and their zero-*g* chemical plants. When liquids were recycled to pure H_2O, the end product, whether designated potable or nonpotable, was mineralized and tasted like uncarbonated Napa Springs water without malt whiskey or brandy to redeem the stuff.

"This goddamn shower tastes like protodefecation," he muttered.

He had had no time for drinking, not when an empress extended her legs in an invitation to undress her. In any event, he had never found enough liquor in any one place or time to beat him into the shape he was in now.

"Nothing I ate," he grumbled.

He lurched, grabbed a door jamb, steadied himself, and pitched to his bunk as the cruiser swerved to evade an oversize meteorite.

The intercom buzzer snarled.

"Screw yourself! *Chinga tu madre!*"

When the buzzer rang again, he got to his feet, stayed right end up, and addressed his tormentor. "Garvin speaking, and what the frigging hell do you want?"

"Space Captain Townley Evans, sir. Aide-de-camp to her Imperial Highness, the Imperatrix. Her Imperial Highness sends her compliments and directs me to inquire whether space sickness prevents my delivering a verbal message."

Garvin had a crude, crisp suggestion for Her Highness, but in view of his own first time with an empress, he'd wish nothing of the sort on a fellow Space Captain. "Orders are orders, and we are stuck with them. Come in without knocking. I'm going to be sitting, and I am not going to the door. Give me time to dress, is that clear?"

"Very well, sir."

He looked at what he was wearing. "Jesus H. Christ! Where'd I dump my clothes?"

Garvin lurched to the locker in the bulkhead. To his surprise, he found brand new skivvies and two space officer uniforms, black, with collar insignia but neither braid nor epaulettes to indicate rank. He thought he detected a hint of Lani's bouquet in the closet.

"Son of a bitch!" he muttered as he undertook the laborious business of dressing. "This Imperial Highness situation—we had a good-bye party—she was going to Mars—I was staying on Terra. What am I doing on this garbage scow bound for who knows where?"

The uniform fit perfectly. He decided against the full-dress outfit with its belt and sword. "Probably could draw it, but returning, I'd cut my hand off at the elbow."

He was comfortably seated before someone knocked at the door.

"Come in."

"I am Captain—"

"Sit down, Captain Evans. Did I get it right?"

"Townley Evans, sir. Quite right."

Rather young for his rank, Garvin thought. But the bland, open face was deceptive: the blue eyes saw more than one would give him credit for. His neat chestnut hair was perfectly styled. He was slick aide-de-camp material. And no stranger to the poop deck. He probably didn't have time to sleep his way to promotion, Garvin mused. Too many nice girls right at hand.

"Mr. Garvin. There are still uncertainties as to your rank. 'Your Excellency' would be appropriate, but it is not yet official that you are Governor-General of Mars."

"Call me shit on a stick, but end the suspense!"

"Her Imperial Highness hopes that when you have recovered from your acute attack of space sickness you will be so kind as to attend an informal reception for her staff and for officers not of the crew."

"*What* am I aboard? *When* is it? Just for ducks, *where*?"

"Sir, you are aboard N.A.S.S. *Garuda Bird*, fifty-seven hours after takeoff."

"So I've been cold meat for more than two days?"

"Purely as an unofficial estimate, sir, that is not entirely improbable."

"When is the reception?"

"Plus twelve hours, sir."

Garvin considered. "Captain Evans, all this 'will I be so kind' stuff is a cargo of crap. An Imperial hint is a command. Ordinary death is no excuse for not producing. It has to be *sudden* death."

"Aptly stated, sir. It is almost as final as a suggestion from the quarterdeck."

"I am not a basket case. But someone has to brief me."

"The Master of Ceremonies prompts the, ah, absent-minded."

"Including the senile, the drugged, the semiambulant drunks?"

"Precisely, sir."

"My respects to her Imperial Highness, and tell her that I'll be there. What is the prescribed uniform?"

"Full dress, sir. With orders, decorations, insignia of rank."

"Captain Evans, I do not have orders, decorations, or insignia. As a war criminal, I was deprived of all such."

"Mmmm . . . In such case, allow me to suggest that you dispense with orders, decorations, and insignia of rank. May I offer other suggestions?"

"Yes! Send me the ship's pharmacist or pharmacist's mate, first class, or the surgeon if he condescends to make stateroom calls. Making a horse's arse of myself at an Imperial reception will be a poor take-off for Governor-General Elect or whatever I am."

Captain Evans smiled discreetly. "May I attend to that at once?"

"Quicker the goddamn better, and bless you, Captain."

The surgeon himself came to Garvin's stateroom with amazingly little time lost. He was ruddy, horse-faced, and until he smiled, grim and foreboding.

"What's your problem, sir? Symptoms and the like."

"Not what I ate or drank. A sort of farewell party." Garvin recited the symptoms.

The surgeon checked him with a gesture. "Sounds like bedroom horizontalitis."

"Now that you mention it, that could be."

"No problem. Laid, needled, and rolled. Probably an unethical R and R girl. Very few such, but you must have had too much cash."

Garvin pounced from his chair and dug deep into his hip pocket. He brought out a wad of hundred and thousand pazor notes that would have choked a pelican.

"All the symptoms of a prod with the hooker's friend," the surgeon said.

Garvin blinked. He gulped. "I'm a son of a bitch!"

"I'm Doctor Forsythe." He extended his hand. "Glad to meet a relative!"

Garvin was busy remembering the night he'd electrocycled from Observation Dome Six, on the prime meridian of Mars, to Dome Five for a few hours with Lani. He'd found Inspector Morgan there, trying to persuade her to share the wealth south of her navel. Garvin had snatched a sharp rock and bashed in the top of Morgan's inspection car. The siren warning had told the Inspector that a fragment, a meteorite, had pierced the shell and that the vehicle was no longer safe. As a disciplined spaceman, he had forgotten romance, grabbed his helmet, and dashed out to check the damage.

Garvin had conked him with the same rock and dragged him back to safety, whereupon Lani had jabbed him with the hooker's friend. He'd been out totally for hours, and no handicap to lovers making up for lost time.

For reasons of her own, Lani had used her only resources—female charm and the needle—to get Garvin on the way to Mars. At least the thought that Morgan had felt this wretchedly ill was gratifying.

"Doctor, how about an antidote?"

Forsythe dissolved two tablets in tap water. "It is none of my goddamn business, but you are the first John who got the needle and was not rolled. According to the ship's log, you were carried aboard in total catatonia. How did you get her too upset to search you?"

"Uh...um..."

"Gentleman to the last. Very well. If time ever releases you from noblesse oblige, I'd like to tape the story. See you in Maritania one of these days."

Garvin's recuperation was interrupted two hours later when someone kicked open the door. "For Christ's sweet sake, didn't you see the no disturb card? Goddammit, I forgot to latch the door!"

"I'm Ham Galbraith, Master of Ceremonies. You are to be presented to Her Imperial—"

"That's why I'm trying to rest up. Worrying about it."

"Mister, they all worry. No problem." He dug into his jacket pocket, got out a pad of printed forms, and tore one off. "Here's a poop sheet."

"Expect me to remember all that crap?"

"Never mind the premature ejaculation! I am here to tell you how to impersonate a gentleman at the Imperial Court. If it weren't for etiquette—"

"Screw you and your etiquette!" Garvin broke in. "You've spent your life memorizing Burke's Peerage, and how to address the wife of the illegitimate third son of a baronet, and how he is seated—how far, I mean—from a grand duke."

The crusty face of an executioner who loves his work became soft, amiable. "Screw me pink! I meet so few gentlemen."

"You passed an examination?"

"And it was a stinker! What I want to make clear is little things like bowing." He pointed a stubby finger at "BOWING," listed on the poop sheet. "You do not kneel.

You do not genuflect. Your bow is more than an inclination of the head, but it is not the ninety-degree bend you produce at the coffin of a Chinese dignitary. You do not clasp your hands like when you bow to a goddamn Chinaman.

"Except in a high-grade Japanese whorehouse, the bowing style of a substantial standard Japanese is peculiar. Trunk a bit rigid. A ten- or fifteen-degree inclination of entire body, from the waist, and snap back, smartly but not with a jerk."

"I've never been in any other sort of Japanese groups," Garvin grumbled. "Too bad we can't compare points."

The MC appraised that one. "Before we get to Maritania, maybe you ought to fill me in."

"Listen, friend, your job is to brief me."

"I work from the sidelines, prompting you. Just practice bowing."

Chapter 14

"YOU LOOK A lot better than you did a couple of hours ago," the MC whispered to Garvin as they halted at the entrance of the saloon.

"I still don't think this is going to have any recreational value."

"Sweat the goddamn business out. It won't be long. Let's take a look. Now, up there—" The MC pointed to the dais. "—on the poop deck, that's where the Imperatrix will sit. Everyone else stands."

The high-backed Spanish chair could not possibly be as uncomfortable as it looked, and whoever sat there could not help but be stately, no matter how she felt.

"Those officers and civilians lolling around along the port bulkhead, pretending they don't know you're here, are not snubbing you." He gestured. "We'll sit over yonder. Officially, you are not here. It's screwed things up. The lines were written for a palace, and the cruiser is cramped.

"One thing more: You're still feeling low. Don't for hell's sweet sake leave the salon until the Imperatrix hauls out. Is that clear?"

Garvin and mentor seated themselves. Space Captain Townley Evans gave the almost-admiral a critical look but remained poker faced as if peering into outer space. Without disturbing his perfectly frozen features, he winked and almost nodded.

A bugle sounded attention. The staff, military and civilian, filed to their stations at the steps of the dais. When each was at his post, the soundtrack played "Ruffles and Flourishes."

Two uniformed equerries stepped through a doorway on the dais and stood at the jambs. "Her Imperial Highness, the Imperatrix, " they heralded in unison.

The Empress of North America came on stage. Since this was informal, she wore a silver brocade hood and a silver lamé gown without a train.

An equerry followed. In his upturned hands he held what appeared to be an attaché case of red leather, fitted with a hand grip. A second equerry came after him.

The Imperatrix remained standing in front of her chair.

A color guard marched in and took its post. When the national flag and the nine-phoenix standard of the Imperator were positioned, the electronic trumpeter sounded "To the Colors" as no human musician had ever been able.

The Imperatrix seated herself.

The MC addressed an equerry. "Sir, be pleased to inform her Imperial Highness that Space Admiral Elect Roderick David Garvin begs leave to pay his respects."

The equerry relayed the news to the Imperatrix, and she answered him in an equally conversational tone. He then proclaimed: "Permission granted. Space Admiral Roderick David Garvin will come forward at once."

Garvin had a moment of dizziness that was not caused by narcotic hangover or the failure of Doctor Forsythe's treatment. Undressing Lani in her private apartment of the Four Seasons Palace had been, after all, only a playback of their first encounter, long ago. But just now their leavetaking, supposedly final, became a reality, and for him a new high.

When I reach a new peak, so will she! It can't fail!

The MC's stern grip steadied him.

"Halt."

Whisper and hand pressure checked Garvin at a mark on the deck forty centimeters from the edge of the dais.

"Your Imperial Highness, I have the honor of presenting His Excellency, Admiral Elect Roderick David Garvin, Governor-General of Mars."

Then, in a whisper: "Goddammit, bow!"

Garvin obeyed. He did not fall on his face.

The woman in silver lamé inclined her head. "Admiral Garvin and Governor-General Garvin, we are happy that you are with us. In addition to meeting our staff and a few of our household officers, it is our pleasure to confirm the rank that was conferred by our Imperial Consort in appreciation of your distinguished services for the Imperium."

She gestured to the equerry at her right. Holding the leather case, he stepped to the edge of the dais. The equerry at the left joined him and lifted the hinged cover of the case.

In response to nudging and an unintelligible whisper, Garvin bellied up to the edge of the dais.

From the case, the equerry took insignia, which the Imperatrix pinned on Garvin's shoulders. Next, she accepted a large envelope from which she took a scroll of genuine sheepskin parchment.

The trumpet sounded "Attention."

Her Imperial Highness read the citation for distinguished service in destroying the enemies of the Imperium in the battles of Kashgar and of the Dzungarian Gap.

Garvin, hearing the words, soaked up another shock: *Alex is telling the Liberal sons of bitches to kiss his arse*

*on the courthouse steps at high noon! He's practically
declaring civil war—which means a fight to the finish—
no goddamn wonder he wanted her and me out of the
country.*

Alexander, planning a suicide mission, had gotten all
the nonmad scientists aboard the *Garuda Bird*; Lani, when
she outlived Alexander, would be Imperatrix Dowager
until her son by Alub Arslan could succeed Alexander.

Garvin wondered for an instant whether Lani was pregnant.

The Imperatrix was concluding: "Our pleasure makes
us impatient for you to meet our staff and our household
officers. You will appoint your staff when you take your
post in Maritania."

The equerry returned the scroll to the case. As Garvin
took the proffered case, a nudge from the MC moved him
to a perfect forty-degree bow, and he heard the final words:
"At that time you will receive our personal message of
congratulation and good wishes."

"I thank Your Imperial Highness."

"Our staff and others may now welcome His Excellency, the Governor-General of Mars," she said then. "It
is our pleasure to present him to you."

The Imperatrix and her attendants withdrew.

"Your Excellency," Captain Townley Evans said. "The
cocktail wagon is coming in. Please lead the way."

"Damn high time."

The MC intervened. "Sir, His Excellency had a grim
package of last-minute duties the final few days before
takeoff. For him to have a glass with each of you, which
he would enjoy, would overtax him." Solemnly, he counted
noses. "Quite too many. Gentlemen, arm yourselves and
give His Excellency a break."

A liter of Old Grandmother, Barrel Proof, peeped from
the wagon.

Garvin raised his glass. "Next time we meet, and that'll be soon, I'll be equal to competition. Until then, your good health!"

He heard the MC's hoarse whisper: "Haul ass, Governor! You did well."

Once in his stateroom, Garvin lost no time gloating over his commission, his citations, and his decorations. He found an envelope. The wax that sealed it had a familiar scent: it smelled like Lani, when she was being Lani instead of the Imperatrix. The bouquet that billowed when he unfolded the penned contents was even more so. The script was Lani's.

The tear blurs had to be genuine. Instead of a signature, a lipstick imprint authenticated the message:

> I hated like snakes doing that to you. He doesn't know, not yet, that I did not go. I promised him I'd get you aboard, regardless of your squawking. Do not come back to fight. Those prehistoric cruisers are fast, but not enough for you to make it in time. His bagpiping was not as crazy as I thought.
>
> One single needle jab *has* been fatal. Two shots and they never wake up. He has been the best and the greatest, but my good-byes to you were not faked. One more thing: I am one of Doc's creations. She told me. She had to get to her island before it was too late. Someday you'll start a new crop of people, selected humans crossed with Simianoids; all humans need is the common sense of monkeys and they'll do wonderfully.

Unsigned, but it smelled like the real Lani.

Garvin had a steward get him a liter of Old Grandmother, Barrel Proof. But before he got stinking drunk, he realized that he was fortunate being marooned on Mars with an imitation Lani. After all, he had three wives. Why complicate life?

Chapter 15

THE CITY WAS worth neither taking nor defending. The armies facing each other sought a finer prize: the other's destruction. If Alexander's forces disintegrated, the Marxists invading from the Caribbean islands, supported and led by Slivovitz troops from the heartland of the plague, would surpass the Imperator's armies. Other Marxist forces, coming up out of Central America, would bypass Megapolis Theta and instead move east and northeast to avoid the almost solidly Oriental and Mexican stretch from San Diego to the Canadian border.

Battle had been joined long enough to fill the air with the stench of war, mingling its reek with the fragrance of burning rubber, smoking oil from what remained of tanks blasted to junk, the haze of fumes from guns defending the ridge, and the acrid breath of high-explosive shells that shredded attacker and defender.

Thus far, high technology had held the advantage. Fire control and superior weaponry, from assault carbines and EHV guns—50-millimeter, two thousand meters per second, accurate as a sniper's rifle—all the way to the 44-centimeter monsters on the heights far behind the line of battle, had massacred the enemy. But the enemy still remained in oversupply.

A red sun half below the horizon cast long shadows of

dead tanks and spotlighted the windrows of gray-clad enemies. Small arms dropped them neatly instead of scat-
tering fragments all over the smoke-veiled field.

"No night attack," a gunner said. "And I'm goddamn
glad."

"So are those Slivovitz bastards."

The troops gargled to rid their throats of the chemical
and putrefaction stench and gulped lukewarm water that
reeked of chlorine. They were enjoying the lull in battle
when one, looking back, coughed and croaked, "For
Christ's sweet sake, what's *he* doing here?"

A staff and command car, heading up the river that
skirted the reverse of the ridge, swung to the north and
halfway up the back slope. There, on a spacious shelf, it
parked.

"No stars on that one."

"That's Alexander's headquarters crate. Driver's taking the camouflage off the nine *gubjas* on the side panel."

"What's he doing in a spot like this?"

"I saw him in Turkistan while you were dodging the
draft. He was close enough to get a good look without
binoculars."

"Even with that eagle covered until he got here, we'll
smell hell from the air."

"Eagle, my ass! That's the nine-phoenix brand."

"What's a bird doing rising out of fire?"

"You idiots mock everything you don't understand,
which is about everything you see. A phoenix lives a
thousand years, then cremates itself in a brush fire and
flies up out of the smoke, good as new."

"Sounds like bull to me."

"The Alleluia Stompers and the Testifiers swallow nonsense that's a lot harder to believe every Sunday in their
churches."

"Well, with lions and eagles and stuff, why'd he pick
a Greek fairy story?"

The old soldier snorted. "It is this way. When the parliamentary government sold out to the Slivovitz bastards, it got burned to cinders with a nuke blast. Alexander came out of the fire with wings spread and shot the looters and loafers. Enough to show he meant what he said about no work, no eat. You learned work never killed anyone, though a lot of you clods wished you were dead.

"Anyway, new government came up out of the fire."

"Uh, I get it now, but I still don't like that wagon— it's close enough to draw air bombing all along the ridge. If he wants to get creamed, why ain't he up here with us?"

Alexander's line, snaking along the ridge that blocked the enemy's advance, had cost the invader twice what "the book" declared to be normal. All that the "liberators" could consider an advantage was that the Imperialists were not counterattacking.

West of Alexander's eight-wheeled headquarters vehicle was a low stretch in the ridge. But this gap, however inviting to the enemy, was not being crashed. General Benjamin Oscar "Hardrock" Pike was one reason; another was the division of Simianoids he commanded. Pike, retired because he had applauded Rod Garvin's effective fighting in Turkistan, was restored to duty, and be damned to parliamentary or democratic routine.

Like their commander, the Simianoids were conscientious objectors: They had moral scruples against letting an enemy survive. Three times the invaders had assaulted the gap, and each time too many of the attackers had lived and escaped. Unfortunately, Pike's brigade was not permitted to pursue and destroy: Pike's mission was to protect the flank of Kerwin's sector.

Despite such restrictions, and thanks to the enemy's ruggedness and downright guts, the Simianoids had cut the three assaults to shreds. They had done all but supply the enemy with chopsticks to pick up the morsels of meat and metal cluttering the approach to the highway leading northward toward Megapolis Alpha and the Four Seasons Palace.

Before hostilities had broken out—before, indeed, he had summoned Garvin from exile—Alexander had explained a few things to his Imperatrix: "There's never in our history been an elected president who took to the field with the troops whose commander in chief he was supposed to be."

"Most of them were clowns who started wars they did not know how to finish," Lani retorted. "But some mighty fine commanders were voted into the top spot."

"And lived to be downgraded as presidents. They beat enemies in war, but they could not beat the homegrown enemy: the politicians."

"And so?"

"As Imperator, I am as sad a mess as any elected executive ever has been. Bad as Grant, for instance. So I ought to be a good commander in chief. With enough good generals to do the work."

"More to this than mocking the elected noncombatants?"

"Right. The Canadians still have a fighting tradition. Still have regimental traditions."

"Still have Highland regiments and pipers?"

Alexander chuckled. "So the soundproofing wasn't proof! All right, my incognito jaunt to Canada for Caledonian Games had a private side. I really love bagpipes, and they knew it, and told me to go ahead and practice no matter how much of a pest I made myself. And I told them that when war broke out, I'd need an ally."

"And now you have?"

There was a long pause. "I'll know when they get here and into it."

"Really think they would?"

"They do not want a Marxist plague spot for a neigh-

bor. I mean, many of them do not. Abraham Lincoln said
something about the impossibility of a nation's being half
slave and half free. We are about fifty-fifty in that respect,
the producing half supporting the parasite portion.

"If Lincoln felt that way about a nation, the Canadians
might feel that way about a continent."

Chapter 16

AN ARMY HEADQUARTERS courier wrestled his four-wheel-drive reconnaissance car along the sheltered face of the ridge, going the entire distance from Hardrock Pike's troops to the wooded eastern flank of Ainsworth's division. Along his route, each general or second in command had signed the "I have read and understood the foregoing" line of an order to report to Army Headquarters, observing all security measures.

No field phones. No walkie-talkie. No bugles. Hence the courier. A simple operation but one that left Courier John Priest wondering how to explain General Pike's refusal to obey the summons he had read and understood.

To censor the words spoken would quench the earnestness, the fire, the right-from-the heart intensity of Hardrock Pike's intent. To render them as spoken—well, one simply did *not* use such language in submitting a report to an officer.

The Imperator's conference and map room, where staff officers worked, was in the front quarter of the trailer; his private work and communications room was in the second quarter; and the remainder was his field residence.

Officers and enlisted staff, widely dispersed in the wooded area through which the creek flowed, had avoided the shelf on which Alexander's trailer was parked. A few generals, sensing that it would be bad for troop morale to find sensible—perhaps cowardly—shelter, had their quarters on the shelf, but well away from the Imperator.

One vehicle sat apart from the others, below the edge of the flat space and inconspicuous in the shelter of a few scrubby oaks. There had been no speculation regarding that isolated vehicle. The Imperator's arrival was a large event. The temporary display of the Imperial Phoenix had signified neither carelessness nor ignorance.

"Friends of the enemy," Alexander had said to his driver, "are bound to notice the Gubja Bird and report it to the enemy they love."

The long-faced sergeant, one of the eccentrics who had not ridiculed history as irrelevant claptrap, saw no good reason for concealing his appreciation. "Sir, we are leaking the news to terrify the enemy, the way Julius Caesar used to do when he wore a conspicuous red cape and stood by the eagles of his favorite legion."

Alexander chuckled. "If they only were sufficiently literate, the enemy would follow the example of Gauls and Germans, and panic. But my being here will let them know that this battle is important."

The local commanders had scarcely greeted the Imperator and taken their seats when he went to the door of his private office and reached for the knob.

"Attention!" He opened the door. "Gentlemen! The Honorable Neville Ingerman, Minister of Defense."

Ingerman, an idealist who had devoted much of his life to promoting the welfare of the underprivileged and the culturally deprived, loved all sentient beings except warmongers and sadists such as Roderick David Garvin and General Hardrock Pike. He also hated all who objected to redistribution of wealth.

Alexander gestured. "Mr. Minister, please sit at the head of the conference table."

This break gave Courier John Priest his chance to report, now that he had marshaled his thoughts. Never having heard of the Minister of Defense, he had not been impressed.

"Sir—Imperial Highness—Courier Priest has a report to render."

"Let me hear it."

Courier Priest tendered a paper begrimed with mud, grease, coffee, and drops of perspiration. "Sir, General Pike didn't put in writing why he is not going to be present. He sort of, well, hollered some reasons, uh . . . um . . ."

Having forgotten his censored version, Courier Priest was groping, plainly embarrassed and helpless. Alexander, in his own way, had a compassionate streak that differed from that of Neville Ingerman, the Great Humanitarian. "Relax, Priest. If you can't remember it, use your own words and give me the sense of it."

Priest blinked, gulped, and then licked his lips. "Sir, he said he'd be good-goddamned if he'd quit his post to listen to a lot of junk—he's chewed the socialists to mincemeat three times, and he wanted a whack at them that had the guts to come back for the fourth meat ration.

"He is holding the key to the whole situation, and he and his second in command are fighting a war, and the Monkey Division is the man-killingest in North America. Tell his Highness to: piss up a rope, this is a war and a goddamn good one, too."

Alexander kept a straight face. The others, except Ingerman, tried to but did not succeed. And Courier Priest made the most of the moment of silence.

"Your Highness, I forgot to tell you, he started with: 'My respects to the Imperator, and tell him'—well, sort of like I done told you."

"Thank you, Priest. You have a good memory. You sound exactly like General Pike. You may leave."

Courier Priest left, looking as if he had never realized

what a nice guy the commander in chief could be.

Once the enlisted man was out in the chilly night, the generals laughed out loud. Although Rod Garvin was not a professional soldier, they knew enough of war to appreciate what he had done in Turkistan, and they despised the humanitarian Ingerman who had converted a sort of war hero into a war criminal.

Since this was somewhat like long-ago meetings of the Consortium, which had once worked for the good of North America, Alexander felt very much at home.

"Mr. Minister, you have had an unrehearsed demonstration of the democracy that prevails in this man's army. We are happy that you have come to share our dangers and hardships, however much we deplore the risks you have accepted.

"Our nation is rotten to the core, rotted by a century and a half of socialism. This is the proving ground. This battle may well be the turning point. For decades, we have been half slave and half slave driver, but now we will either be free men again or totally the slave race we have been striving to be.

"Mr. Ingerman, accord us the privilege of hearing your message."

The Minister of Defense beamed amiably, as if the Imperator had not flayed him alive. He rose and regarded the deeply lined faces of officers as weary as enlisted men holding the ridge. A seasoned speaker, Ingerman had learned to pick from a group the believers he would address, and thus personalize his words for each member of the audience. He needed, in addition to himself, at least one other believer. His glance shifted.

Alexander, who could without malice condemn a man to death or, like Garvin, could without unkindness kill a human menace, felt sorry for Neville Ingerman. Since it was not practical to exterminate the enemy, temporary compassion was permissible.

The eyes of the audience projected daggers that, after slashing, after sinking, must be twisted. As professional soldiers, each had brushed aside as childish whimsy the value set on a man's own life, and could scarcely consider an enemy's life more valuable than his own. Amateurs, slimy civilian slobs, had to hate the enemy in order to work well. The professional was devoid of hatred, devoid of pity. The enemy was not even disliked. He was simply to be destroyed.

Alexander knew that not even Ingerman's deadly, undeniable sincerity could soften those faces. Alexander, however, could not sell short the deadliest of all masters, one who believed in what he sought to sell others.

Beatitude glowed from Ingerman's face. His voice rang true, mellow and reverential, when he began. "Gentlemen, thank you. Applause would have embarrassed me. I could not have believed it came from the heart, however genuine the courtesy that moved you."

The upraised arms spread in an embracing gesture. "All—all, from battle-seasoned officer to drafted enlisted man—are driven by the knowledge that however futile it is to win a war, it is far worse to lose one.

"We in Megapolis Alpha pray for a negotiated peace, an honorable peace, so that neither side is driven to victory or to surrender. We implore the Almighty to bless both sides so that fraternity may combine with differences resolved, with the awareness that neither can be wholly right or wholly wrong.

"So that the highest in command on each side has no feeling that he is failing in duty or surrendering ignobly. Finally, that there is neither victor nor vanquished."

This was not organ music with vox humana tremolo. It was rather the Chinese seven-stringed *cheng*, which only a philosopher or a scholar, one who had lived long and fully and deeply, could coax to deep, rich life.

The Imperator was thinking: *That son of a bitch is*

dangerous. He means every word, believes every word. If he keeps this up, he will find a believer.

Alexander Heflin was speaking for himself and for the iron men with whom he had soldiered during their earlier years, when they were winning the start of their hectares of campaign ribbons and decorations. Now they would reject, yet when it was time to put every reserve on the line, each psyche that was warped now might waver.

Alexander fingered the grip of his pistol.

General Kerwin's eyes had softened, and his mouth was relaxed a little, until it was no longer thin as the edge of a saber and twice as hard. And then Alexander saw Kerwin become himself again, having fought and beaten the seven-stringed enchantment.

A flash of whimsy darted through the Imperator's mind: *Wonder how Hardrock Pike would respond to this.*

Alexander no longer caressed the grip of his 11-millimeter automatic, but the touch had reminded him of other options not as dramatic or as scandalous as driving a slug through the fine loop of golden chain that secured the Defense Minister's maroon brocade tie of natural silk.

He could kill Ingerman and declare civil war, or think of something else, and in a hurry.

Duty demanded that as a soldier in uniform he subordinate himself to civil law and authority.

A chair scraped. Men who had not twitched when a shell burst near at hand jerked as though prodded by hot iron. The rasp of wood had torn them from a half trance. Hatched-faced Harrington was on his feet; he had his service automatic at his hip. Trained hand and trigger finger would direct the bullet where his bitter cold eyes looked.

"One more word and I will blow your ass from your appetite. We are here to win this war. We are going to kill every Socialist son of a bitch in the country, and if you're not out of my sight—"

"General Harrington," the Imperator said, "I relieve you of command, and I place you under arrest. We who are in uniform are subject to civilian authority. I am in uniform, you observe."

Harrington holstered his pistol. Being under arrest, he did not salute. He unbuckled his belt and laid it on the table. "Very well, sir."

"Since you are under arrest," Alexander said, "you cannot properly give an order to your second in command. You may, however, deliver my written order."

He fumbled at his tunic pocket. His aide-de-camp emerged from the private office, bringing a notepad with the phoenix insignia and one of the Imperator's twenty or more mislaid pens.

After penning a few words, Alexander handed the slip to Harrington. "My compliments to your second in command. General Austin, I presume?"

"Very well, sir."

Leaving the belt and pistol he was no longer entitled to wear, Harrington stalked from the conference. A door slammed.

"Mr. Ingerman," Alexander said. "I apologize for this unseemly and grossly unmilitary interruption. At the same time, I must suggest with all respect that you absent yourself from the combat area at once. Without attempting to condone General Harrington's offense, I must warn you that a soldier less disciplined might fire first and express indignation later. Officers and men under fire are prone to forget political theory."

"I cannot quit my post and my duties any more than General Harrington can forsake what he earnestly believes," the minister countered. "I am aware of the danger of my position." He meant what he said; he was genuine.

Alexander drew a deep breath. "General Ainsworth, be so kind as to remove my shoulder insignia."

Ainsworth did so.

Alexander beckoned to a brigadier general. "Timmie, pull my belt."

The one-star officer stepped up to disarm the Imperator.

Alexander peeled out of his tunic and handed it to another BG. "Red, take charge of this. May need it soon."

Neville Ingerman was perplexed. Glancing about, he saw only menacing faces: the silent contempt that once had been, but no longer was, a military offense. If he lived long enough, he would demand revision of the Articles of War.

Ingerman peeled out of his cashmere jacket and flipped it to a chair. He lost no dignity standing there in shirt-sleeves.

Alexander took the discarded jacket. "Mr. Ingerman, let me assist. Please get into this garment. This is not going to end in fisticuffs! I have killed too many men in battle to have any taste for loutish brawlings." He smiled winningly. "As a retired professional, I could not ethically challenge you to a meeting with man's weapons. Furthermore, the Articles of War prohibit such."

The officers waiting on the Imperator were not at attention, but their silence and rigidity made it seem that they were.

"Divested of uniform jacket, insignia, decorations and orders, belt and side arms," Alexander continued, "I am now a civilian. As Imperator of North America, the ultimate authority, I command you to leave this area at once. Please spare me the awkwardness of putting you under civilian guard.

"The Provost Marshal has a staff of Imperial Marshals to arrest civilians not immediately dangerous, and thus not liable to court-martial and immediate execution if found guilty."

After a long silent confrontation, Ingerman said, "To

avoid an awkward clash, it is my duty to waver from duty and to defer to civilian authority. But before I take my leave, may I have a few words with you in private, perhaps a written memorandum to justify my withdrawing from my tour of inspection?"

Alexander opened the door to his private office. "Please wait a moment while I dismiss my staff and other officers."

Once the door closed behind the Minister of Defense, Alexander said, "Gentlemen, I summoned you only because of our distinguished visitor and his high status. While I am putting on my tunic, my insignia, and so forth, and resuming my pulled belt—" He glanced about and picked his man. "Red, tell General Harrington that he is released from arrest and restored to command. I'll confirm it in writing. Tell Hardrock Pike he was quite right even if a bit insubordinate.

"Go ahead and win this battle, while I cope—" He gestured. "—with intangible enemies."

Chapter 17

ALEXANDER'S AIDE-DE-CAMP OFFERED his chief an official envelope. "Sir, an Amazon sergeant with credentials that got her a parking space quite near your trailer gave me this. I would not have disturbed you, but the imprint—" He indicated the embossed gilt circle in the upper left corner. "—looks like a Turkestani emblem: nine yak tails. The script stops me. Ethiopic or Armenian, purely as a guess. We tested it with infrared, but the way it was folded, we couldn't make much of the message. As a matter of routine, we used x-rays, laser, and finally compression to see whether it'd explode. With your permission, I'll open—"

"Thank you, no. It's time I begin accepting nonexistent risks. For starters, I might question the courier and see how she contrived to commandeer a trailer and park it so near mine."

Apparently security had been so busy checking for danger that no one had noticed the hint of Lani's perfume. When the ADC ushered Lani into the trailer and departed, Alexander was not surprised that however little his visitor looked like an Imperatrix, she smelled like the only one in the known world.

Unveiled in public as she had never been, from her first official appearance until she had quit Four Seasons

Palace, wearing defeminizing makeup and permissible earrings, she was a most un-Imperial frump.

"One of Rod's semilegitimate friends made the seal and the rest of the documents," she said. "I think the text is Armenian, and the seal, that's nine yak tails, stylized, and Ethiopic characters from a collector's stamp of Menelik's time. Naturally, nobody dared admit he'd never seen anything like it. Hamlin Daly says his productions are better than genuine."

"Probably are. And when he undertakes a ticklish job, he forges a habeas corpus, or whatever is needed to release him. In advance, I mean."

"Lover, you still don't believe I am really real."

He came close and whispered in her ear. "I'm almost sure that the trailer is not bugged, but until I have it rechecked, we'd better go to your wagon."

Alexander snatched a belt and a holstered pistol, flung a dark cape over his shoulders, and stepped to a side door.

Lani pointed. "Yonder, near that clump of scrub oak."

Once within the road-muddied vehicle, Lani snapped on the bluish lights. As his eyes became accustomed to blackout, Alexander picked out the field desk, Pullman bunk, and ultracompact shower and accessories. The galley was tiny. There was a lot of cargo in crates. The field desk was anchored to the deck. The two chairs were not secured.

She snatched a bottle from the galley and poured dollops into paper cups. "Oh, quit looking at me that way!"

"What way?"

"So puzzled."

"Your look-alike, in the New Palace, Maritania. What a job of planning, arranging! And look at you, after all your practicing to walk and stand like an empress!"

"Am I really as awful as all that?"

"If I didn't have so many memories of earlier days, I'd

be running and hiding in the woods. What the hell brings you here?"

"Trickery, latrine rumors, gossip, female intellectuals' chitchat when they didn't know who they were talking to. Testing my disguise, you know. Some Amazons are attractive undressed. Some are sleeping around with loyal generals, and others with members of Parliament who have sold out to the enemy. Oh, it's a mess!"

"Your being here is the only surprise. Intelligence briefings are longer, but yours is more pointed."

"I can't prove a flake of it. But Neville Ingerman is out to promote 'understanding' and 'basic humanitarian principles' and 'the humane idealism which can and must prevail.' Meaning a negotiated peace, with the enemy taking all the chips."

"That son of a bitch tried to snow a staff meeting an hour ago."

"That's his dish! He's a true patriot. I'm not being funny! He believes that selling out his country will save it."

"You're anything but funny!"

He sketched the conference and its termination. "Kerwin stood fast, all day, holding the line. Murdered two waves of tanks. Hardrock Pike—he cut the conference, sent me a snotty message saying this was no time for talk. Too busy getting ready to massacre the enemy that escaped his first counterattack."

Lani nodded. "I drove along the river, or is it a creek? It's a long line they're trying to crack. Which they have to, or bust."

"Which is why I'm here. The generals are doing the work. I never commanded more than a battalion. I'm for troop morale."

"You suppose Ingerman is here to pick the moment when Kerwin is hurting seriously, and Pike and Hatchet Face Harrington are worn out before they get the enemy whittled to size, and then call for a truce, a parley, or something?"

Alexander's sigh testified to the weariness of his days and his nights. "Foxy and foolproof. So reasonable, you know. And the troops are tired, the new ones especially. A rest for talking, and they'll cool down. Getting them fired up again, they'd have to limber up, once they feel their aches.

"Meanwhile, the divisions rolling in from the southwest could get between us and Megapolis Alpha. You're here to tell me to watch out for a giveaway truce?"

"Alex, I've got no facts you can use."

"Then why are you here? You never looked so good! I had reasons for sending you—trying to send you—to Mars."

"I had mine for not going."

"Don't get out of that uniform until you've told me why, and be sure you make it good. I can't afford to have you in North America. Someone might recognize you, and if you were a prisoner of war, a hostage—"

"The enemy would bend you into line?"

"The Veiled Imperatrix, the Glamour Empress, the Girl of Marvelous Mystery—the idiot public would revolt. I'd lose the considerable support that I have. The North American is a sentimental imbecile incapable of saying, 'Carry on and win the war.'

"This woman-ruled nation, this land of Momism! Martial law checked looting, public rape, even drove lard-bottom bastards to work, but—are you crazy? They could win the war if they had you as a POW."

"You sound like Rod Garvin! Why not have him send for the flotilla of destruction sprayers to incinerate these whelps?"

Alexander shook his head. "The cleanup at Kashgar was backed up by the submarine fleet that obliterated the one important city in Slivovitz Land. Civil war, assassinations, and Moslem revolts in the Caucasus and all the way into Mongolia did critical damage. Now the Moslem world has written us off.

"And as long as the enemy does not use tactical nuclear weapons, I could not put Rod to work. Finally, fast as they are, those cruisers are on an asteroid—the Asteroid—a far piece from Mars. Before they can get here to nuke the enemy out of existence, we have to win this war, or lose it."

Lani was not as dismayed as she should have been. "Well, that does take care of Admiral Governor-General Garvin, autocrat of Mars, ruling the Red Planet and three wives, and with an iron hand, whenever he isn't sleeping with the Imitation Imperatrix."

"Goddammit, woman! Why this idiotic risk?"

"I sensed that the last chip was on the line. I wanted us to have a final honeymoon before our world fell apart. That was most important. But there was another reason."

"Before you get out of that rape-preventing uniform and slip into something comfortable, make *that* reason clear!"

Her voice and eyes were sweet mockery. "If you really cannot wait, close your eyes. The perfume is genuine Martian Mist."

"Don't waste too much time!"

"Alex, you are here because this is the last roundup, the end of the trail. For you or the enemy, it is payday. Our country is rotten to the core, and I am full to the brim and puking over.

"You are not King Arthur, and Ingerman is not Mordred, your son by your half sister. But this is *our* Barham Down, our last battle, not with honest enemies but with traitors, homegrown."

He caught her by the shoulders and thrust her from him. "So you're here to talk me away from it."

Lani broke from his grasp. Though he drew back no

more than a centimeter, the gap felt like a kilometer. The Amazon frump was an empress with nothing lacking but a nine-deck parasol and a standard with nine phoenix— or nine yak—tails.

"Alex, darling, I am here to stay. I am not leaving until you leave. My look-alike is doing a beautiful job."

Having dealt with many people, Alexander was slow, but finally he understood. "This is a finish fight, and *therefore* you came here, and *therefore* you will not leave."

Lani's accumulated weariness dissolved as an inner glow made the surface radiant. "Lady Wu," she said, her voice soft and happy now that she knew that he knew, "escaped from a Buddhist monastery, became empress of China, made the T'ang Dynasty greater than it had been. She died of old age and whoring around before she could set up a new dynasty all her own.

"Theodora, the after-banquet fun and games girl, married the Imperator of Byzantium. She was empress in form until he and she faced the mob that came to kill her and him.

"Instead of backing down, she said to her husband, 'Once you wear imperial purple, you can die wearing it, but you cannot take it off. It has to be your shroud.'

"Loyal troops, arriving in time, dispersed the mob, and until *her* final breath, Justinian was emperor in form and *she* was empress in fact."

Alexander looked renewed and years younger. He hammed a Roman gesture of salute. *"Ave, Augusta! Morituri—"*

"Morituri be damned! You'll bugger them through their oilskins, and they'll furnish the barrel to bend over.

"You and I are in this up to our chins. If you pitched a circus tent over North America, you'd have one magnificent madhouse of idealists, narcotics addicts, courts that love criminals, parole boards that turn child rapers and child killers loose to do it again, with recidivism hailed as advancement!

"You are not running out. You have become too real to quit." Lani dipped into her droopy tunic and produced a chrome syringe. "One jab and an enemy is out. Two jabs and he is dead. For self-inflicted wounds it is perfect."

The Imperator blinked and then passed his hand over his eyes.

"Get out of that uniform and never mind slipping into something comfortable. Time I found out what it is like with an empress."

Chapter 18

ALEXANDER'S ARMY FACED southward, holding eight or ten kilometers of ridge that overlooked rolling terrain seamed by dry runs and dotted by clumps of oak and scrub. Massive desertions, occurring during preparations to block the road to Megapolis Alpha and the nearby city that nobody wanted, had left the army with a fighting Simianoid division, seasoned regular army forces, and a substantial residue of drafted men who responded to good leadership.

Three-star General Dennis Kerwin was in command. From the experience of commanding a battalion, Alexander had learned that the handiest way to lose a war was to have an army subject to a civilian commander in chief.

"Dennis," he said to Kerwin, "a civilian C in C is almost always a chap whose only talent is getting votes by charming an electorate as ignorant as he is. Meanwhile, it would be a good idea for us to discuss matters of general policy. Or supply problems."

"How about updating me on policy?"

"No change. Do not use nuclear tactical weapons unless the enemy does so. Destroy the enemy or see the nation finished. There is not enough transportation for escape to Mars. Our job is to exterminate the liberators—this first installment, I mean—and give Martian Mining, Manufacturing, & Tech time to build up a defense and, finally, a counterattacking potential.

Dennis Kerwin eyed the C in C: grim, gray, and sharp-eyed, this was the man whose presence made the highest ranking officer the number two man. His squarish face made him resemble a sculptor's preliminary sketch of the son of a bull bitch and a battle-ax. Then the sun-blasted face became amiable.

"Sir, I am happy to meet an optimist," the general said. "I have heard nothing but long-faced crap about the entire world's trend toward socialism, the wave of the future. With the nonmad scientists you herded to Mars, there is a chance that MMM&T will have time to cook up weaponry and accessories to blast the believers out of their opium dream, the silly-ass notion that a man's going to bust his tail to earn enough to support several lardass loafers."

Behind and north of the defenders' line, well beyond the creek and the wooded area near which Lani's trailer was parked, a horseshoe-shaped formation rose from a stretch of open country broken by dry runs, swales, and wooded patches. The tips of this crescent tapered off instead of joining the distant rocky palisades in which the heaviest army artillery lurked, with lighter guns to blast such invaders as might turn the flank of the Imperial line and drive northward to Megapolis Alpha.

Air Force and satellite reports were keeping Kerwin's headquarters busy. Infrared sensors picked up the heat radiation of armor and aircraft. Projectors searched the gloom with IR beams. Screens converted those invisible rays to visual images.

Satellites projected the scrambled images of distant armored columns, of troop carriers, "sightseeing buses," coming out of the deserts and mountains of Arizona and

New Mexico. Computers extrapolated the probable path and progress of the Liberators on their way to reinforce General Igor Kuropatkin's army, which had been brought to a disastrous halt by Kerwin's battered troops.

On each screen there was a calculated point. As images of leading enemy units, some a good three thousand kilometers west of Alexander's line, neared their predicted points or overshot them, actual time, distance, and bearings were fed into computers, and new prediction points were established. Bit by bit, intelligence reports on the enemy contributed to convert plausible into probable direction, progress, and plans.

Alexander's silence heartened the technicians. He was busy seeing the war as tridimensional chess on a board bounded by two oceans. He had no suggestions on how the general should wage the war. Counting each military unit of regimental size as a pawn and larger outfits as pieces, he knew as never before that a civilian chief executive who fancied himself as commander in chief was the enemy's best friend.

Late that night, when Alexander broke from his round-the-clock vigil, Lani said, "You look as though you'd won the war. Experts give you some happy answers?"

"Better than that! I quit the chess game and talked to a farmer who complained about stray shells scaring his cows and cutting down on the village milk supply."

"Couldn't he move his cows and family?"

"I remember, ages ago, we were getting artillery practice. Missed a target on Mount Boracho and dropped a two-hundred-ten-millimeter shell a hundred meters beyond where Stinson Beach quit and the Pacific Ocean began. No swimmers or recreation boats were hit. Too many hands fooling with the deflection adjustment."

"Quit holding out!" She sniffed. "Battle stink blended with Martian Mist. No trace of the GI cologne that dissolute and immoral Amazons splash all over strategic areas."

"Her'n or his'n?"

"Oh, you bastard: Tell me about the farmer."

"He was perfect except for chewing Copenhagen snuff instead of Miners & Puddlers. I told him to watch trifles like that. If the wrong people notice such a boner, I might have to find a new operator."

Lani made a slicing gesture just below her chin.

"Right! The enemy sends operators from the big cities, probably intellectuals majoring in social studies and dramatics. Anyway, this intelligence man said he'd take my hint, but this time he'd been just plodding along, minding his own business. All of it night work."

"So there was a farmer who had a daughter?"

"Confidentially, there were Canadian troops, wearing Imperial uniforms and marching by night. Enemy satellites and planes would miss them. No motor transport, no IR radiation. The only risk they faced was from the ground. Being fired on by National Guard units."

"Not really!"

"Devilish confusion. Snafu prevails. Between enemy-owned outfits and trigger-happy loyalists, it's almost as sticky as a civil war. COs are firing from ambush at National Guard companies."

"Conscientious objectors?"

"Well, of course! Darling, you'd led a sheltered life until now. Pacifists bombed a university science building because there was research suspected of being war-oriented. Nobody in the building but three or four mathematics students, all killed. The bombers said they were political activists and couldn't be tried as criminals. Highest court sustained their plea.

"And the conscientious objectors who fired on National Guard warmongers had a similar demurrer: Sure they fired, but it was not a crime, it was political activism."

"The courts sustained *that*?"

"Get out of your dream world! You're the most innocent girl I've ever had. The NG fired back, did a better
job. Killed a few, wounded a few, captured some. They
hanged the wounded and the uninjured who couldn't run
fast enough. Ran out of rope, so didn't hang the dead.

"And marched on, real warmongers. There is still a
grain of hope in the land. Some of the civil disorder really
helps free people to carry on against organized treason."

"Don't forget the Canadians, darling."

"This imitation farmhand looking for a job as a hay
pitcher or a teat puller—on a dairy, of course—saw them
forming for muster. In their own country. And, of course,
for war games. Glenlivet Fusiliers. Islay Guards. Glen-
fiddich Grenadiers. To make it look traditional, for the
newshounds and so forth, they all turned out wearing
kilts, and each outfit had its pipers."

"Pipers? Not really!"

"Really, and not for the media. For business. They
changed to our uniforms, of course. We had so many draft
dodgers that there was an enormous surplus, and a supposedly corrupt QM officer outfitted the Canadians. Little
chance of the shortage being noticed."

"Now why not admit that their taking bagpipes along
is part of a grand feature story. Or would that be too
crazy?"

"Not as bad as your staying here!"

"Alex, this isn't Caledonian Games! They're on their
way to help us decontaminate—delouse—North America. This isn't the Kaiser War when the White Watch and
the Hotstream Guards routed crack Prussian regiments."

"Evidently you never heard of the assault at Dargai a
couple of centuries ago."

"I'm not as old as all that!"

"You must be to be so bitchy-smart! Mix us a drink."

"Not unless you tell me about Dargai!"

"British outfit on the way out of Afghanistan, going to join a division needing reinforcements for oppressing poor but honest border bandits.

"A tough pack of mountaineers held a mud-brick fort on a summit, way up a steep slope. They broke up two assaults. A lieutenant said to the Important Man, 'Sir, if we mounted an attack with two regiments, all out, there'd be a lot of us the bastards couldn't kill. So we'd exterminate them, you know.'

"This made sense. The general had a Highland regiment and a Gurkha regiment. The Scots were the world's greatest fighting men. Then the command: *Officers and pipers to the front!* Each regiment a challenge to the other. The bright lieutenant survived but was not so tactless as to say, 'What'd I tell you!'

"The assault cleared the pass. The troops marched to the rendezvous, getting there on time, and with the skirl of pipes."

Apparently Alexander had done a lot of homework in Canada.

Chapter 19

A HARD-FOUGHT NASTY day: chilly drizzle and drifting fog hampered observation from ground and air. The Liberators tried to turn Alexander's eastern flank, and on the face of things it seemed that they had worked on inside information. Perhaps they had. But, though correct to the minute and to the meter, the apparently brilliant coup was a failure.

The Imperial tanks that burst splendidly into tall flame and billowing smoke were dummies. The attackers bogged down in traps that held them until the 420s on the far-off ridge blew them to fiery junk. Artillery from the Imperial right enfiladed those who tried to retreat.

So few succeeded that Dennis Kerwin shouted, "Coffee break!"

The general's grin was convincing. He did a grand job of keeping staff and other officers from suspecting that he was concealing something bordering on worry. Kerwin got the Imperator into the raw, blasting wind of the great unbugged outdoors. There he shared his suspicions.

"I still say, a fine day's work," Alexander replied.

"I still do not like it. That drive against Pike was a feint. The objective: to break through and turn our left and hold us long enough for their main body to get well on the road to the capital.

"They were betting on information that had everything but one nasty little fact: that from the start, we had had traps deep enough to stall armor, and dummies with fuel to set off a grand blaze, shell blasts, and trimmings."

Alexander frowned. "Firm information or just a hunch about a leak from our side of the fence?"

"Whatever you call it, it jibes with some regimental commanders who are not as glowingly happy as they ought to be. The enemy was too damn sure he could not lose."

"Denny, keep going this way and learn the art."

"My staff is busting its collective tail to analyze scraps of fact and see how they tie in with hunches. Next coffee break—"

A staff sergeant interrupted. "Sir, the enemy commander, General Kuropatkin, would like to speak to the Imperator. He is on hold."

"Sergeant Billings," Alexander replied, "the Imperator has not been available since—oh, hell, since we started a junkyard of Slivovitz armor. And now that clown tries to go over General Kerwin's head. Denny, the sergeant's boss wants to hear from you."

Kerwin took over. "Sergeant Billings, my compliments to Colonel Whitfield, and say I would like to have him rig a circuit so the Imperator can listen in. If he wants to comment, it must be as though we were in touch with him at a spot rather distant from here. Tell General Kuropatkin I am taking a coffee break. Will call him presently. Meaning when Colonel Whitfield has made the arrangements I want."

"Sir, Army Signal has already made such an arrangement."

"Very good. I am still taking a coffee break."

"Coffee keeps me awake," Alexander said. "Let's look at the screens and get a satellite view of things."

"I'm another insomniac," Kerwin declared. "Keep

that son of a bitch waiting while we find out if the staff has confirmed or negatived my hunch about the enemy's getting too much information from our side of the fence."

The staff had a recommendation: army to corps to division, and to regiment, written orders only, from commander to subordinate. Regiment to company, usual signal corps communication.

When Alexander and Kerwin had time to call the Slivovitz general, he was, as anticipated, taking a coffee or vodka break. During the face-saving delay, Kerwin got a message from staff. But before he could discuss an elaboration of security measures and opinions, General Kuropatkin was on the wire.

After formal courtesies, the invading general said, "Yesterday and today our armies acquitted themselves gallantly. You and I and the Imperator can honorably discuss the situation."

"His Imperial Highness," Kerwin answered, "is not present."

"With your most modern communication facilities you could make His Imperial Highness a party to a three-cornered conference."

"I could, but I do not care to do so."

"I could," Kuropatkin countered, "arrange for my supreme commander in Slivovitzgrad to take part in this conversation. He and His Imperial Highness could communicate while you and I stand by, to give details as required."

"I have all required details," Kerwin retorted. "The Imperator has ordered me to destroy your invasion force. He said nothing about debating. I am fighting until my mission is accomplished." He paused and then continued amiably: "If you have something to say, I shall hear it with interest."

"General Kerwin, you are relying far too much on your Canadian allies."

"If we had had allies today, we would be pursuing the survivors of your army. When we have dealt with you, we move to our capital, where you have more friends than you have in your entire empire."

"Since so many North Americans are friendly is precisely why I requested this parley. We do not wish this rich and beautiful country to be harmed. The land is more important than the individuals who live on it. If we must fight, one army destroys the other, if they do not destroy each other. So let us spare the country. Armies are easily replaced. Land never is."

"Spoken like a soldier, General Kuropatkin!" Kerwin's applause was hearty. "The only question is, How do we spare the land?"

"Neither you nor I will use nuclear weaponry."

Kerwin demurred. "You and I can bind each other, one professional soldier to the other, and for this battle. Perhaps for this campaign. You cannot bind your country. I cannot bind mine. You and I agree, no nuclear weaponry on either side. Neither tactical nor strategic. Is that understood?"

"That is understood," Kuropatkin answered. "Tomorrow we destroy each other without nuclear weaponry."

"Nice work if we can get it. Over and out." Kerwin hitched about and addressed the Imperator. "He may mean what he says."

"You are congenitally skeptical. Do you smell a booby trap?"

"If they fling tactical nukes at us, we'll field-test some of ours. What he said about not devastating a rich country, he spoke total truth. Under the czars, the empire exported grain. Under Marxism, they import from us to make up for what their system cannot produce. Of course they'd love to take over a country with American puppets to keep the socialist fieldmice from starving."

"So," Alexander persisted, "no risk of nuclear weapons?"

Kerwin shrugged. "Socialism is a religion. No matter how smart a religionist is in everything else, he is a pure fool where his creed is concerned! Every Sunday, some of our brightest scientists recite creeds that would get them into the nearest insane asylum if they spoke their lines during the other six days! There is only one answer."

"I can guess."

"You've already said it: Exterminate them. The alternative is national suicide."

Chapter 20

A RAW, NASTY dawn of drizzle and mist, each chilly and short of freezing. Enemy armor roared its course, swerving to avoid shell-blasted wrecks, outcroppings of rock, and the enormous craters made by the 420s high up on the granite palisades. The left stood fast. So did the center. Hardrock Pike, on the right, patiently stood fast, fighting for the big event, the counterattack and pursuit.

Security had been tightened, and lest the enemy wonder at an abrupt radio silence, the air was riddled with junk messages relating to the action but giving the invaders nothing of value.

Rocket teams popped up from trenches and broadsided armor; other teams, working downgrade from cover to cover, plastered the enemy with shaped plastic. Gunners in the trench network hosed the troop carriers that no longer had protection.

Assault carbines nailed whoever got clear of his crippled vehicle.

A busy day, but the enemy's superior numbers made it tough going for the defenders. When an attack wavered or was simply shot to shreds, a fresh column came storming up, roaring and eager. And the men holding the ridge were just as tough: Retreat, they knew, would be more dangerous than facing the fire, and never mind whose finish it was going to be.

Alexander, declaring that for him to jeep or cycle along the line could make him a conspicuous target, stretched his long legs to stalk through greasy red clay. Although he had taken off his insignia and was wearing a tin hat, he looked commanding and stately.

Kerwin, sloshing along, came to a halt. "Goddammit, sir! What're you doing here?"

"I am sightseeing. And why aren't you at headquarters running the show?"

"Balls! Second in command is doing that."

Wind-driven sleet and rain that could not make up its mind whether to be hail or water made small arms fire erratic. A brigadier general, second in command, who had probably hounded his chief back to division, was hailed by men along the line.

"For Christ's sake, Jingles, take cover, you're drawing fire on us."

Jingles Wilson made a derisive sound. "Nothing but their seventy-sevens can shoot straight in this goddamn drizzle!"

Wilson stalked on. He knew the morale was okay. And it had to be: Stretcher men were taking casualties to ambulances waiting below the rim rock. An entire company emerged from mud and muck to take care of Liberators crawling from their sight-seeing bus.

Jingles Wilson stopped, hunched his shoulders, bunched up the collar of his hip-length jacket, and outwitted the twisting wind long enough to fire up a fresh cigar. He looked downgrade. Newly arrived Liberators made way for demoralized fugitives who were escaping the kill-crazy capitalists.

Wilson sighed and shook his head. "Get nowhere," he

grumbled to the roar and rumble, "till we whittle them down some more."

He was nearly at the boundary of the division area when he checked himself sharply.

"Crazy bastards!"

Newspaper men. The quicker they got shot up, the better. Lacking sense enough to take cover.

"Got to see the horrors of war, get the slimy civilians more pacifistic and CO than ever."

Then, squinting into the drizzle, he saw that one was a soldier, head bandaged, helping the other fellow up from a pratfall.

A 50-millimeter shell, missing a tank turret slot, grazed the general's tin hat and went elsewhere to burst. Thanks to the chin strap, the helmet stayed in place. The impact folded Jingles Wilson. One of the figures that had attracted his attention jerked back, twisted, and then crumpled and clawed mud, as did the general. There was one difference: Wilson would get back to headquarters.

The survivor of the reckless pair, the one with his head so crudely bandaged, slip-slopped his way toward Hardrock Pike's sector, the gap through which the enemy had vainly tried to pass.

Meanwhile, the center of the long line was getting the worst hammering thus far. Kerwin and Alexander were carrying on with their depressing promenade.

"Overworked stretcher-bearers," the former grumbled. "When they unionize the armed forces, the troops won't fight in the rain."

"Correction, General! If I know unions, they'd have the troops strike for double pay and—hell's bells! That's Jingles Wilson they're bringing from the far west."

They followed, overtaking. "Did he get it bad?" they asked at the ambulance.

"Probably nothing but concussion," the pill roller

answered. "Something creased his hat."

The ambulance rolled on.

"Off the record, Denny, how bad a day is this?" Alexander asked.

"Stinking weather. If the next attack is with submarines, I'd not be too surprised."

"That'd be good for the troops to hear. Old Kerwin sloshing knee-deep in gruel and quipping bright words. *How bad is this?*"

They eyed each other. "You have been places," Kerwin said. "I do not have to tell you."

"It is as bad as all that?"

"It is worse. The visiting team is running fresh players into the game. You'd think this is football. We don't have fresh outfits. Lucky that Pike is a nasty package. They want no more of that gap."

"You mean Pike's outfit is tail-sitting and bitching because there's no hot buttered rum issue?"

"If they had it that way, they'd rate it."

"Quiet back there."

They looked westward toward the gap. No muzzle blasts. The wind brought no fumes, no reek of hot lube, no smoking metal.

"Suppose Kuropatkin is using anesthetic gas?" A pause, though no answer was required. "Jumping Jehovah!"

A red flare, high up; two green flares, lower; three spectral blues making a triangle against the sky. Kerwin had night glasses to offset the murky overcast. Alexander, startled, snapped binoculars to his eyes.

"Enemy armor pouring in. Making like this is war games."

There was no fire from the gap. This could not be one of Pike's capers, an ambush for an overconfident attacker. If so intended, the Liberators would be through and out of the trap before it could be sprung.

Pike's force was not defending the gap. What had been

the right wing of Alexander's army was elsewhere. The center had become the right flank, and the enemy was turning it to cut communications and strike from the rear.

Bugles and sirens sounded along the center, signal flares went up—everything but bosuns piping general quarters. Kerwin set out at a dead run, with Alexander just behind him. The general shouted, "Get to your headquarters truck. Make for that horseshoe!" He caught the Imperator's shoulder and pointed. "Pike's outfit's going to reinforce ours. What a screw-up! Get out of here! We can form the horseshoe—yes, damn it, my assistant worked that one out, just in case. Whatever you do, don't get captured . . ."

Pike's Thirty-seventh Armored, bringing up the rear of the pullout from the gap, was swinging to meet the invaders. They had already gotten the message and were changing their front. The unopposed Marxist breakthrough had jammed up in the woods of the flat stretch separating the ridge and the horseshoe. Their reforming was blocked by Pike's Thirty-seventh. Concerted action became impossible.

Armored platoon battled armored platoon. Artillery from the high palisade shelled the gap, blocking it with blazing armor, and blasted troop carriers on their way to follow the first wave.

Meanwhile, the division at the extreme left of the ridge had swung into the valley to fight its way westward to meet any who evaded Pike's Thirty-seventh. And all along the ridge, Kerwin's reinforced center withdrew unit after unit toward the left, some to hold the enemy, others to establish a new position on the horseshoe's rim.

With flares and microwave, Alexander signaled his arrival on the new line. Searchlights reaching from the palisades began to pick targets as the confusion between the former line and the new one was hammered into order and the mutually destructive dogfights of total chaos subsided.

Effective artillery fire drove the reorganized enemy back to and over the rim of the ridge. What they had for several days assailed was now their shelter.

On the crescent, with a line much shorter and with forces depleted, Hardrock Pike faced a chance to prove that being surrounded was the supreme blessing: No matter which way the fighting soldier faced, there was an enemy to be exterminated. Although the Imperial Army was not yet surrounded, reinforcements coming from the southwest promised to supply the ingredients that Pike's prescription demanded. At the moment, however, he faced a more immediate test: Lieutenant General Dennis Kerwin.

General Pike, once commandant of the Imperial Corps of Marines, was getting an eating out that went beyond the history of the armed forces of the Imperium or of the Parliamentary Republic that came before it.

When at last Kerwin paused for breath, Pike asked, "Sir, have I had it, or is there a rest of it?" Pike, dogtired, dirty, with mud, sweat, and a blend of exhaust fumes and the nitrous breath of artillery adding to the military aura, was not as disturbed as the situation and sound effects warranted.

"General, you have something to say?"

"No, sir. I have something to show you." He dug into an inner pocket and produced a paper. Deliberately he unfolded the grimy and sweat-soaked product of the army field press. He handed it to Kerwin.

"This order, apparently signed by you, explains why my division left the gap wide open and went to reinforce your line, which was actually smelling hell."

Kerwin snatched the paper. He shifted to get the best light on it. He gulped, rereading. His index finger followed each line, a shaky finger that found it hard to keep on the typing.

"Ben, where'd you get this goddamned order? Fooled

me for a moment, Army Headquarters form, but I never signed it."

"A wounded aide-de-camp lurched through shit and corruption, poked it into my hand, then nearly folded."

"Who was it?"

"Your ADCs have been so expendable lately. This fellow had a head wound. Damnedest bungle of bandaging I ever saw. He mumbled something about a shell sliver. Didn't have the sliver, so he could not ask me to autograph it. Christ, no, I don't mean he was one of those glory hunters. He was out on his feet. I said, 'Son, for Christ's sweet sake, have a pill roller do it right.' He lost no time staggering away."

"You obeyed this idiot order!"

"General, last time I ad-libbed, I got an eating out that was impressive. I got moderately chewed out, by an ADC, for not attending the conference with the Honorable Neville Ingerman. And then comes the general order, in writing, about no more verbal transmission from corps to division.

"So I executed this order. Before I could help or hinder the center, the Slivovitz bastards were through the gap as if they'd gotten engraved invitations."

"They practically did." Kerwin made a sour grimace. "They barreled through so fast, they jammed themselves into a muddle."

"I'd like to have a word in private with that ADC, so-called."

"Not if I get at him first." Kerwin chewed air for a moment. He extended his hand. "Ben, my apologies. I walked into that one. I am telling the Imperator that our retreat is not cut off. Mainly because we are not figuring on a retreat. And when the Canadians get here—" He grinned and hammed it up. "—you'll counterattack, and we'll have the sons of bitches at our mercy. They can't escape."

Chapter 21

WHEN ROD GARVIN included the scientific community in his tours of inspection as Governor-General of Mars, he found that glass blowers, tool- and diemakers, machinists, and chemists were more comprehensible than the grand masters of so-called pure science. He was baffled by their descriptions of theory and experimentation. At the Prosthetics Development Department, despite the demand for repairs for victims of industrial accidents, there was time for experimentation.

In the Prosthetics Development Department, he tried to make a show of following the remarks of his guide. "Uh, Dr. Wittmer," he began. "Fitting people with artificial hands that are, uh, more dextrous than natural ones seems most humanitarian."

"Humanitarian, hell! The hands you applaud are actually in the interests of robotics. Though I grant that survivors are more inclined to observe the so-called piddling and nonsensical safety precautions that even the sensible Simianoids sometimes ignore. Bit by bit, they learn that explosions here are more disastrous than in Terrestrian plants. If the blast does not finish you, the thin atmosphere of a dome blown open will do the job."

The floor shuddered. A siren wailed. Greenish-brown

fumes poured from a ventilator. The odor was like rotten eggs blended with skunk essence. Visitor and guide headed for a more salubrious compartment.

"Be damned if I can see anything constructive about that stuff, whatever it is," Garvin commented.

"Admiral, you miss the point entirely. The phenomenon that drove us to cover is not a manifestation of any specific investigation. We are not devising a new perfume or a new explosive. This is what you might call brainstorming. Random starts, abstractions."

"I begin to get it. You might've come up with a Chanel Number Ninety-one or with something that eats holes through glass or tastes like vanilla."

"Exactly! That is the lure of pure science."

"How's the fertility hormone project getting along? I mean, for female Simianoids." Seeing that Dr. Wittmer was still groping and looking perplexed, like a zombie trying to decide whether he is alive, dead, or both, Garvin prompted him: "The sociologists and the psychologists are working on the causes that drive so many male Simianoids to the recruiting stations, bribing the sergeants to accept them for military duty in combat zones. Nobody gives a good goddamn *why*—"

"Insofar as you might regard them as scientists, theirs is the attitude of pure science."

"Sweet Jesus, Doctor! If someone takes his thumb out and develops that hormone, no one will be interested in reasons."

One simply did not—repeat, *not*—give the Governor-General of Mars a snotty-sarcastic answer. "Ah . . . Admiral, seems to me that we do have one of the trainees or interns or whatever at work on the purely empirical aspects of the question. I'll get a report and submit it."

"That'd be nice, but see if you can get him/her to take his/her thumb out and do something!"

Garvin's inspection was not without merit. At the Imperial Palace of Maritania, there was the pilot model of the greatest 3-D audio-video viewer ever designed. And on his return from the science area, some fifteen kilometers out of the city, he found waiting for him an invitation to a private presentation of the war news, which he had banned because of its effect on the Martian work force.

The screen Garvin faced was two and a half by three and a half meters. Until the buzz and hum of warmup blossomed into light and sound, he was sure that he and the Imperatrix were quite too far from the screen. Finally, the showing was as private as it could have been; he and Pseudo-Lani had the room to themselves.

The dark-eyed, tawny-haired impostor smelled and sounded as Lani-ish as she looked. She was quite at ease, having perfected her act.

Garvin recognized the terrain west of the city that no one wanted. The illusion of depth was so convincing that at times he felt as if he were sitting on the distant heights from which howitzers dropped shells behind the long ridge that now sheltered the enemy who had so persistently assaulted it.

A personnel carrier was making an end run, apparently to turn the western tip of the horseshoe along which Alexander's hard-pressed desperadoes stood fast.

Garvin pounced from his chair. "Nail the son of a bitch before he reaches the dead space!"

He sank back to his seat. "Sorry, madame. That's realistic camera work. If he makes the dead space, the gunners on the ridge can't touch him and he's no target for a howitzer. What're they up to, making for behind the lines..."

"Maybe to get at Alexander's command post. I got a glimpse of his flag."

Her voice was not as controlled as it should have been.

Although an imitation Imperatrix, she had a stake in that moment of danger; that much was clear enough. Then one of the EHV guns got into action, spitting flame from the left flank. Flat trajectory and extremely high velocity succeeded: The shell reached into the supposedly safe area.

Flame and purple-green smoke blotted the screen as if a volcano had erupted from the foot of the horseshoe. As the cloud thinned, a telephoto zoomed into line on a deep crater. Alexander's phoenix reached up through wind-torn smoke.

"Damn idiot, raising his flag!"

His exhalation of breath long held hid Eileen's gasp. Her voice was steady when she said, "Admiral, you're sixty-five million kilometers from there."

"Watching is tough. When you're in it, you're too busy for suspense."

The Imperatrix picked up a decanter from the side table. "You need a drink. I need two or three."

Three-dimensional realism with sound was bringing them to the verge of shell shock.

The voice of battle had changed. Small arms fire from the horseshoe was lagging. There were pauses, then short bursts, then longer breaks. The enemy was venturing from cover. Troop carriers were coming through the gap. And then a shift of scene: a close-up of Alexander. His eyes dark fires, his lean face clean shaven, he radiated power. Iris out, and pause to get combat ribbons and decorations; a camera shift, and the red and gold phoenix on each shoulder filled the screen. And then the lens zoomed back, half figure, and the Imperator spoke. He was addressing Terra and Mars, and his words were for the troops who manned the menaced crescent.

"Satellite told us a small arms munitions drop was about to be made. There is no need to fix bayonets. My compliments to the gunners and battery commander of the One Fifty-five, which took care of the enemy's attempt to destroy the parachute drop of munitions we needed badly.

"This proved not—repeat, *not*—to be a suicide mission by enemy heroes. Our magnificent gun crew killed them. The enemy may have intercepted our satellite message. They are committing themselves.

"Food for assault carbines is being manhandled upgrade. General Benjamin Hardrock Pike may or may not command *Fix Bayonets*. If he does, the Liberators are in for a new experience: meeting the new North American, the North American of the future, a man devoid of conscience like the fighting man of long ago, and the Simianoid North American—the happy man killer who will welcome our Liberators."

Garvin choked. "Pure Smithfield ham! But that long-legged son of a bitch makes me wish I were on the line with his troops—" He gulped a sob. "I'm almost sorry for the poor silly bastards when they tackle that horseshoe and try to clear the deck before ball cartridges get to the line!"

The imitation empress sank her nails into his arm. "Rod, you're so happy, you're crying. Good God!"

"Sure I'm happy! Here's a man who isn't telling Americans it's not nice to kill the enemy, that you should try to understand the bastards—once you've killed them, you've got lots of time to understand!"

The tremendous blast intended to blow up the parachuted munitions dump before it could be taken to the firing line made more than a crater. Although mud did not make a cloud as did dust, smoke and steam burned out of wet earth blurred the scene, covering the attackers as they came from cover to close in on the eastern flank. This was their chance to take the horseshoe before machine guns laced them with belt after belt of cartridges, and the survivors met at close range, face to face, riddling fire from assault carbines.

And then something sneaked into the audio, and Garvin had no time to think. He broke from Eileen-Lani's claws, knocked the refilled glass to smash against the deck, and was on his feet, half crouched, *en garde* with a nonexistent claymore.

Somewhere, pipers were at work—the skirl that makes mighty man slayers of Milquetoasts—and the drone, mimicking and going beyond drums, moving mice to defy lions, to kill tigers.

When the Roman legions met the Scythians and their pipers, it was tough going for both sides. But the Romans learned. They brought pipes and piping into Spain, into Ireland, and into Scotland, where fighting men were invented: dedicated man killers who were experts with the pipes.

The attack had to clear the line before cartridges came from where they had dropped, parachuting helter-skelter to the flatland. The cases had to be hauled upgrade and broken open, and then the contents must be served to gunners, machine and carbine.

The spot from which the attack took off was not much more than a kilometer distant; the men in gray knew that for many it was a lifetime away. And there was hope for those who lived to close in before cartridges were issued, a chance of reaching their goal, even if Imperial troops did get small arms cartridges with seconds to spare. The open ground was dotted by trees and what was left of trees toppled by gunfire. There was a clutter of armor blown by rockets, by HE shells, by plastic stuff.

The Liberators knew pretty much what they were doing, but the best information is rarely perfect. A tank and a personnel carrier took the lead, and others followed, somewhat in echelon. The main assault was more outdistanced than it should have been, but whether that was good for the rugged men in gray was a question never answered.

The mines the Imperial sappers had planted by night let go as the vehicles touched them off. Flaming junk joined the cold remains of yesterday's armor. Infantry poured out of sight, seeing buses torn by eruptions from the muddy slope. But those scrambling up the grade were outnumbered by those who had taken their final ride.

Good soldiers, they knew that however fatal it was to advance, it would be sure death to retreat.

They had resisted panic. Now they had to reorganize.

A supporting wave of Liberators was deploying.

Somewhere an AV operator was on the job; again, Garvin could hear the skirl of pipes, the drumbeat of drones. Far down the misty depths of the narrow valley, emerging from windblown smoke rising from the red earth, a line of troops was advancing. They wore the Imperial uniform; officers were in the line, without insignia. The pipers were not in front: Pipers were too valuable.

In the thickest fog, the wail of pipes, the menacing drones, and the eerie interference beat could be heard, like the saddle drums when the Golden Horde of Genghis Khan rode out to exterminate all living things so foolish as to oppose them.

A ripple of flame raced along the line of defenders. Small arms were eating their cartridge ration again, and the assault wave coming to sustain the stubborn survivors of the first attempt slacked off, becoming ragged but never stopping. If they knew that Highland troops were on the way to hose them from the flank, they gave no sign. Fire from the front was giving them a full-time career.

"Admiral, don't bash your head through the screen, that's the pilot model!"

Garvin backed off, yanking his arm free of her grasp. "Goddammit, madame!"

"Well, it *is* realistic!"

During the moment of spectator distraction, the scene changed to show Alexander, meticulously turned out, wearing insignia, orders, and decorations. For a second or two the camera caught him full face. No swagger stick. No pistol. Nothing but a bagpipe. He cleared the crest and the line of men who fired from cover as prudence and good soldiering demanded.

"Flatten out, you silly son of a bitch!" Garvin screamed. "Nobody's following you!"

For a few seconds, Garvin was right—and then dead wrong.

Alexander Heflin, the Imperator who had learned too late that Democracy and Socialism were fool's dreams, had fighting men behind him. Not an idealist in the pack, not one intellectual: These were men quitting their proper line, men moved by the ultimate truth that the final judgment is not from sitting on your tail, fondling ideologies.

Some had drawn pistols. Others, at a running crouch, followed with carbines. Some in their trace fed clips of twenty, clips of forty, into the nasty little 556s as they ran.

Alexander's piping was not as bad as it should have been. And though his strutting would never have won a place among the finalists at Caledonian Games, no contest in modern history had taken place on a downhill pull, in the face of enemy fire.

Coming from the west, the disguised Canadians heard the piper, and then saw him. Charging, they caught the enemy wave as it swung to face the counterattack coming from the crescent rim.

The 155s and lighter artillery on the left flank plastered the enemy until the visiting team from Canada was near enough to grab its meat ration. Veteran pipers drove them beyond fighting—massacre was the mood of men who would rather be dead than red. They had decided to be neither.

Correction: It was the pipes that drove them. The decision came later.

A lens zoomed in.

Alexander was ahead of the counterattacking defenders, who raced downgrade, carbines crackling.

When Imperial piping cut short, Canadian pipes urged the homicidal maniacs who needed no further inspiration.

The camera caught stretcher men, a three-star general without his stars, and a frowzy Amazon, muddy, ragged from lurching through thorns and slipping on jagged rocks.

"Lani! Oh, my God!" the woman beside Rod Garvin screamed.

Camera and sound closed in on Alexander Imperator and the woman soon to be Dowager Imperatrix of North America. Lani dropped a carbine too hot to be handled. She knelt.

Alexander made an impatient gesture. "Goddammit, let her alone, I don't need help!" He coughed. He drooled blood, wiped his mouth with his sleeve, and tried to support himself.

Lani held him upright and waved away the stretcher men. "Let him talk while he can! It's important."

Although not knowing that an empress was speaking, the hospital corpsmen obeyed, and they heard:

"Lani, get out, right away. Don't let them catch you, not alive, and not dead!" He addressed General Kerwin: "Denny, get her on the road. She has confidential statements, things I taped."

"Will do."

"They must be delivered. To Garvin. You stay—in command—of North America. Dictator—warlord—"

"I hear you." Though kneeling, the general straightened up. He stretched his arm in an ancient salute. "Hail, Caesar! We'll murder the bastards, hunt and kill to the last man!"

"You and Pike." Alexander's gray grin was happy. "Lani, carry on..."

Kerwin nudged Lani. He supported Alexander until she could catch him with both arms.

Audio failed to get what she said or what Alexander answered before he coughed, choked, and slumped and Kerwin gestured.

The corpsmen closed in. Lani got to her feet. The general took her arm. She straightened and half turned.

"Hail, Caesar, and good-bye."

Sixty-five million kilometers distant, Garvin said, "Madame, she won't have a good cry until she is awfully alone."

"Quit pretending you don't—you didn't—know the difference between her and an imitation," Eileen said. "Rod, I'll need help carrying on."

"As long as Lani is undercover, you are going to need help staying alive. Habeas corpus is here and now a dead letter. Martial law for Mars, and a one-man court with a few advisers to decide if someone does or does not get a life sentence to the radioactive mines or is lucky enough to face a firing squad.

"If they catch Lani and quietly finish her, you are in just as tough a fix."

"Is it as bad as all that?"

"Madame, it is a damn sight worse. I can tighten security. Sneaking into Maritania is a job, but North America is a grand property. It's going to be your hide or Lani's when the next move is made."

"Next?"

"Heraclitus was right when he said that praying for peace is asking for the end of all things. Until the plectrum twangs the strings, a guitar is dead. Being a widowed empress with Lani's history leaves you in a nasty fix. Our country was born out of war; it grew out of many wars! You've seen the *start* of something."

Chapter 22

MARITANIA'S LOCAL LOOKIE-SQUAWKIE processed the Terrestrian transmissions and broadcast them to the entire developed area of Mars. Little time had been lost in editing the AV clips from the cameras of newsmen covering the climactic scenes. Intersplicing not only eliminated duplication but also heightened drama by means of order of presentation and the illusion of continuity.

General Kerwin and his division commanders made their bows on the screens of Mars. For reasons of their own, the Canadian commanders of the expedition to prevent the "liberation" of their country preferred to have their names and the names of their units kept out of the broadcast. This was a matter of policy; General Kuropatkin, in his parley with Kerwin, clearly had been aware that Canadians would participate.

"Thanks to the unexpected arrival of reinforcements and small arms munitions," General Kerwin began, "Generals Harrigan and Pike pursued the routed invaders, overtook and destroyed most of them before they could join the so-called Liberators who had taken Megapolis Alpha.

"Minister of Defense, the Honorable Neville Ingerman, endangered the entire army with his treason. Head and face bandaged as if he had been wounded on his way to deliver a message, he impersonated an aide-de-camp newly assigned to the Imperator. He handed General Pike a forgery written on the Imperator's stationery. Obeying this order, Pike moved his division from the gap he would otherwise have defended and went to reinforce the army's hard-pressed center. Circumstantial evidence against Ingerman is sustained by his fingerprints on the stolen message form.

"At a critical moment when victory depended on minutes and the enemy still had a chance of taking our line, Canadian troops approaching through dense fog closed in and enfiladed the enemy's left flank. Caledonian pipers convinced the invaders that reinforcements had arrived.

"At the same time, an airborne unit closing in from the Marxist right rear heightened the desperation of our so-called Liberators. It is presumed that panic moved a responsible officer to violate General Kuropatkin's covenant, where he had promised not to use either tactical or strategic nuclear weapons.

"This violation of the covenant gave the Imperator cause to anticipate that strategic nuclear weaponry would follow. You will now hear the late Imperator's words, recorded when he learned that our allies were charging into terrain and a situation already menaced by nuclear weaponry.

"Citizens of North America and Mars, friends and enemies, at home and abroad, hear Alexander Imperator speak for himself!"

Alexander's image and voice: "The enemy's violation of our covenant made during a truce in this very battle leaves no alternative. Rather than wait for them to obliterate key cities and industrial areas, leaving the remainder of our land and population unharmed, to be exploited as a rich prize, I strike now and invite reprisal!

"For several generations, a scarcely concealed movement in our country has made us subservient to the Socialist Empire, inviting ever further encroachment by tolerating the intolerable. Not content with this, they seek to make their dominance de jure.

"We and they have scarcely recovered from their earlier attempt, a narrow miss. Now they try again. This, their second attempt, is about to fail. We will destroy their power for war. They no doubt will attempt to destroy ours. General Kerwin, Supreme Warlord, will marshal guerrillas to hunt and destroy the invaders who hope to live off the country once their homeland can no longer supply them.

"Friends north of our border will do as much for any who escape the rural citizens who want no so-called Liberators.

"I have closed the switch. I have given the order. Many innocent people will perish, but during these three days of battle I have seen the deaths of soldiers guilty only of defending their betrayed country.

"Now I go to lead the counterattack, until I join those men."

General Kerwin stepped from the row of warlords to be and faced the video and mike. "Now hear this! It is well for all to understand clearly that Lani, Imperatrix, assisted by counselors and a corps of scientists we relocated in the Martian Development Project, will rule a decontaminated North America.

"She is protected not only by the technology and armament production potential of Maritania. There is at her command the squadron of prehistoric cruisers that won the critical battle of Kashgar. Had that flotilla been on Mars instead of at its home on a friendly asteroid, there would be no invaders left for rural guerrillas to hunt and kill.

"Subject to direction from Maritania, with Admiral

Garvin, Governor-General of Mars, her chief adviser, this consortium of warlords will administer the law.

"The total failure of seven generations of Egalitarianism, the progressive growth and power of so-called Democracy which at last became tyranny, a Mediocracy which swamped the original good designed by the founders of our onetime republic, demands the elimination of what ruined the primitive excellent plan.

"Government henceforth will confine itself to waging war and to negotiating treaties with foreign friends and foreign enemies. If ever again we can maintain rivers and harbors and a postal system, such is to be done. Barter must prevail until we coin money which is money, not the fraudulent skivvy paper the Bureau of Printing and Engraving foisted off.

"Legislators rarely if ever know any art or science other than that of getting votes. Accordingly, business and industry, when there be such, will be managed by today's equivalent of those who during the nineteenth century made our country great and powerful, prosperous and respected. When we have such again, they are not to be hampered into futility and nonfeasance!

"There are those who have condemned the late Imperator for lacking social conscience, for disregarding the woes of the 'common' man and woman. Such of them who survive the grim days ahead of us will mourn Alexander.

"This, I repeat, is no drill." Kerwin's grim face crinkled in an amiable and sun-blasted smile. "Now I present onetime war criminal and exile, now Admiral the Governor-General of Mars, Roderick David Garvin."

There was perfect synchronism to allow for the twelve minutes required for the light-speed transmission of radio and visual images from Terra to Mars.

Garvin, speaking from the Imperial Palace of Maritania, wore full-dress black, space black, with cocked hat, gilt belt, and symbolic sword. Campaign medals and orders, decorations recently conferred by Eileen-Lani, made a big patch of color on his tunic. Having little confidence in symbols of rank, he also wore his 11-millimeter magnum.

He knew the weapon would be none the less deadly for being gold-plated.

That his height was only one meter seventy centimeters was not what kept him from being as stately as his rank demanded. He moved with feline smoothness. When the lens zoomed for a close-up, a space squint and other lines about the gray-green eyes and those at the corners of his mouth made him look older than his years, until he grinned amiably. He neither slouched nor carried himself as a professional soldier, largely because he was nothing of the sort. But a master of kung fu would never have been fooled. Such a master would have known that the Governor-General of Mars was too deadly, whether with handgun or with empty hands, ever to be stately.

"One or two or maybe three percent of the population, Martian or Terrestrian, are a valuable elite. These will be welcome as trainees, student engineers, you name it. The rest of the pack, ranging from goddamn good to low-grade morons, will find their own level if they are not starved or trampled in a busy world.

"Egalitarianism, lack of an elite recognized as such, is what got us into this fix. Between sociology, psychology, and theology, too many forgot all about human nature, what will and what will not work. That and too much brainwashing. Before I get fouled up in my own theories and doctrines, I present all Martians, original settlers, and Terrestrian newcomers, all Asteroidians, and all friendly North Americans, to our final speaker of the day, Her Highness, Lani, Imperatrix of North America."

He gestured, and curtains parted, revealing to local Martians and all viewers, from Terra to the Asteroid, the woman they were to hail, to curse, to accept—or to condemn—as the symbol of liberation from *ologies* and opium dreams.

She stood, as elegant and stately as her prototype. Her headgear towered, making her seem taller than the ladies-in-waiting who held the train of her sea-green gown, a thing of stark simplicity adorned by the wearer instead of adorning her.

The gown and the long ear pendants of "emerald" jade from Burma made her tawny-ruddy hair glowing and almost red.

To one side and somewhat ahead of her, a bearer stood holding a golden parasol with nine decks, each fringed with tiny golden bells. A pace to the rear stood a second bearer, holding a similar parasol, but of a single stage only.

She stood, waiting for the audience to lean forward; she knew when she would speak her first word, and she knew what that word would be. But they knew neither. Her dark eyes moved, picking out "believers." The smile she leveled at each of those congenitally credulous ones was accepted as well by the several on either side of the individuals being singled out.

Finally she began. "Before I address you, I must ask for changes of detail." Eileen-Lani gestured. "If you please."

Ladies-in-waiting unhooked the Imperial cape-train. Another took off the stately headgear of silver brocade and kingfisher plumes, exposing high-piled, magnificent hair.

The leading bearer stepped off camera with the nine-stage parasol.

She nodded contentedly and smiled more to herself than to those who sat wondering. Garvin considered her to be more Lani than Lani herself.

"As the widow of Alexander Imperator and as your

fellow exile, I set the Imperial insignia aside until it is earned and rightfully goes to whosoever decontaminates North America. Warlords may do this by hunting and exterminating fools and the traitors who duped them. New insights and evolving wisdom may enable less drastic modes to get as good or better results. Or we may reject doctrine and dogma and act as each situation demands.

"We have here most of the world's elite in science. Already we can defend Mars and ourselves, which is to say, in due course restore North America, once the envy of the world, and to be made so again.

"We of the nominally Christian West have been an offense to our onetime Islamic friends. Whether justly or unjustly, our cultures thus far have found each other incompatible. A great Moslem invader failed to conquer Europe when he met that *Frangi,* Charles Martel, at Tours. Four centuries later came the Crusaders, fanatics and war criminals if ever there were such, to invade Syria and Egypt.

"Since our people are the most recent offenders, the Moslems hate and despise us more than we do them. Mohammed, the Prophet, considered Moslem, Christian, and Jew to be 'Children of the Book' and bade them be brothers. Until his advice is honored, we can only accept that which is.

"The heartland of the Earth, that Middle Kingdom, that China which has absorbed every invader these past six thousand years, and ignored him until he became Chinese and civilized, has with its common sense reconverted Marxism until Marx would have called it rank heresy; they took human nature and realism into account.

"History assures you that China has no urge to conquest, that passion which ruined our not-totally-destroyed enemy. As for the surviving island kingdoms, prophecy is ridiculous when our immediate present demands total attention."

She inclined her head and raised her hand. Curtains drew to conceal the Imperatrix whose single-decked parasol betokened her only pretension to rank: princess by marriage and divorced wife of Alub Arslan, the Gur Khan, whose prehistoric cruisers had destroyed the enemy at the battle of Kashgar.

Chapter 23

THE IMPERATRIX FACSIMILE made clear to the world that Mars was the capital of the North American Empire; the Governor-General had nothing to do but translate communications from the warlords into terms she and her counselors could understand. In his spare time, Garvin wheedled the corps of hyperscientists into letting their dreams of pure science wander into channels such as devising hormones to increase the fertility of the Simianoids, or systems for destroying the missiles of Terrestrian powers who fancied themselves entitled to Martian minerals and technologies because of the treaty that made Mars, like the Moon, an international property.

None but the Empire and its ill-fated predecessor had financed the Martian Development Projects, "Eck & Ag," as well as Mining and Manufacturing. As Garvin and the warlords saw things, if any other country so desperately wanted a share, it could come and take it—if it could survive the attempt.

Then there were the spies sent to learn all about the doings of the relocated elite of elite Terrestrian scientists. Security caught one, ostensibly a space tramp dissatisfied with working conditions on Luna. His story was convincing. His possession of that dangerous synthetic narcotic which had bemuddled many North American and enemy scientists was not as easily talked away. Garvin and a menacing security man terrified the fellow by convincing him that pushing that narcotic was a capital offense and then leaving him for a solitary sweating in the pokey. After some hours, a kindly security operator cheered him up:

"No problem. The Governor-General used to be addicted, and he had a tough time of it, so he is a pure fanatic against that drug. He means it: death, and no copping a plea." After a long pause, the kindly security man went on. "Tell him what you *really* came to Mars for. No one believes your job-hunting yarn. Nobody looking for work ever could afford so much of that drug. Someone important sent you on an important job. It's got to be pretty damn important. No petty larceny."

"There's no law against this drug," the chump declared. "It's not well enough known to attract legislative attention."

The other man sighed. "You are right, but the Governor-General declared martial law, and you are stuck with it."

Spying in peacetime had never been a capital offense, not in Human Rights countries at least. The visitor confessed. Once name, rank, serial number, and confession were taped, he got a neat whack with a blackjack. He was unconscious and unterrified when the muzzle of an 11-millimeter magnum was put to his ear. One shot did it. With national security at stake, losers had no rights.

They held a private burial, over the rim of a crevasse two thousand meters deep, which Garvin had discovered during his months of working from Dome Number Six, Prime Meridian, making a geological survey fourteen years earlier.

There would be other spies, Garvin told himself. *But*

all you need is a classical education. That trick worked
when Odysseus and another Greek caught a Trojan spy
at work. Soft talk and then—off with his head. An old
gag even in Homer's day.

Garvin's life, however crowded, had room for domestic problems. Felicity in the home, that rarest of blessings, had gone beyond plausible harmony, and this was beginning to disturb him. Flora, Azadeh, and Aljai for some weeks had been operating on a perfectly tuned idyllic vibration. Normally, at least one of the trio should have had pensive moments, periods of abstraction, phases of moodiness.

When at last Garvin realized that Camille, Alexander's natural daughter, was harmonizing with her elders, he knew that he was not imagining things. The beautiful brat's facial structure and coloring were so much her mother's that there had never been any of those hassles as to which of her parents or kindred she "took after." Camille, a miniature Flora, became ever more his own, not an adopted, daughter.

"Psychologists claim that every male has a submerged female side," Flora had explained, "and every woman has a below-the-surface masculine portion in her psyche."

"Uh, you mean like that yang and yin circle symbol? The white curlicue has a tiny black dot, and the black one has a white spot?"

"Never thought of that, but that's the idea. There was more than my fatal female fascination that baited you into a needlessly hasty wedding. What made my talkie-squawkie show a million-pazor project wasn't female or male; it was simply plain human basics. And the same goes for you. Those were qualities that kept us together after the honeymoon."

He nodded. "So we settled down to battle mooning. Once you had your shoes on and makeup in place, you went completely incomprehensible. Only time in our first half dozen years was that night of truth in Maritania. Hating space like snakes, but spacing all the way to wish me bon voyage. But what happened to those neither male nor female qualities that made the original bedroom opium dream an accessory to something more important? And what's it to do with Camille?"

"The only way I could express those basics was in female thinkings and words, which you simply couldn't understand. And you've been just as incomprehensible to me. When we did contrive to communicate, it must have been by telepathy, instinct, intuition."

"I still don't see what this has to do with Camille."

"You and Alexander didn't look alike, but you were two of a kind."

"Now I begin to get it. She has your looks and a disposition like mine or her father's. You had it figured out from the start."

"Oh, but I didn't, not really. I just sensed it in no time, and it's taken you about eight years to notice and wonder."

All this had been clarified quite a few months before Garvin had begun to be disturbed by unusual domestic sweetness. Recalling Flora's labyrinth of logic, when Camille began to mime mother and two surrogates, he dismissed spies, hyperscientists, and warlords, to devote himself to ponderings.

I am being marinated for grilling, he thought. *Being buttered up like a roasting ear.*

Garvin had once counted on female bitchiness, with each wife competing, knifing the other two, only to learn that a firm alliance confronted him. It was no use questioning Flora.

Finally inspiration struck, when she asked, "Today's April fourteenth—what's tomorrow bring to mind?"

"Those IRS bastards, but the joke's on them," he answered. "There's not enough income to report." But it

put him on the hook. April 15 was the date of their first
and only North American wedding. And there was the
inspiration: He would shock her into talking by remembering an anniversary. To double the impact, he would
pick one that Flora certainly would not have remembered.
Moreover, it would be one that would not include Azadeh
or Aljai. He would get her isolated and then give her the
emotional blast.

The Maritania Historical Museum had both props and
dates. Eck & Ag would furnish the locale: an experiment
to determine atmospheric loss because of the low escape
velocity of Mars. In this, the Asteroid was unique: Despite
its insignificant size, its tremendous veins of iridium and
other metals of the platinum series gave it a mass that
raised the escape velocity sufficiently to retain atmosphere.

The artificial Martian atmosphere, a blend of oxygen
and inert gases liberated by electrolysis of minerals, was
being released in ravines of relatively low elevation.
Weekend cabins had been set up there. Instead of Gooks,
Simianoids, and North Americans disgruntled by serving
as guinea pigs, there was a waiting list of customers.

Garvin's arrangements were all in the line of scientific
and sociological duty. He had discussed details only with
technicians. The Governor-General had done his homework, and in the mode of Genesis, he saw it and it was
good. But his optimism was terminated when he hurried
home from the office to find eight-year-old Camille, the
beautiful brunette brat also known as devoted daughter,
awaiting his arrival.

She held a tray carrying two absinthe drips. Garvin
was willing to bet that they were a perfect duplicate of
the mix Mona had prepared in the manner of the late Doc
Brandon of Nameless Island. Garvin hoped they were not.

"Thank you, darling. But shouldn't you offer one to
Mommie first?"

"Oh, of course I should." She turned to Flora but added as she did so, "This is special. I mixed these myself."

Garvin raised his glass, and before Flora could hoist hers, he toasted. "Ladies, your good health."

The late Avery Jarvis "Doc" Brandon could not have told the difference between this and one concocted by his late steward, Isaiah Winthrop, Litt D, PhD, and a master's in bartending.

"Rod!" Flora exclaimed. "Don't look so amazed! *Your* Mommie whaled the daylights out of you for guzzling Duffy's Malt Whiskey out of the for-medicinal-purposes bottle."

"Did you whale Camille?"

"She wasn't drinking the vile stuff, or I would have."

"Mommie says it's hereditary. Grandma said you'd be a wine bibber and a whoremonger like your great-granddaddy. How would I learn how to be a whoremonger?"

It was not the question that made him gulp and grope; it was the drink. He was trying to find a rational explanation for what savored of black magic. Also, he was glad that he was in the era of science; otherwise, Alexander's impish daughter would, at an early age, be burned at the stake. Camille made the most of the pause.

"Where would I learn to be a whoremonger?" Getting no answer, she conceded, "I don't have to be one, but I ought to learn how and what."

"You simply couldn't be one. That is a man's job."

"The Imperatrix used to be a whore," the puzzled child protested. Resigned, she shrugged. "I suppose I'll never be an Imperatrix."

"I'll drink to that. This is marvelous. Thank you."

That concluded the children's hour until after dinner. After Camille had made her bow, Garvin said to Flora, "For Christ's sweet sake, mix me another."

Dream Girl, Senior Grade, reached for the decanter.

"I must be psychic, hoarding this all these years, until you had what must have been a hideous day."

"Uh—*hoarded?*"

"Of course! A liter Mona gave me. From the steward's stock, all ready except for shaved ice. When we stopped at the island. But you'd not remember your first long trip with three wives, two newly wedded."

So Camille wasn't a juvenile witch. Nevertheless, Garvin remained uneasy. "I still think Camille ought to go to Miss Hawkins's school," he said. "The public—well, their parents, ah, fathers anyway—a pack of thieves, pimps, cutthroats, soldiers, spacers, and scum of the earth!"

"Lover, you skipped the Marines," she reproved, and her voice was an enchantment. "If you weren't Governor-General, I'd be all for it! But it'd look so awfully undemocratic. You *do* have so much rank, you shouldn't throw it, not even at, ah, such people. Noblesse oblige, you know." She paused and then abruptly shifted subject, emphasis, and voice. "I've been having the most persistent gnawing notions, sneaking up, building up . . . I know it'll sound crazy—"

His thought made his glance shift to her waistline.

"No, I am not pregnant! It's just become an obsession with me—you and I have got to make a tour all over Eck & Ag. Start out with one of those original observation domes. Get the spirit of Mars the way you did ages ago."

Garvin took command. "Madame, be damned to noblesse oblige. I know a better spot." After winning every bout, she had walked right into a knockout. "And a real surprise."

"Azadeh and Aljai were hoping you'd not mind if they went to the Gook—ah, Aborigines Festival, a whole week of traditional tribal doings, really prehistoric. Are you sure you could get away for a whole week?"

"I'd make it ten days if you could convince our daughter that referring to the Imperatrix as an ex-whore constitutes lèse majesté."

"Easier than you think! Oh, marvelous! We'll forget that either of us was ever married to anyone, and having almost been Imperatrix, I'll be immoral and dissolute and—"

"Let's pack up!"

Chapter 24

GARVIN AND FLORA drove through a succession of dome-sheltered meadows, tilled fields, lakes, and uncultivated stretches where partridges and pheasants spread their wings. She finally gave up trying to guess or to bait him into telling her what anniversary they were about to observe.

"I forgot our wedding anniversary," he countered. "Finally we're even. You forgot something more important."

That reduced her to silence, which Garvin eventually broke by saying, "Over yonder. Those ponies from Turkistan."

"They're full-grown horses!" she retorted.

"They are for polo, which makes them ponies. I'm finally shipping three stallions and some brood mares to the Asteroid to square things for the cruisers that won a battle. Alub Arslan isn't interested in cash."

Presently the road wound into slopes of sheep range enclosed in areas watered by a stream trickling from a far-off snowcap.

"No dome, Mommie. Synthetic air, natural water."

There were seedling conifers. Squirrels chattered, bounding from tree to stunted tree.

"That grass. The greenest green I ever saw!"

"Sun's low and ruddy, and bouncing from the red desert

makes it more so. So the grass is nearer spectral green than you're used to."

Someday, Flora might quit craving Terra and be content with Mars.

Then she saw the dome.

Garvin cut the power a bit. "Entrance to the park. Keeper tends instruments. Reads barometers, checking and recording loss of atmosphere and how the humidity is holding out. And looks at customers' IDs."

The custodian-recorder confirmed their reservation. "Governor, we hope you like everything. Here's your keys. Lodge Twenty-seven. Can't miss it."

Rising from stream level, the road skirted the edge of a shelf on which a lodge of ruddy stone squatted among young spruce trees.

"Our reunion honeymoon spot on the Kizil Ssu!" Flora exclaimed.

"Reasonable facsimile, but not the date."

"Oh, this idiotic Martian calendar with two moons and years twice as long as ours!"

"Quit griping, darling. You'll catch on, maybe."

A key twist and a deft boot opened the door. A fanny pat urged her over the threshold.

"Touch up your makeup while I get our gear."

There was more luggage than a week of outdoor living called for. After dumping two suitcases he went back for a hamper.

The all-purpose room had Martian-crafted, Chinese-style furniture. Garvin touched light to vegetable-wax tapers and then fired up briquettes of carbonized wood pulp to cut the chill and broil the marinated mutton *satay* packed in the hamper.

Peeled down to her shantung slip, with chrysanthemums breast-distance apart, Flora busied herself stirring up curry.

Garvin bounded to the car and returned with a folding garment case, which he heaved through the sleeping alcove curtains to land on what Flora called a two-hectare mattress.

"What's that?"

"Unpack it and find out. I'll stir the curry and keep the *satay* from busting into flames while your're dressing for dinner." He snatched the chopsticks from her fingers and set to work. "If you don't guess the anniversary, you get no chow."

"Don't tell me you brought full-dress uniform, cutlass, and cocked hat!"

"I brought special gear. Take a look. I'm busy."

He stirred sliced onions and spices into hot oil. He turned the wooden skewers on which cubes of mutton were impaled for broiling. At the same time, he kept an eye on the kneeling girl who was grappling with the folding case. He had never figured which of his wives was the best shaped, either front or rear.

Flora outwitted the case, unzipped it, and flipped it up. Her cry of amazement ended in a choke and a sob. "Where'd you ever get this?"

She displayed a formal gown, a replica of the one she had worn at the cocktail party in Maritania on the eve of his takeoff to circle Saturn fourteen years before.

"Dressmaker copied it from the one in the museum. Only no train. Not in this little lodge."

"This time you can carry me to the alcove for imaginary cameramen to get a panorama all the way to my navel."

"Well, screw me blind! You do remember my quip when I took the place of a team of maids of honor and kept your train from dragging all the way to our suite."

"You sentimental idiot! I can't eat a bite. Take that stuff off the fire! Skip the louder music, and let's have stronger wine!"

Instead of hot *shao hsing*, he poured *kao liang*. Flora choked on the fiery millet spirit and coughed it all over her slip.

"Don't you dare strike a match! I'd burst into flames."

"First honeymoon I tore your slip off. Why not burn this one?"

"Where's the one that goes with the formal?"

"Sweet Jesus! I forgot you'd need a matching one."

"And a matching bra! But take a top mark for effort. Didn't I see champagne?"

"See? Hell, you can smell Paul Masson Brut a kilometer away."

He got frosted glasses from the hamper, set them on the taboret, and eased the cork stopper from the bottle. There was barely an audible sigh; no vulgar pop. For a long moment they watched bubbles rise in the antique-style hollow stems.

"Sometimes it's a century ago, then it's like last night. But why'd you pick this instead of a wedding date?"

"They way you hated space and still came to wish me bon voyage before I took off for what they'd planned as a one-way trip. Our night of truth. We'd never been able to communicate. Seems we loused it up every time we tried, and battled instead."

"And so?" She thought a moment. "Make this a night like that one. What's been cooking, these past two or three weeks? You did see through me! Oh, all right! But don't make me tell all, not until we're done with emotional wallowings.

"I didn't put Camille up to that caper. I have to get away from Mars. For keeps. Try to live long enough to retire, and we may spend our final years together. And don't blame Camille. She just sensed the spirit of things and ad-libbed her act. I'd have to get away, even without her future to consider.

"Between Labor and socialism, England's crazy, but the French still have common sense. Their country's the only civilized one left."

She paused. "Mind if I keep the rest of it till honeymoon's end?"

"The rest? Is there something left to say?"

"You'll let me go?"

"I hate it like snakes, but yes, I will."

"Night of truth, Rod?"

They regarded each other for an everlasting moment, reliving flashes of their first experience of what promised to be final leave-takings.

"Give you my word."

"Oh, you darling!" Flora caught him with both arms, kissed him as she had not—not since their reunion after his return from the Asteroid. "It's crazy! I don't know when I've been so awfully happy and so awfully sad."

She wriggled clear and found her handbag. From it she took an envelope. "I wasn't supposed to give you this until later."

He sniffed it. "Smells like Azadeh."

"Read it while I dress for the night of truth."

Although the envelope was unsealed, Garvin fumbled with the flap. He fumbled getting the thin paper out and unfolded. He heard the rustle of the gown but for once failed to watch Flora dress or undress. Finally, Garvin read the message:

> . . . Aljai and I are going to a festival of aborigines, but on the Asteroid, not in Gooktown. We are going as horse tenders and we have your message of thanks to Alub Arslan.
>
> We gave Flora a jar of fertility hormone capsules and a course of shots to last till we come back. We are staying long enough to make sure you have no distractions and lots of urges to give her something to remember you by. Happy honeymoon and don't fool around with your favorite Imperatrix, or you'll have us to reckon with.

The note was signed by Azadeh and Aljai. Each had sealed it with a lipsticked kiss.

Garvin read it a second time, slowly.

"I'll be a son of a *bitch*."

"Always have been, but an awfully nice one."

Haste had kept Flora from the slick job that woman and dress rated.

Garvin turned. "The three of you rigged this deal?"

"How often have I told you that women are not always bitches bent on knifing each other!

"You always said it was bad to eat on an empty stomach. Well, we've had a couple of drinks."

"Warmed-over chow is better than warmed-over girl. Remember what happened to the gown that night?"

"Just watch."

Garvin had ordered minor structural changes. Flora's quick move tore the garment all the way to the hem. When she stepped from the wreckage and flipped it into the corner, Garvin saw that Flora had not followed the routine of the first night of truth. She was not going to fling slip and bra after the torn gown.

"Of course I improvised! Do you think I'd wear those liquor-soaked things under my night of truth dress?"

Chapter 25

AT ALEXANDER'S DEATH, the Warlords ruled the Empire, with Eileen a glamour symbol, somewhat after the British monarchical model. No one was fooled; each general saw through it all. Nevertheless, each joined the others in pledging allegiance to the Imperatrix. This was ancient tradition and made for esprit de corps, unifying form and organization. Although Dennis Kerwin was supreme warlord, he, too, was a vassal, and this limited his autocratic power, keeping him from going beyond merely ranking his subordinates. All this prevented the persistent enemy from taking control, bit by bit, of the rich lands that once had supplied them with wheat produced by white, black, and Simianoid farmers. The other great deprivation was the lack of Megapolitan Utopians, idealists, academicians, and intellectuals who had for years exported high technology, strategic material, and manufactured goods for war. The doctrine of sharing scientific knowledge was gone, destroyed by realists who recognized an enemy and killed rather than loved him.

Professionally supervised guerrillas supplied by Martian arsenals took care of persistent infiltration and the dreary-deadly-dull drivel of Marxist radio propaganda. The shortage of gullibles and the ever increasing popularity of "hunt and kill" gave zest to rural life and kept would-be agrarian reformers and Liberators from making significant headway.

Garvin's business was governing Mars. Tall, stooped Caspar Tweed, ever brushing back his cowlick when he was not tucking snuff behind his molars, assisted by Hamlin Daly, whose forged documents were better than originals, and two other survivors of the Saturnian Circumnavigation, served as unofficial security assistants. Since they worked unnoticed, there was never an objection to their methods, if only because the spy or other menace always got an attorney to appeal the sentence. Garvin handled appeals.

Because of Azadeh, selected Gooks kept the Governor-General well informed.

Despite Eileen's repeated invitations, he steadfastly balked at sitting in on meetings of her counselors. However, the Imperatrix sent him taped reports of those discussions and invited him to private consultation.

"I need your off-the-record advice," Eileen once told him, smiling wearily. "You do not have degrees in political science."

"Madame, that is precisely why I will not get within smelling distance of your council. If I meddled in your business, they'd contrive to screw mine up totally."

"Oh, how could they? You are the actual power here, and my suspicion is, you are absolute and appeal proof. They and I, we in fact, are refugees."

"Alexander was supreme power screwed up by democracy and bureaucracy. They fouled him up at every turn. Your staff would try to do the same with me. First false move they made, I'd have to invite them to a strictly stag cocktail party, confidential of course, in the Big Lodge of Experimental Outdoors Area. Get them plastered and then dump them into one of those thousand-meter-deep crevasses."

"Rod, you are crazy!" Eileen exclaimed when she realized that he meant precisely what he said.

"I know human nature. It would be me or them. When a Persian padishah or Turkish sultan came to power, he had to dispose of all or most of his male relatives. That left him with nothing but foreign enemies, and he could take care of those. By the time Alexander came to power, there were too many bureaucrats and not enough ravines."

The Imperatrix looked peaked, run through the wringer, and on the verge of tears. She pulled herself together, but her voice control was not as secure as it should have been.

"You're not feeling any too well," Garvin added when she had herself reorganized. "My answer was a bit strong, but in principle there's no argument. Have you heard of any spies in Maritania?"

She had not. He told her of the space tramp and his parcel of dangerous narcotic. "There is so little atmosphere outside the domes that vultures won't be circling and picking out the carrion. That fellow is not, and he never was." He paused. "Honey, what the hell *is* troubling you?" he asked with genuine solicitude.

"I didn't ask for this job!"

Misery had sharpened her usually low-pitched voice.

"Neither did I. But we are stuck with it. You've done a grand job not looking worried in public or when you're on camera. But if I'm to help you, I have to have a free hand, no questions answered, none asked.

"Whatever—whoever it is, it's them or you! There's not an empress in history who served her time by being a sweet little girl. Theodora was a tough package, though not as bad as they claim. The widow of Augustus Caesar was dangerous till she died. Frail Carlotta, ex-empress of Mexico, died in an insane asylum. No iron in her soul. I'm handicapped, but maybe I can help you."

"I'm another Carlotta."

"Sweet Jesus, woman!"

"That battle movie, Alexander's final words."

"That was private, when you recognized Lani and sounded off."

"He called her Lani, don't you remember?"

"I scrubbed that soundtrack before the public showing."

"We don't know who caught it before it came to me."

"Alex was not speaking too clearly. There was battle noise and staff officers and medical corpsmen sounding off. A dying man might've thought of his far-off Lani, not knowing who was kneeling beside him."

"That's been eating at me ever since."

"If you're suspected of being ersatz, your staff will defend you to the end. If they don't, they'd lose their jobs. It is not every slob who is household or official staff to an Imperial Highness. Anyway, if Lani is still alive, she is the one who is in a tough spot if you're exposed as her look-alike."

"You've helped a lot. I'm just in a low phase."

"Quit crapping me! You are mourning for Alexander."

She nodded. "And getting ulcers. Nothing but pains."

"Alex was the best! But you're letting grief go way too far! Six years now. The most devoted wife doesn't become a career widow that way. Well, very rarely, and if she does, she's plain demented!

"Nature has a grand cure for things like that."

"Tell me."

"Nature, time—they're the same, I guess. *It* always has new griefs to bury the old ones, always new losses to shovel earth into the graves of past woes. Wonderful, what?

"Your impersonation of Lani was so fine-tuned, you fell in love with Alex for keeps!"

"I used to sleep with him, and he didn't know the difference. That didn't make me a wonder girl. He was so weary trying to stave off war until defense could be built up."

Garvin patted her shoulder. "You must have been an unreasonably good facsimile. There were quite a few women in his life, but he was never casual about them."

She gulped, choked, and then poured out her worries.

"What's driving me sick and crazy is loving his memory and trying to ignore the horror he turned loose when he closed the switch that wiped out a lot of enemy cities and drew their destruction on half a dozen of our most important Megapolises. He killed more people than Hitler and all the Marxist monsters put together."

That brought Garvin to his feet. Eileen shrank from the fury in his eyes and the iron in his voice. "You're crazy as a coot! Socialism, great society, scientific thought control, psychologists and sociologists masquerading as scientists, with science the new cult. Six or seven generations of trained seals. All told *what* to think, never *how* to think! Democracy, a phony word for mediocracy! Redistribution of wealth, the schools full of it, the punks loving it! It's a Christ's crying wonder Alex didn't close the switch long before he did.

"The nation's been rotten to the core. Good thing the Megapolises were blotted out: They were the heart of it all. The Slivovitz bombs finished our homegrown traitors and coddled criminals; we did the same for them. We may not live to see the day, but with humans and Simianoids with common monkey sense, and no one protesting or chanting slogans or loving our enemies, a new America will be built up.

"The phoenix rising out of the flames, honey!"

"I wish I could believe it. Dr. Forsythe says there's nothing wrong with me. Just worrying too much."

"Dead right! A good MD is better than a battery of headshrinkers wired up to swear a multiple rape and murder defendant is insane, should not be exterminated, ought to be rehabilitated. But put the same psychiatrist on the DA's payroll, and he'll swear that the defendant is as sane as we are, and get the cyanide Easter eggs ready for the gas chamber.

"You stick with Dr. Forsythe and quit brooding. Alexander's the all-time American hero!"

Chapter 26

SINCE BEAUFORT WAS booming with postwar recovery and job hunters from all over the country had found work in the relocated tractor assembly plant, sweltering Sunday made the beach exactly what the two conspirators needed. Only a Rolls-Royce or a Benson limousine could be conspicuous; private transportation ranged from smoking heaps held together by prayer and masking tape to gleaming American imitations of Italian body styling. All were there, and with passengers as diversified as their vehicles. And finally, it was not practical to bug a couple of miles of beach.

Harry Offendorf, after advancing from Chairman of the Welfare and Education Committee to Secretary of International Spatial Relations, had resigned shortly before the Liberators invaded North America. Since the Warlords had evaluated him and found him liberal but harmless, they reduced his budget to Harry's salary, plus zero.

Being too conscientious to accept any such sinecure, he tendered his resignation. In view of his established harmlessness, his resignation was not accepted; he was retired on three-quarter pay, leaving a vacancy that remained unfilled.

Having private means, the Emeritus Chairman protested by contributing his retirement allowance to the poor. Harry Offendorf enjoyed the role of Lord Bountiful, meeting the underprivileged and brightening their lives. Being gross materialists, the Warlords had not fully grasped the fact that Harry Offendorf's sincerity was in many instances an indication of dedication and fanaticism far more dangerous than the greed for power and cash of the professionals whose bureaucratic empires were peopled by altruists bent on serving causes.

The Warlords, however, were often right. There was the case of Neville Ingerman, Minister of Defense, the dedicated idealist who had disguised himself as an aide-de-camp and handed General Pike the forged order to pull his division from a vulnerable gap in a hard-fought line.

Although treason had failed and Ingerman's escape was covered by the immediate confusion and the successful counterattack by the Imperial forces, there was a price on the idealistic head: one hundred thousand pazors, gold, for the arrest and conviction of the traitor.

This was an exception to the practical "hunt and kill" that took care of Marxist friends of the domestic breed. Ingerman's once-high position called for formal trial, maximum publicity, and public execution of the sentence as a hint to idealists. There would be a fair trial, then a hanging, followed by a classical California pit barbecue, public invited, guests of the Imperium de facto.

Despite the danger, Neville Ingerman had quit his Caribbean hideout, and despite the peril of being nailed as an accessory after the fact, Harry Offendorf had come from retirement to conspire with a fellow Marxist.

The conspirators wore robes and swimming suits. The rented parasol, table, and four chairs suggested an invitation to sylphs on the prowl for fun, refreshments, or cash business. Hot dogs and cold beer were set out and waiting.

Aside from his beach garb, Offendorf had changed little if any since he and Neville Ingerman had called Garvin to account for the stationing of Asteroidal battle cruisers. Dark hair with scarcely a touch of gray, ruddy face with hardly a line, the onetime bureaucrat evidently relished retirement, and he tried to reassure his colleague. "If any would-be pickups try to move in, tell them we already have dates. Relax, this is foolproof. This crowd is the best cover we could possibly have."

Neville Ingerman, on the other hand, hid behind greenish glasses. Caribbean sun had tanned him deeply since his daring appearance at Alexander's headquarters shortly before the coup that failed. He had lost weight; his features, under sun-blasted hair, were sharper than in earlier days, and his postwar beard, though by no means bushy, had through neglect lost its neat Vandyke styling.

"Of course I'm twitchy! Right to the last, I was facing camera. Those goddamned newsmen and my position. And you are risking your life by being here with me. No reward on you, no publicity, which is why I got in touch with you.

"If you are remembered at all, it's because you wept for the poor and smiled on everyone, the Empire's nice guy."

Offendorf nodded. "I know it's been rugged! But I could not let you down. You're still a real hero. If it hadn't been for the Canadians, Alexander would have been routed." He paused and sighed. "Am I here to tell you things for our Caribbean friends, or are you here to brief me? Need a hideout, or are you short of cash?"

"As of right now, the answer is no to all but the briefing. We are stuck with a task, and you are the only one who can do the job."

"And what might that be?"

"I'll give you the background first. Once you get that clearly, there is nothing to do but get to work.

"Two of our operators, our best ones in Maritania, have faded out. Garvin's way, you know.

"And Lani sending her son by Alub Arslan to the Asteroid to visit with his father. Letting the little devil and two of his playmates get into the barroom of a Maritania whorehouse, and with newspaper men hustling the kids home—well, that was bait.

"We just recently got a straight story. Lani's illness and her going to France or North America for treatment was a pure fake. Lani never went to Mars—she sent a look-alike. An audio-video technician heard Alexander call an Amazon sergeant 'Lani' in the death scene. That bit was scrubbed before the intersplicing and putting the show on the air."

"A dying man might have been muddled and called any woman Lani."

"It took a long while for the rumor to leak to us," Ingerman continued, ignoring the interruption. "Meanwhile, we had been watching Nameless Island. A Caribbean boat making soundings for us off that island never returned. And somehow, the Imperialists discovered Calabasas Cay and obliterated it.

"The Imperatrix and Mona Smith, Doc Brandon's girl, were friends. Smith was a guest at Four Seasons Palace right before the war broke out. That woman and that teak plantation became more interesting. Well before Alexander's death, Mona Smith began going to the mainland more often than she used to. Sometimes the 'shore birds' saw her, and sometimes our people saw her driving around the country, but the shore birds had not seen her come from the teak forest to the mainland."

"Mmmm..." Offendorf was becoming more interested. "You mean evading notice because she was on the mainland for matters other than shopping?"

"Harry, you should have been in our private surveillance and intelligence instead of weeping about and with the poor! But doing the way you have remains grand."

"My intelligence has reached its limit! Clarify a bit!"

"Smith has been prowling and looking at Trappick— or is it Trappist?—retreats."

"Getting religion?"

"About the one thing that bitch could never get—she is immune! If the hurricane did not destroy our sounding boat and crew, she and her headhunting natives did. And if Mona Smith had anything to do with wiping out a crew, she and her friends probably had a hand in that Calabasas Cay job."

"I still am groping. This religious business?"

"Mona Smith seems to have been hunting for a hideout for herself or her accomplices. The Imperialists won that round, but at the time nobody was sure." He paused and then spoke fiercely. "And right now, no one is sure, no matter how the War Criminals oppress the country. According to firm evidence, the Imperatrix is in hiding at a nonsectarian Christian retreat. We sent an imitation novice to that spot. Very reliable chap, George Wolf. He never met Lani face to face, and she always appeared in public wearing a veil, but he is sure that Sister Zenia is not a bona fide recluse. She works in the fields, but not very often. She eats in the refectory but skips a lot of meals.

"And Mona Smith is not prowling the land looking for better retreats."

"Why would an Imperatrix go for such a Christian ascetic spot?"

Ingerman snorted. "Her class has oppressed the working people for so many centuries that in spite of seeing through the ecclesiastical fraud and swindle, they and their victims are addicted to the opium of the people."

Offendorf sat up straight. He beamed. "Now I get it. And where do I come in?"

"Right in the pocket of my robe, I have maps and a briefing. Memorize the briefing and destroy it. Then go to that retreat and persuade Lani that it is her duty to the Empire to emerge and declare herself to the Warlords. They need her as the dedicated widow of an imperial hero or their coup cannot succeed.

"Drive by night in an official-looking car. Rough country, and a motel stop is imperative. Tough driving conditions. Put a sedative in her coffee.

"Put a vacuum cleaner hose to the tailpipe of the official-looking limousine. A black one is best. Secure your getaway, of course, and give maximum publicity, by phony phone calls to the motel, to the mystery death. There will be all sorts of evidence before the Warlords can squelch or refute.

"Let the world know that the Imperatrix, the real Imperatrix, is as dead as Alexander."

Offendorf sat up straight. He chewed air. His color had bleached out. "I could not do that. Outright murder—Neville—"

"I risked my life to get Pike's division out of the gap," Ingerman said. "I intended to destroy sixty or seventy thousand American soldiers. I did not make it. Kuropatkin did not make it. But goddammit, we did our best.

"Are you chicken, weeping for the poor, or are you for the oppressed victims of imperialism?"

There was a long pause before Harry Offendorf finally answered, "Give me those papers and drive me to my clothes. They are in an airport locker."

As they headed for Offendorf's car, Ingerman said, "Four beers, eight unhot dogs abandoned to prowling sylphs!"

Chapter 27

FLORA TOOK OFF for France a few days before Azadeh returned from delivering the horses that would give Alub Arslan and the neighboring princes polo teams for fun and cavalry for their friendly little wars. While waiting for takeoff, the enlightened ruler shared some thoughts with Azadeh, who in turn was to pass them along to Garvin, one of the few sane North Americans.

"Science makes such a nasty mess of war. Quarter of a million years ago, we had a higher culture than Rod's barbarians. We ruined it like those Terrestrian idiots are doing today with theirs.

"People like to fight; otherwise there wouldn't be wars. We keep it a gentleman's business. Don't ruin the country. Never fight until the plowing is done and the crops started. And peace before harvest time. Each side lets discontented wives and daughters go to the other side as a war indemnity. Everyone is happy, well, for a little while. Seems as if Rod's people never are."

There were other messages, but the first one Azadeh shared with Garvin was, "Aljai sends her love and says she just got so homesick seeing the Asteroid again that she decided to stay. Her parents are getting old, and being a virgin, she can make a good marriage and settle down."

186

"Shoot that one again," Garvin demanded. "Six years she was my long-haired dictionary, teaching me Proto-Uighur Turki. Before then, she was a sort of sleeping hostess for distinguished visitors."

"Oh, Rod! Our customs still seem to confuse you! She wasn't ever pregnant, and that makes her a virgin, doesn't it?"

"Between Martian Aborigines and Asteroidians, one seems to get a lot of civilizing viewpoints."

"And Aljai told me," Azadeh resumed, "to be sure and not let your barbarian fascinations make me forget to give you her love."

"Could you settle for standard fascination?"

"With only one wife left, even that'd be fatal for one or both!"

Then they received Flora's radiogram:

EN ROUTE. DESTINATION, PREGNANT IN PARIS. LOVE TO AZADEH. RELAY SAME TO ALJAI.

Garvin gave his remaining wife a long look. "You three wenches had everything planned."

"We did have good teamwork. If those North American females ever learned to be women, they'd not be screaming for lib, they'd have it the way we always had it. Speaking of teamwork, Alub Arslan's astrologer figured that Flora will deliver a son while the Sun is in the second dekan of Leo. Converting Terrestrian tables to. Asteroidan, and no computer, he couldn't get it closer than that."

Two days after her return, Azadeh tuned in on the Gook Town grapevine. Although the Aborigines did not yet know the diagnosis, they were certain that the Imperatrix was sadly off her feed.

"You neglected Lani," Azadeh said reproachfully. "You

and Flora monopolizing each other."

Whether she was fishing or actually informing him, Garvin could not guess. Ever since their reunion, after six years of severance, there had been two other wives, one senior, one junior; now, finally, the only pillow talks would be with Azadeh, as it had been for a little while fourteen years ago. Her innate female wisdom would not be confused with Flora's magnetism or with Aljai's. It would be a fair exchange; they knew that she would get as much as she gave. It could not be otherwise.

"The Gooks of Gook Town," he told her, "might give me more than I could offer them. But the Imperatrix is a soul-sick woman. Sick because Alexander, the peak and high spot of her life, closed a switch and exterminated more humans, many of them harmless and innocent, than Genghis Khan, Tamerlane, Napoleon, Stalin, and Hitler killed."

"Lani was a woman far more realistic than the standard North American female."

This left Garvin wondering whether Azadeh had told him something or whether he had given her new facts. Not mentioning Lani's Simianoid component or entirety, he said to his wife, "She is realistic, yes."

"Amazing that realistic Lani is impressed by bombing casualties. Dinosaurs trampled the earth for longer years than humans have. Scientists speculate about why they became extinct. Interesting but academic. The cosmos did not skip a beat when the dinosaur no longer was. The cosmos was no more impressed when all but a handful of my race obliterated themselves. Aside from Gooks, there were sufficient numbers, breeding like flies in a manure pile, to overcrowd the earth. How can Lani be so concerned?

"How can any of you barbarians be concerned when you are so indifferent to lives other than of your own kind?

"You intensive cattle breeders feel deprived if ever there is a meal without meat. Since no other animal race can kill and eat you, why should not war exterminate you? Living on the flesh of others, something must live by eating your flesh.

"Lover, isn't it simple? Mix us a drink and let the Imperatrix brood, and your good friends, Tweed and Daly, and others who lived to quit the Asteroid with you—let them tend to security while you and I get used to there being only you and I, as it was when we first met in Maritania."

"That's gospel, Madame."

But as he stepped to the bar, he wondered whether Azadeh had suggested that the Imperatrix was not that Lani, the call girl who had married Alexander.

With sufficient pillow talks, Azadeh would tell much without ever saying anything.

A week must have elapsed before Azadeh got around to projecting the audio-video tapes of her excursions about the Asteroid. The return cargo of thorium isotopes and crude iridium and other metals of the platinum series were routine for Martian Mining & Smelting. The first-named was superlative for spaceship propellant; the heavy metals broke several Terrestrian monopolies. Thus, by barter, the Warlords got military and technological supplies that North America could no longer produce. Disposing of precious cargo and getting accustomed to Azadeh as One and Only Wife put the Imperatrix on a back burner, though Garvin could not get that critical talk out of his mind. Optimism, however, assured him that Eileen would in due course snap out of her dark mood.

He wondered if it might have been a lover's quarrel—Space Captain Townley Evans or equivalent. She wasn't old enough to be reaching what in New Orleans was called "a certain age." But he knew that something climactic had happened when Azadeh said, casually as if it happened every day, "Dr. Gatchell Forsythe would like to have you come to the Imperial palace soon as you can. The Imperatrix wants to talk to you."

However well known the Governor-General was, he had never gotten into the Imperial apartment as rapidly as he did this time: neat, swift, perfect as general quarters on a first-class ship. Nothing missing but the bosun's piping.

Gatchell Forsythe was waiting for him. "She's got a lot on her mind," the doctor said. "Whatever you do, don't interrupt. If she has a question, answer in as few words as possible."

Garvin knelt beside Eileen's bed. He caught her hand. While it was not as cold as it looked, there was something wrong about the feel of it. Beads of sweat gleamed on wrists and forearms. The expression in her eyes shocked him. That and the way she looked reminded him of one who had taken an overdose of sleeping pills. Every dragging second, he liked the scenario less and less.

He could not decide whether Eileen was present and accounted for or AWOL. When she finally spoke, he was not reassured.

"Rod. I am awfully sick. Do you hear me?"

"Got every word."

"Absolutely—nobody—except Dr. Forsythe—must know—I am so—promise me—"

The rest he could not get. "Try again."

She beckoned. Forsythe caught her under the arms and helped her to sit up and catch Garvin's shoulder. Her speech became clear and labored. "Promise to bury me beside Alexander."

"I promise. Keep telling me."

"If Lani is alive, help her back to Mars. If dead—"

Silence. Garvin began to sweat. She still breathed.

"—bury her beside—Alexander."

Garvin grimaced and twisted his head. The doctor

whispered, "She needs a promise more than anything I can do."

"I'm listening," Garvin said.

"Rod." After a pause, her voice was low but clear. "Pray for me."

"Will do."

Whether her arms went limp or her words and his promise had shocked him, he did not quite know. She twisted, and before he could check her, she slumped and lay on her side.

"For Christ's sake, Doctor!"

After a moment Forsythe straightened up. He glanced at his watch. "She died twenty-one fifty-three Martian daylight saving. She had been responding to treatment."

"Anything to get you to knock off treatment and call me?"

"Right. What she said to you jibes with things she told me. Getting your promise was more important than treatment. But handling it the way I did was malpractice."

"Horse dung, Doctor! Handling it the way you did puts me on the hook in a nice new way." Garvin extended his hand. "But you were right. Now I have some more malpractice for you.

"Nobody is to know she is dead until I think this out. Scare them with any yarn that'll ring true and plausible. Tell the household staff she broke out with herpes, AIDS, leprosy, and German measles. She'll get isolation as if she'd invented it. This business has political complications."

Dr. Forsythe pondered for a moment. "Governor, you're going to do a bit of malpractice yourself before your mission is accomplished."

They wished each other luck.

Chapter 28

WHILE GATCHELL FORSYTHE, MD, was releasing scientifically plausible but expertly falsified press reports concerning the illness of the Imperatrix, Garvin exchanged scrambled-frequency messages with the Supreme Warlord, General Dennis Kerwin. The communication related to landing heavy equipment consigned to Kerwin's headquarters in the City That Nobody Wanted. Details would be discussed by microwave after landing.

While these preliminaries were being settled, a crew of shipwrights fabricated sheet metal to make the silhouette of a prehistoric battle cruiser resemble that of the *Martian Princess*, designed for luxury rather than speed.

Medical science completed the snow job while Simianoid craftsmen were welding and dressing the final seams of the body styling. The last bulletin truthfully stated that the Imperatrix would not be taking undue risks in seeking a Terrestrian resort whose atmosphere would be more salubrious than that of Maritania.

According to the local announcement, "Her Imperial Highness hopes that there will be no demonstrations at the spaceport. In lieu of flowers, candy, books, or other bon voyage gifts she would prefer contributions to the

Space Widows and Orphan Fund. Being piped aboard will suffice."

This was all in accord with her love of simplicity, which had moved her to case the nine-phoenix standard and break out the single-deck golden parasol of an Asteroidan princess.

For at least a week, stark simplicity characterized bon voyage parties. This kept the social column and the "Who-Is-Which" column of the *Maritania Gazette* quite too crowded for mention of the young heir apparent's departure for the Asteroid to visit his father, Lani's former husband, the Gur Khan.

The Khanlet, however, was not neglected by the Gook Town-Maritania grapevine. Terrestrian spacers got stories in the dancehalls and whorehouses, and Garvin's crew returned for duty moderately sober and primed with gossip.

The nice thing about pioneer spacing was that skipper and crew could be stumbling drunk: with low Martian g, take-off speed was low, there was no space congestion, and it was rare for an asteroid's orbit to intercept that of Mars. There was always someone among the officers who could get her off the ground and pointed toward her destination.

The crew, however, was bellyaching and sullen while sobering up. Owing to the gravity of the cruiser's mission, ostensibly transporting dangerous and highly classified cargo, there would not—repeat, *not*—be any space concubines aboard.

As Garvin informed the officers in the ward room, "If you find a blare of strumpets, so to speak, stowed away, pretend you suspect nothing. Grounding them would make this mission conspicuous. Once we're under way and you discover them, if any, there will be one for the skipper, one for the officers, and one or more for the crew."

"Suppose there aren't at least three?"

"Caspar, you know the union would never let that happen!"

Somehow, that got the wardroom talk synchronized with that of the crew.

There was a good deal of speculation regarding Lani's eight-year-old son. The media had ignored him, which was odd. Garvin cursed bitterly, using not only four-letter Anglo-Saxon but polysyllabic obscenities in Proto-Uighur Turki, Tagalog, and Gujarati.

"Skipper, what's cooking with you?" Tweed demanded.

"You—" He fixed his glare on Tweed and then on Barrett; Ames was on the bridge. "—know goddamn well as I do what is top secret about this mission. Everything we have done so far has been right. It is what I did not do. Lani kept her son offstage so totally that I forgot him in my reckoning. He should have gotten a good press. Hustling to the Asteroid to tell his father that Mommie is going to be all right. You and Ames know as well as I do that the Gur Khan never wanted to divorce Lani. Now those Terrestrian sons of bitches are smart enough to wonder if the khanlet really is Lani's son, and if not, where he is."

Tweed dipped a pinch of snuff and forgot to whip his cowlick from his eyes. "Relax, skipper. The junior Gur Khan got a better interview than you realize."

"Scuttlebutt at Big May's, I guess."

"No, it was at Irish Annie's. A Gook said a newspaper fellow, a big, hearty bastard, peace to all living things, one of that benevolent type of do-gooders, was buying the kid gumdrops and chocolate bars and asking him things."

That sketchy description did not prove that Harry Offendorf, one of the two Garvin had promised himself to kill on sight, had come to Mars, but the idea could not be excluded.

"You mean Irish Annie let kids eight years old into her whorehouse?"

Barrett shrugged. "Well, it's unusual, but it's a good house, and the kids weren't molesting anyone, nobody molesting the kids."

"Get to that interview!" Garvin's voice could have commanded a thousand men in battle.

"Well, it wasn't much. It didn't last long. All the Gook that talked to me heard was that the kid said, 'I'm glad to go home to see my daddy. I am damn well fed up with Mars. North Americans are assholes.' Well, that's about all."

"All?"

"I was wondering that too, when the Gook said two palace security men in uniform and a Gook nursemaid came in, grabbed the brat, and hustled him away. Come to think about it, I never heard kids talking like that on the Asteroid."

"Maybe Ham will nail the guy, and if it was Offendorf, I hope Ham dumps the body into a deep crevasse."

When they had Mars a week or ten days astern, the officers, and undoubtedly the crew, had gotten from Irish Annie's and Big May's to women in general, with time for politics and wars.

"If people could only get their thinking into modern channels, this chore would have real meaning."

Tweed wondered about the amendment the skipper had in mind.

"It is this way," Garvin explained. "Alex ought to be aboard. We'd secure his and Lani's coffins together, flip them into space, and they'd be in orbit until the cosmos went black and waiting for the next big bang. And then, things start all over, world without end, amen, with all hands waking up to a new life, a better one."

"Jesus, skipper! You're getting tuned up. You'd fit in, preaching where we're going."

"Who, me?"

"Religion is in again according to scuttlebutt. Every so often they climb down out of the trees. You were stately and sonorous when you sounded off."

Garvin frowned. "You mean Alleluia Stompers?"

"Sure, and the Testifiers. Bombing a lot of the Megapolises all to hell and gone, that was divine punishment for sins."

"Whose sins?"

"The Stompers claim it was the Testifiers and the Sodom and Gomorrah big city people. The Testifiers, they say the same, except it is the Stompers sinning. Feuds are getting ready to break out, and strangers with no religions are going to choose sides, or else.

"Everyone's getting pious. No working on the Sabbath, and on that day you have to drink your own corn whiskey in private and pretend you are reading scripture. No profane cursing or swearing at any time. Flinch, Pitch, and Rook and suchlike, okay, but no decks of regular cards—like it used to be, couple of centuries ago."

Barrett, who had risen from warrant rank to officer's ticket, snapped out of his reverie. "They ought to be having camp meetings and revivals, which would be good."

"What's so good about Stompers hollering and cutting up like half-witted children?" Tweed demanded.

"It does something to the women. Farm girls are getting knocked up more often than they used to."

"Meaning the preaching is more emotional?"

"Condom factory machinery getting rickety," Garvin cut in.

"One of war's by-products," the philosopher contributed.

The red blinker on the port bulkhead blazed. Tweed reached for the intercom. After a moment he said, "Keep reading while I ask the skipper." He hitched about. "Lookout spotted infrared quite a piece away on our starboard bow. Radiation hotter'n the hobs. Speed about half ours. Course seems to be to intercept us. What are your thoughts?"

"Look like she is bent on hailing us?"

Barrett poured a question into the mike and cut in the squawk box.

"She's speeding up," the lookout answered.

Ames spoke from the bridge. "We have the choice of action."

Garvin addressed the mike. "Look out, keep reading. Ames, order gun crews to stations. Load with HV plastic homing charges."

"They've never been used against live game," Tweed observed.

Garvin nodded. "This is in the interest of science."

Impatient, Garvin paced the deck. He wanted a look, but he did not want to make the third officer feel that the skipper did not trust his judgment.

Then, from the bridge: "Ames to CO. Approaching cruiser signals international code: 'Stand by for inspection.'"

"Negative," Garvin answered. "Tell the son of a bitch to keep off our course. Thirty seconds to comply or we fire."

"Rocket across our bow," Ames reported.

"Can you hold your fire till I get topside? This I've got to see!"

"Can do."

Garvin made a dive for the elevator. When he emerged, he saw that gunnery had discharged a rocket spitting red and green stars.

"Just to keep the bastard interested till you got a look."

Gunnery's pilot light blinked "Ready: on target and tracking."

Ames jabbed a switch.

The camouflaged battle cruiser shuddered. Seconds

later, there was another jolt. Garvin's nails dug deeply
into his palms. Presently he realized that he had been
holding his breath. The seasoned gunners probably were
relaxed and grinning like apes.

"Keno!" The shout was a blast, and he drew a deep
breath. "Their damage control's busier than a cat on a
slate roof!"

The tremendous blob of flame that lighted the enemy
cruiser justified him. Seconds later, another self-directed
missile struck. The flare made it clear that the antitank
stuff worked nicely when the target was a space cruiser.

There was more to see. Perhaps ten kilometers off the
starboard beam, glowing blobs raced into space, all the
while responding to lunar and terrestrial gravity.

"Tell the gunners well done," Garvin shouted, and made
for the ward room. There he addressed the first officer.
"Nice work, Captain, and my apologies. This whole business right from the start got me all fouled up. Admiral the
Governor-General had no business taking command. From
now on, she's yours. I'm responsible up to here and now."

Tweed took a pinch of chewing snuff. "Meaning I'm
skipper and standing a watch as first officer, and responsible."

"We're too close to landing to have a mutiny aboard.
I've got a lot of thinking ahead of me. That funeral, you
know. You take command, and if I am in any way disabled,
take this cruiser home."

"Admiral, did you have any confidential briefing on
the chances of being tackled by pirates? Or did you figure
that the news releases were overdone? And then this matter of Lani's son?"

"Not mentioning names, Caspar, but you suggest that
someone might have been careless in clearing broadcasts
and other releases?"

"Sir, not mentioning names, but what some people might

have figured for carelessness was bait the silly bastards snapped at."

The Admiral grinned, and the glint of his greenish-gray eyes was as good as an affirmative. "That is none of your goddamn business, Captain, but now that you mention it, setting out bait is better than being caught with your pants at half mast."

"Admiral, any guesses as to the identity of the, uh, orbiting junk? What odds in favor of a few survivors?"

"In the first place, the Imperatrix and General Kerwin did not try to halt us for inspection. That is sure.

"In the second place, I could not care less who we shot down in flames. They were acting like the Internal Revenue Service, which they had no right to do.

"In the third place, if the silly bastards didn't have emergency escape gear, this is a lesson to them and they'll know better next time. Caspar, you better stow the questions. I feel faint, and I need a drink."

The new skipper's first command related to splicing the main brace. The Admiral did not go over his head.

Chapter 29

PENSACOLA HAD NOT been bombed. After looting the abandoned city more thoroughly than would any invading army, fishermen and farmers got back to shrimp, oysters, fish, and farming. There being no telephone upkeep, radio and the gossip of teamsters and itinerant traders were the major modes of communication.

Garvin had a microwave talk with General Kerwin, reporting all but the attempted hijacking and the actual purpose in returning to Terra. He concluded, "General, I brought you something from the Martian scientists. A self-propelled hundred-and-five-millimeter EHV rifle, Mark One. Martian proving-ground tables have been converted for Terrestrian g and atmospheric density. Trajectory is so flat, a battery commander's problem is keeping the men from using the gun for deer, turkey, and squirrel."

"The reason for your really being here is going to hit a new high in Garvinizing!" the general retorted. "Meanwhile, you leave your crew to see that the natives don't scrap your ship for junk. I'll send you a couple of platoons of Simianoids, a staff car, and a personal flag for the fender. That'll facilitate requisitioning subsistence."

Officers and men fished on the gulf and swam. They

learned how homegrown talent can become as rapacious and vandalistic as Sherman's army in the vicinity of Atlanta, circa 1865 A.D.

Despite the encroachment of scrubby pines, no one was wasting energy cutting wood. Crawfish, shrimp, and other marine goodies were cooked in fifty-liter copper kettles. The water was heated on fires fed by wrecking buildings.

The Floridian shore birds were amiable people. It did them good to see strangers who enjoyed seafood. The men from Mars got along beautifully with the local folk, and when the staff car and Garvin's Simianoid escort arrived, he had no qualms about leaving the Asteroidian battle cruiser in the charge of Captain Tweed.

The Imperial coffin found a spot in the munitions caisson and was neatly disguised as high explosive for EHV shells.

Garvin's personal flag, three small phoenixes embroidered on purple, fluttered in the pine-scented breeze. Each bird of immortality and rejuvenation through fire rose from small embroidered flames. As he jounced over the deeply rutted road, it was easier for Garvin to visualize the resurrection of Alexander and of Eileen than to picture the revival of the North America he remembered.

He was concerned about Lani. The attempted hijacking suggested that a significant group of enemies had seen through the reports of Pseudo-Lani's serious illness, but whether they had meant to seize her as a hostage, put her to death, or otherwise deprive the Warlords of their symbolic figurehead, he could not guess. No news of Lani would be a sore letdown; news of her, from whatever source, would set him worrying that enemies also had information.

The staff car's trailer carried petroleum fuel. The self-propelled gun's diesel burned soybean oil, peanut oil, and other oils listed in the manual. Filters and jets, quickly interchangeable, accommodated diverse vegetable oils and petroleum diesel.

A day's march depended on the space between settlements. Protocol was simple: Call on the mayor, present ID, request permission to camp, and requisition food and supplies. Country sausages, barbecued ribs, real pies, and fried pies were entered on the requisitions as inflated quantities of soldier food. Reasonable amounts of potable motor fuel—distilled from corn—were billed as ersatz coffee. The Armed Forces had not changed during Garvin's short life.

As for motor fuel, His Honor, Cyrus Buford, Mayor of Jump Off, explained to Garvin, "Some is methanol, some is ethanol. First named is cooked off out of garbage, barnyard and chicken droppings, and sawdust. This ain't fit to drink, but it burns good.

"What's cooked off out of corn and the like, it's good to burn in your engine and it's good to drink. And some ain't fit to drink and ain't fit for even an engine."

Garvin conceded that things got complicated for a stranger.

"General, that is gospel."

"You all mean you ain't got no real petroleum fuel?"

"There's a little wildcat drilling here and yonder. They use what you call a Fort Worth spudder. You get an engine from a car that got totaled and rig it to raise and drop the spudder. That is right, you don't drill, it's the old fashioned *chomp-chomp-whup-whack*, plugging and bailing. Ain't any good for more than a couple hundred yards; we don't talk the meter language out here.

"So we cook it off, and if you diddle around with the carburetor and jets, the engines will burn about anything you can light with a match." The mayor paused to knife a chaw from a plug of tobacco. Then he gestured. "Out yonder, that's where the tax collectors and suchlike camp.

You are right welcome, not being one of them lawful robbers."

"I have a couple platoons of troops. Hate to impose on you folks, but I hear the army gives you receipts the revenue people take in place of tax payment in money or goods."

The Honorable Mr. Buford chuckled. "Lord, Lord! Even a sinner and a publican, like Jesus said, is a country mile ahead of them Bureaucrats that plucked us down to pinfeathers and bare skin. The Warlords don't begin to rob us like the Emperor's thieves did."

"Roman tax fellows never thought of the tricks you've got in mind," Garvin pointed out. "But it wasn't the Emperor's fault. Jesus was broad-minded about sinners and publicans, but I bet he never met a bureaucrat of Alexander's time."

"General, you sound God-fearing."

"Uh...um...when a man lives through a couple of battles, there is nothing much left to fear except someone or something awfully powerful."

The mayor considered that carefully. "That makes sense, but a lot of soldiers got to lusting and whoring around, and with profane cursing and swearing."

"Your Honor, the pure cussedness of battle does make a man take the Lord's name in vain. Even on the Sabbath."

Having inadvertently established himself as God-fearing and pious, in a rough way, Garvin settled down to discussing rations for evening mess and for the following day's march to the City That Nobody Wanted.

"Speaking of rations for the troops, I ain't been in this part of the country for years. We've been getting grits and pone and sowbelly and okra, and stuff, but I haven't seen some of the things we used to eat. Like peach and watermelon rind preserves, and dried-apple pie and fried apples and fried green tomatoes."

"They're hard to fix in large messes, but there's plenty of staples. You send your carryall back, and I'll tend to issuing vittles. Maybe I could find special odds and ends for the officers."

Being God-fearing might get some good grub out of hiding, and Garvin's memory had been active. "Didn't General Leonidas Pike come from somewhere around here? Started out as a bishop. Sort of a praying general."

The mayor brightened. "That religious gentleman set up a university maybe forty, fifty miles from here, and he fought only a hop, skip, and a jump from where you're standing. He got killed before he went back to being a bishop.

"If you'd relish some of them things I can't get for a couple of platoons, you ought to go to the preaching tonight. Barbecue and basket lunches. You all would be mighty welcome. We don't often have visiting generals."

This clinched it for Garvin. The more he learned about the regional religious fundamentalists, the better he could tackle his next task, that of tracing Lani. Mona and the Imperatrix had become quite friendly during the days before Garvin had been shanghaied to Mars, and since Lani had evidently been thinking for some while on sticking with Alexander and the Empire to the end and beyond, she would have explored the possibility of needing a refuge if she were separated from him. Nameless Island would not be safe.

A retreat, religious, cultist, coed or not, would be a temporary or permanent hideout for a political refugee. That this had become a historically sustained move indicated that despite its being a standard response, it succeeded much more frequently than it failed.

"That's mighty tempting. Seems to me I passed a church on my way trying to find you."

"You sure did, but the meeting is going to be outdoors."

"Real revival, sort of a camp meeting?"

"Peace breaking out betwixt us and the Testifiers."

"So you folks here in Jump Off are Alleluia Praise and Glory Church."

"Bless you, brother! Strangers most always call us Stompers."

"So did I, till I learned better. How come you and the Testifiers quit feuding?"

"Ever since the Lord punished all the Cities of Iniquity with fires from heaven and spared us God-fearing country folk and most of the Testifiers, we decided to be more strictly righteous, loving our enemies. I mean the Testifiers. Redeeming them out of their wickedness and folly."

"You figure it'd be proper for me to sit in on that sort of conference for an uncertain peace?"

"We aim to tromp out works of Satan that's worse'n the Testifiers ever dreamed up."

"You mean the Harlot of Rome is getting so sinful that good Christians are, um ... getting offended?"

"They, in a way of speaking, *pertends* to be Christian. This I'm telling you about is plum heathen, an abomination."

"They worship graven images?"

"Worse yet. It's blasphemy out of Egypt."

"Druther not meddle in what isn't my business. I'm a foreigner."

"I'll tell Reverend Mr. Galen Thatcher I told you about the meeting. Having a distinguished visitor is bound to stir up the backsliders that never show up for divine worship. I notice you got a little scouting vehicle."

"Reconnaissance car."

"Put your flag on it and have a soldier drive it for you. That'd make it stylish."

Chapter 30

THE TROOPS PITCHED pup tents in the meadow near a creek and not far from a tobacco barn. Aside from cured leaf for local use, there was barter with traveling peddlers; in addition, baled leaf went to Savannah for shipment to England and the Continent. Factories had one by one gone out of action because of lack of routine maintenance. Nobody had had the gumption to set up equipment of the sort that had served before the early industrial era had taken hold.

"Captain Wilson," Garvin said to the commander of his escort company. "No change in standing orders, but conditions have changed. We are near a settlement that appears to be larger than its odd name suggests. They are having a camp meeting that is bound to draw people from miles around. General Kerwin may have overcorrected in fitting me out with a three-phoenix personal flag."

"Sir, general officers rating three philley-loo birds are quite uncommon."

"Precisely! We are getting special attention, which he intended. We are also arousing more interest than he would care for: Farmers and other religious fanatics recently coming down out of the trees to keep sinners and publicans in their places. As someone remarked to me, 'You army folk are mighty welcome. You ain't got no religion. It's them with the wrong religion we can't put up with.'"

General and captain found it increasingly difficult to keep things straight-faced and military.

"Goddammit, Harvey, relax. To put it into English, just because some apple knocker acts the perfect 'Mountain Boy,' with an indentation on his nose from drinking pop skull out of a mason jar, does not mean he is a congenital horse's arse, nor as wide-eyed and gaping as he looks. Someone looking a shade too stupid may be overplaying his act."

"Sir, so far I am with you."

"Curiosity is likely to get us visitors. If you make too much of a point about running them off their own meadow or challenge them for getting within ten meters of that EHV gun, you'll be as good as telling a spy that the equipment is red hot. I am putting you into a can't-win situation."

The captain grinned. "Sir, you mean it is my ass if I am too strict, and the same if I am not tough enough." This was an assertion, not a question.

"Your savvy is beyond your age and grade. Brief the officer of the day and the sergeant of the guard. Now, my jeep?"

"Waiting, sir."

"Just an afterthought, Harvey."

"Sir?"

"Dogs trained to detect narcotics or other contraband might sniff an odor of solvent exhalation from propellant charges for that EHV gun. It's not fixed ammunition. Special alloy bore, but even so, not to be punished by a heavier charge than range requires.

"Dog sniffing around to make up his-her-its mind. If sentry shoots dog, the owner is alive and remembering the sniffing. If sentry shoots man, dog is not going to tell what made him sniff and whine, but our public will wonder about quick-trigger sentry."

"Very well, sir."

"What is so goddamn well? Please explain—I'd feel better."

"I am responsible for the sentry's judgment."

"You are, until there is an incident while I am at the camp meeting. I am responsible for what the sentry does after the officer of the day instructs the sergeant of the guard and the sergeant instructs the corporal and the corporal instructs the sentry.

"Captain, nothing for you but to do the right thing and refrain from doing the wrong ones."

Some of the camp meeting lights were glass-enclosed. Others wavered in the chilly breeze that stirred the second-growth conifers. The milling crowd, the voices, and the wood smoke of cooking fires welcomed Garvin as his driver pulled up at the edge of the clearing. Well away from the improvised podium, men were turning the spits on which young pigs and sides of beef ribs were broiling over beds of coals.

Some of the women wore drab homespun or dresses dyed in home-cooked indigo or whatever herbs, roots, and leaves they fancied. They dipped swabs into bowls of marinade to baste the meat.

Although only a couple of hundred meters from the encampment, Garvin set his feet on the ground and entered another time and another world, one in which there were no EHV rifles or the embalmed body even of one Imperatrix, genuine or spurious. He recalled his childhood in an isolated rural area and what he had read of farm life a century or two before his birth.

If Eileen had seen this, he mused, *she'd not have had her qualms about Alexander's giving the signal to wipe out a dozen megapolises.* To the driver, he said, "Higgins, case my flag. They've seen enough rank for one evening."

The unpretentious democratic touch never failed.

"See those three young fellows heading for the barbecue department and edging off, making for the woods?" Garvin asked.

"Sort of looking over their shoulders, halfway sneaking?"

"That's the three."

"Probably going to meet some girls," the driver said.

"Could be but not likely. Not until their religious emotions—I mean, the girls—get honed up. Always a lot of talk about camp meetings, and girls getting foxtails and leaves in their hair, and grass stains on the backsides of their skirts. Certain amount of truth, but that's in the family, and we are foreigners. Those young fellows are probably being polite about sneaking into the woods for a snort of pop skull and—looks like the preacher is heading our way."

The approaching man wore a store coat and pants black as his low-crowned hat. The laymen in white shirts and blue denim pants followed him. One carried a wicker tray. Both wore badges.

"Good evening, gentlemen. Welcome to our revival. I'm the pastor, Galen Thatcher. It is not often that the military attend our meetings."

"Reverend—"

"Please omit honorifics. Brother Galen is the Christian address."

"Thank you. I am Brother Roderick. This young man who drives my jeep is Brother Gary. The mayor said you'd not set the dogs on us, but I didn't expect so cordial a welcome."

Galen Thatcher was probably nudging forty. His longish, narrow face, weather-beaten and deeply lined, was kindly and seconded his voice when he resumed. "Mighty happy to have you with us. But I should not assume the duties of the deacons." He gestured. "The lay committee is waiting to bid you welcome."

"Deacons—*laymen?*"

The pastor's amiable face became stern and impersonally hostile. "With the Harlot of Rome, deacons are members of the clergy. Such is not the case here."

"Put my foot in it that time! Sorry."

Cordiality at once resumed command. "General—"

"*Brother* Roderick if you please. My flag is cased."

The pastor chuckled. "Physician, heal thyself! Now that both have been caught off base, let's give the committee a chance."

Brothers Amos and Joel stepped forward. The latter had a wicker tray of badges, each neatly embroidered: "VISITOR". Brother Amos tagged the newcomers, saying to each as he did so, "Welcome, and God bless you, brother."

Their duty performed, the deacons led the way to benches in the front row. Garvin and the pastor followed them. Brother Gary Higgins, remembering parade ground protocol, trailed along three paces to the rear and one pace to the left of his "chief."

"Brother Galen, I left my escort at camp. Soldiers tend to be a profane lot. If you could find time to brief me before I leave, I could give them an idea of what you are offering. Once I put it into military terms, they'll understand."

"We have no theology. We follow the Gospels. Their language is plain. Servants of Satan have complicated divine simplicities. I came to this region to settle the differences between the Stompers and the Testifiers. My message tonight is directed against the works of Satan. The problem has become international."

"General Kerwin did nicely enough the last time we had such problems."

"This is not the menace he is accustomed to cope with. Although the troublemaker has a British passport and he has not yet done anything unlawful, Ernest Albert Wallis Budge has far too many followers. And he is quite insane."

Garvin frowned. "Seems to me I've heard that name before—sure! He wrote books about ancient Egypt. Translated the *Book of the Dead* into English."

"Precisely! He was born in England, 1857. He was knighted, 1920. He died, 1934."

"Wait a minute! He seems to have died about a century and a half ago or more. You're getting me all confused. I don't mean to be wisecracking funny, but is his ghost kicking up trouble?"

The pastor smiled wryly. "I do not intend to be wise-cracking funny, but in a sense you are correct. He has convinced his followers that he is a reincarnation of Sir Ernest, born again to bring the ancient religion back to a devastated world."

"Good many Christians," Garvin pointed out, "back around 300 A.D. accepted reincarnation. The Gnostics, you know. With very few exceptions, fellow Christians killed them off. Sir Ernest, even if he is a phony, isn't hurting anyone. This is a free country."

"Brother Roderick, so many Americans believed in Marxism, which is a species of religion, that the late Imperator closed a switch and in a way of speaking called fire from heaven to the Marxists and their devilish cult."

Garvin grimaced. "Brother Galen, you leave me well up the creek and without a paddle. Please carry on."

The pastor smiled, not in triumph but in good fellow-ship.

"Sir Ernest, ghost or reincarnation, is preaching a new religion. The blasphemous and heathenish Isis cult. Isis, the so-called Virgin Goddess, an incestuous monster. Having had carnal knowledge of her brother, Osiris, she gave birth to a son, Horus.

"That is a mere hint of what this foreigner is preaching."

Brother Galen glanced at his watch. "Well, here I've been gossiping like a house afire. After the services, I'll answer your questions." He headed for the podium.

"Higgins," Garvin said, "judging from the smell, those are the best beef ribs in many a day. Isis and Osiris be damned! These people won't wait longer than we can for mess call."

Chapter 31

THE SERMON BROTHER GALEN delivered to people who came from as far away as Fiery Gizzard and Salvation Run emphasized the fraternity that had always linked the Alleluia Stompers and the Testifiers: primitive, unspoiled Christians, brothers all. No sense in this feuding. Every Testifier in the gathering was welcome.

"Inasmuch as some of those present came on impulse, we will dispense with Holy Communion. It would be unfraternal of us to have a period of departure, the duration of singing a stanza of 'Bringing in the Sheaves,' for the benefit of those not in a state of grace."

Garvin recognized tact and genuine kindness in the speaker's heart. No Testifier could possibly be sanctified, no matter how hard he tried—his heretical pack dished out unfermented grape juice instead of wine that was *wine*. The Testifiers reviled the Stompers for guzzling pop skull six days a week. And then there were serious differences in defining unleavened bread. Any way you sliced it, Brother Galen was a man of goodwill, one able to cut corners and truly avoid theological hairsplitting as the first step toward establishing genuine fraternity.

Setting theology aside, Brother Galen was the sort of man you could take along when you were putting the last chip on the line: that was Garvin's estimate. There might not be any atheists in any foxholes, but when you were out of ammunition, it was time to fix bayonets and counterattack. As General Hardrock Pike would put it, "Leave theology in the foxholes and don't let a panic-stricken enemy escape!"

No more quibbling, backbiting, faultfinding. All men and women of goodwill would team up to exterminate the blasphemy that was creeping southward, spearheaded by an insane nobleman, Sir Ernest Albert Wallis Budge, the self-styled reincarnation of an actual scholar who had translated the Egyptian *Book of the Dead* one hundred seventy-eight or so years ago and then was struck dead.

"This man may not be insane. Old Satan has wily tricks at his command. Pretending to be insane so folks will dismiss him as harmless, an amusing idiot. Whilst we have been cursing the Harlot of Rome, the Whore of Old Egypt is invading the land. The Children of Israel fled from Egypt and the abominations of Pharaoh. We will not flee. We will stand and fight."

On that note, the little foot-pumped portable organ sounded off. The tune was neither "Rock of Ages" nor "The Ninety and Nine" nor any of the hymns that evoked Garvin's childhood memories. Instead, the organ played martial music without a trace of "Onward Christian Soldiers." That funny little box was operated by one with the agility, dexterity, and resourcefulness of a one-man band. And the insignificant-looking fellow who pumped wind into its pipes must have been born in the land where war had been invented.

There was nothing funny about that braying, squealing thing. It sang of battle and fire, of pillage, of raping the nuns, hanging mayor and city council, burning courthouse and cathedral.

Neither bass nor snare drums hid in the darkness of the pines. The magician plying pedals and stops and keys simulated percussion instruments, the snarl, the rattle, the relentless *thump-thump-thump* of Mongol drums when the Great Khan had hung out the black flag, day and night, unceasing attack, until not a defender survived or there was not a man left to press the siege.

Garvin fought what he heard without even knowing what he was resisting. The music was dangerous, hypnotic. He was glad that he had left his escort in camp. Whether their presence here would have resulted in mutiny or mass conversion was a question he was glad to sidestep.

Brother Galen has bit off more than he can chew. This is not for a man of goodwill and peace, Garvin thought.

He glanced about him. Higgins sat there gaping, staring.

In spite of being internationally famous for minding my own business, I am sorely tempted to tell Brother Galen a thing or two. Bible-thumping honest vegetarian missionary going into cannibal territory, aiming to serve man—

And then Garvin learned how the Alleluia Praise and Glory folks stomped when they settled down to stomping.

All but Garvin and Higgins had quit the front row. Behind them, the benches were vacated as locals and visitors scrambled to join those who jammed up in columns of fours, fives, sixes, and more. There was no segregation. The shapeless mass of Testifiers and Stompers, glassy-eyed and gaping, thinned into a column four or five thick and continued in a clockwise course, skirting the far edge of the clearing and circling all the while.

Brother Galen had backed off, a hint that sanity had not entirely vanished.

The podium crashed to the shuddering earth. Visitors and locals *stomped* past.

They chanted.

Speaking tongues?

Pure gibberish?

Or what?

The rush became an orderly column. The gait was not a goose step; it was something akin to the stylized rhythmic step of riot-control police or special-duty troops in the early stages of quelling a demonstration.

Deliberate short steps; the footfalls at intervals long enough to create suspense that dragged into uncertainty and unease and that, by repetition, grew into menace. The *smack...slap...thump...whop*...insidious shuffle...*thud*...pause...suggested the trained swordsman wearing down a novice until he was just right for a fatal thrust. It hinted at the deliberate leopard waiting to drop from overhead, the lioness stalking on ground.

thud, shuffle, whop—remorseless, inexorable.

A hundred people...two hundred...and more, and from farther out than from Fiery Gizzard—the ground quivered as the impacts became ever more synchronized.

Crazy bastards are hypnotized. Garvin pounced, a long lunge, toward Brother Galen, who sat hunched forward, tense. Raising his voice above the wordless chant, he yelled into the pastor's ear, "Brother Galen, I want to tell you something!"

The pastor turned. He blinked. He oriented himself.

"You've got a tiger by the tail! This is dangerous!"

Belated understanding brought Brother Galen's eyes and attention to focus. He groped for words. It was clear that he more than half agreed. In another moment he would have spoken. Garvin sensed that there would be justified admission that letting go of a tiger's tail was ticklish work.

The chauffeur raced into view as though he had been blocked by the tail of the stomping column. "General, for Christ's sweet sake, ain't you heard nothing? Some son of a bitch is shooting around camp!"

Chapter 32

REDHEADED PRIVATE OSCAR EMBERG, although one hundred percent North American human, was so quick-witted, practical, and devoid of qualms and ideologies that he had gotten away with impersonating a Simianoid when he voluntarily applied for enlistment in an outfit liable to combat duty. He had tried school until he was thoroughly fed up with compulsory protests and demonstrations, had become a dropout, and had gone to associate with a better class of people. With his unusually quick reaction time and common sense approaching that of a chimpanzee, he did well.

Emberg listened to every word when the corporal recited the special orders for post number three, at the self-propelled EHV rifle, Mark I, and accompanying caissons of shells with various detonating charges. There were, in separate caissons, premeasured parcels of propelling charges. Because of the idiosyncrasies of such propellants, the cannisters in which they were packed had one-way "breathing" valves to prevent spontaneous explosion.

Finally on post, Private Emberg could recite his special orders perfectly: he had heard the troop commander, Captain Wilson, brief the officer of the guard, who briefed the sergeant of the guard. Finally, Emberg had heard the first relief get its briefing.

Although Emberg had special orders bubbling from his ears, he had a more detailed picture of the situation than did Admiral the Governor-General of Mars, who had given the captain a sketch, with the details to be filled in by the hierarchy.

This, he cogitated as he walked his post and sized up the EHV rifle and the neatly parked personnel carriers, *is dull stuff, waiting for an imaginary rube with an imaginary dog to come sniffing at propellant charges to see if there is something new for this gun or just more of the old stuff*.

As an experienced soldier who had a combat ribbon for service in the Kashgar area, where most of his time had been spent learning modern Uighur from his long-haired dictionary, Emberg instantly dismissed the notion of sneaking off post to see if what they had said about camp meetings was true. Trimmed to essentials, his thought was, *A quick piece in the woods is not worth risking a year in the hoosegow, forfeiting two-thirds of pay and allowances for a like period*.

Unlike country girls, country chow would sneak into camp and right to post number three—and this did relieve the fornicating stupidity of walking post. A buddy brought him a pint mess cup brim full of steaming hot coffee, almost boiling.

To drink while walking post was not practical. Any officer of the day, when prowling by night to inspect the guard, would be stealthy lest he awaken a sleeping sentry. With horses long abolished except for polo and shows, there was no longer the *tock-tock* of hooves, the jingle of curb chains, or the tinkle of saber chains to herald an officer's approach. But the old methods of outwitting the OD could be modernized.

Emberg recalled yarns dating back generation after

generation, originating with his own or someone else's great-great-great-great-grandfather—the goddamnedest liars on earth, but every so often they slipped and spoke gospel.

Sleeping on post was simple. The space beneath an escort wagon was no treat, but for a soldier, sleep was sleep whenever he could find time. Wagons parked, hub to hub, almost. Squish of mud, jingle of curb chains, and all you did was dive from cover and into the clear space between wagons, step forward, and challenge the son of a bitch.

Military as could be.

"Dismount and be recognized!"

The officer was always surprised. The sentry, never.

The troop carriers were far too close to the ground to offer overhead cover. However, within the limits of Emberg's post were darkly shadowed spaces between vehicles. He placed his carbine against the body panel and tackled the snack. In addition to coffee, he had two chicken legs, southern fried, and a slab of dried apple pie. He seated himself on the ground. The arch of the fender made a good backrest.

Someone, seducing a farm girl, had evidently pleased her greatly.

The chicken might indeed have been finger-licking good, but the soldier wiped fingers on shirt. He had to take care not to get grease on his carbine when he reached for it.

And that pie, finally. Someone had met the right girl.

Thinking of the right girl got Emberg's mind on the risks he had jeered away as imaginary. His first awareness that he had not been as alert as he should came when footsteps quite too near startled him. He scented a dog. Something moved near the caisson containing the propellant.

Twisting to grab his carbine and come up out of darkness was no problem for the agile sentry, but girl wonderings had spoiled his coordination. Instead of getting a good grasp on his weapon, he knocked it away.

The clatter startled the prowler. The soldier's abrupt move got him out of gloom and into skyglow; he saw not the OD but a civilian drawing a handgun. There was scarcely a glint of blued metal; that bit, and motion, was more than enough.

Emberg wasted no time scrambling for his carbine. He scooped the coffee and heaved it. The stranger's reaction time was slow. Startled, he jerked a shot before coffee drenched him. Blinded and scalded, he had no chance against Emberg's lunge, and he did not regain the pistol he had lost when the soldier knocked him down.

The handgun had the voice of the 11.2-millimeter model the Army had used before someone had displaced it with the picayunish 9-millimeter. Once he had the prize stuffed into his hip pocket, Emberg got his carbine.

He ripped off three shots.

"Halt or I fire! Corporal of the guard, number three! Halt, you son of a bitch!"

Another short burst, just for luck.

Before he could wonder whether either prowler or dog had committed a nuisance on or about Private Emberg's post, the snooper was well on his way and the soldier was being interviewed by the corporal of the guard.

The arrival of the sergeant of the guard made for a fresh start and an improvement in the narrative. By the time the officer of the day came on stage, Private Emberg had a story that contained not a word relating to fried chicken and apple pie. He rearranged the sequence of action, getting the challenge where the book said it belonged.

His tale was interrupted when someone bawled, "Halt! Who's there?"

"You damn fool, can't you see the general's flag?"

"Carry on, carry on," Garvin grumbled. "What's been going on?"

Garvin heard the explanations of the hierarchy until, each in turn having been dismissed by a curt gesture, he gave Private Emberg a chance.

The redheaded soldier got off to a good start, but Gavin cut him short. "That pistol in your hip pocket. It is non-regulation."

"Sir, I didn't notice when I confiscated it." He gave his version of a remote ancestor's trick of sleeping on post and never failing to halt the OD.

"With everyone else buying your story, I'll do the same," Garvin concluded. "Some of them must have been playing dumb." After a long pause, he continued. "Your quick reaction time did not give the prowler reason to suspect that his dog had scented something classified. You did not kill the man or the dog. The way you followed Captain Wilson's briefing was most effective. Meanwhile, keep that unauthorized handgun out of sight."

"Very well, sir."

"Walk your post."

Chapter 33

NOW THAT THEY had taken Alexander's body from the battlefield grave for reinterment, this time beside Eileen, Garvin sat with the Number One Warlord. The emotional aftermath of the funeral had left them disturbed. Inasmuch as death is only another facet of life, a professional soldier is inclined to have beneath his weather-beaten hide a stratum of sentiment different from that fear of the hereafter that drives so many career civilians to divine worship for a booster shot of salvation-reassurance. So they sat in General Dennis Kerwin's headquarters, from which they could see the towering granite palisades overlooking the horseshoe ridge from which the Imperator had touched off the charge that had routed the Liberators.

They sat, and they said old things over again.

Each had assured the other that "You look good as new," which evoked realistic retorts such as, "Balls! I am damned well as weary as you are."

On each face the lines had deepened, especially at the corners of the mouth and about the eyes, with sun squint and frown ravines; but the tiredness was internal, disguised as resolution and perceived only by those of comparable experience.

Another repetition: "Only three stars, Denny. When's Lani promoting you?"

The retort, rephrased: "Every *other* son of a bitch would yell for another star, and that'd screw up the budget. And the public recognizes true humility and dedication."

Spaceman's prescribed retort: "Bullshit! But the suckers buy it."

Two topics remained untouched: Which drink was to be the stirrup cup, and where was Lani? They had shied from the latter, for it was she who had heard Alexander's final words.

Rather than continue with that sadness, Kerwin made a detour. "That EHV Alexander Mark I is beautiful for reducing spots of organized resistance. And your idea of firing live projectiles as salutes, each with a different bursting charge, hitting that horseshoe ridge—nice touch, Rod. High explosive nearly leveled the ridge, and incendiary spewed liquid fire the length of what was left." He smiled, a twisted, bitter grimace. "By now enemy infiltration in our southwest knows the ballistics of our new gun."

Garvin shrugged. "Just like old times. I still can't figure which is the underground, they or we."

"Never heard it put that way, but whichever it is, we have them groping."

Garvin sat straight up. "Clarify that one. Funerals always leave me a bit muddled."

"When someone signaled a supposed freighter to heave to for inspection and you turned it into an orbiting incandescent junk heap, someone was wondering whether you were freighting high-tech material, a seriously sick Lani, or a dead Eileen."

"Speaking of high tech, why not analyze Eileen's broadcasts, graph her voice curves, get new speeches, a new girl, and modulate the wave pattern till it passes for Eileen's. With good makeup, we wouldn't even need a look-alike. Use film clips and make a plastic 'breathing' texture mask for the new speaker."

Kerwin frowned. "Can they do that?"

"Nothing like trying it." He paused. "But every gimmick like that makes more work for Security, more risk. Better to find Lani."

"Rod, you are as good as asking me where she is. I do not know. I do not want to know. Last thing I said to her was to get going until she could dump the service transportation and get a civilian crate. Keep going until she was sure she had not been traced. She knew all about Neville Ingerman's caper, and you can bet she took my advice."

"You don't want to know where she is."

"Anyone three grades higher than a lance corporal's dog robber runs the risk of being kidnapped and questioned or held to be exchanged for someone we are holding—or something we know. The processing the enemy would give any of us would be more than we could take. So, what I do not know, I cannot tell."

"If you find her, get her back to Mars."

"So you think she'd be a meaningful symbol? Like the British royal family?"

Garvin nodded. "Could not miss. And with Momism a North American invention, she'd be the Great Mother Goddess.

"Now that we've picked a rallying symbol, a palladium, you might say, and no more Moslem allies to worry about, she can take off her veil. Bedazzle them the way Flora used to. Even in Slivovitz Land, they manufacture counterfeit Sudzo, with an imitation Flora waggling phony pink panties with forget-me-nots in an area no one ever forgets."

Kerwin sighed. "Those were the days when American culture was *American*."

"Denny, sometimes I think you have a sour touch, or

is it bitter? Now that we have done with weeping for
Alexander, let us get at the state of the nation. When I
am back on the job, I have to know everything. Which
calls for a guessing department that works most of the
time. Far as I've gone, it looks—the country, I mean—
like a whore's bedroom on Monday morning."

"You've been going through backward agricultural
country. Little communities, each with its own way of
doing things. Communication falling apart. Groups are
separated. Each has its own laws. We collect a lot of our
taxes in produce and export the stuff. Hides, tobacco,
copper, and silver, and with labor costs way down, they
export quicksilver. Even Arkansas diamonds and Navajo
blankets!"

"All that home industry and one-man mining and a lot
of mule-pulled ploughs; there are shortages in some lines,
where they once were in oversupply."

Kerwin nodded. "Wartime emergency drove a lot of
people to every known do-it-yourself gimmick. And barter. Now they have no jobs to go back to. Some gripe and
yelp. Others, lots of them, think it's fun. Plenty of guns,
and what the arsenals can't supply, Mars does. They grow
their own law. Between hunting foreign enemy hideouts
and homegrown renegades, subsistence farming is not so
dull. When the shooting is slack, there is feuding growing
popular."

"In these postwar years, a new culture is building up.
Religion and cults are building up. The Stompers and the
Testifiers are making peace to combine against Oriental
heathenism. But you have been giving me the idea these
past couple of days that my glimpses of mint julep land
is by no means the nationwide picture."

"It is not. The industrial stretch in Ohio, from West
Virginia all the way into Indiana, is hanging on. The enemy
didn't want the country destroyed, and they picked on
nerve centers.

"Up to a point they were right, from their side. But the silly bastards did not realize that our rural people are an ornery pack. Cussed and quarrelsome. Lead their own lives. They'd kill a commissar for fun and marbles or to see him squirm. They are different from the intellectuals who'll believe anything as long as it is silly enough.

"And free ammunition does something for people."

"But as an industrial nation we have retrograded a century."

"Maybe more. A century and a half ago we were primitive, but no government was breathing down our necks, so a great nation built up. But too many lardass loafers went to school when they barely had sense enough to come in out of the rain. Gullibles who did not get brighter sitting eight hours a day in front of the boob tube."

"Are the courts still favoring the criminal class?"

Kerwin chuckled. "Don't even know whether there is a court working at being supreme. If you get out of step, friends and public opinion may save you. The second boner is your last. If your neighbors do not love you, you do not live long enough to worry about your old age, your golden years."

"Not building more jails?"

Garvin's heavy-footed irony made Kerwin laugh out loud. "We may refit the jails to be lodgings for the poor. Those who can work, produce rations, get paid in kind and share with the disabled folks."

Garvin frowned. "Socialism again?"

"Not by a country kilometer! No cash, no stamps for cash, liquor, narcotics, or women. Just beans, rice, sowbelly, and prunes when available. So, damn few on welfare. Staying home and working for subsistence is better when you're with neighbors."

"You begin to tempt me."

"You'd soon get weary of being inspector general or works manager or the like of a half-ass harvester or tractor or truck factory, or an open cast copper mine or iron diggings when the crew goes on strike because the Moral Minority ran all the whores out of town to keep God from blasting the country with fire again.

"Your job, *Admiral*—" The old soldier made that seagoing and space-wafting tag sound like a dirty word. He grinned amiably. "—is to inspire elit*er* scientists to cook up a technology to shoot Third or Fourth World invasions down in flames when they try to take Mars to liberate the planet enslaved by Imperialists."

"That's on the agenda?"

Kerwin wagged his head. "Naturally. The dopes and dreamers have to be encouraged while they are getting shellacked by rural snipers who do not want to be liberated."

Garvin sighed. "The school system didn't suffer too much when divine wrath gave the too-many survivors a religious revival. Nobody but a moron fed into the assembly line that turns out PhD intellectuals can be dumb enough to believe that after all these millennia, he is the first one to suspect that the world is less than perfect, and that he is the first one to make it a real utopia.

"Like in Morocco—damned if I can think of that Arabic which is spoken without vowels—but it means, 'head in the clouds, arse in the mud.' General, dump the intellectuals and tell me things about energy, which is what makes someone or something else do all the work."

"It is this way," Kerwin explained. "Now that the antinuke fanatics can't demonstrate, there is more power than you'd expect. And more windmill farms, and geyser area turbines grinding it out by the multi-megawatt-hours."

"We're tapping Martian volcanoes," Garvin interjected. "With electrolytic tricks and synthesis, we're breaking down minerals and building a breathable atmosphere and water you can drink without whiskey in it, and it does not kill horses or fish. Carry on, Denny."

"If your mad scientists could turn water into whiskey that wouldn't kill a horse, I'd ask for a transfer. Anyway, there is quite a bit of oil drilling. What you sweated out is mint-julep-belt clannishness and loving agriculture."

Garvin saw the sun touch fire to the distant palisades and cast long shadows. It was almost time for a stirrup cup and a night march. Time for sadness and fun was running out.

"Denny, there seem to be bits of government aside from your martial order maintenance patrols."

"There are." His face tightened. "The same damn bureaucratic hierarchy that screwed things up for Alex and during the century or more before him. Sometimes when it is a bona fide traffic accident or street crime, the bureaucratic empire figures that Security was executing someone sentenced after a five-minute general court-martial, and the whole machine of government goes into compound complex catatonia. Like the time the QM could not get flour but finally, yes, buckwheat is available."

"Buckwheat?" Garvin frowned. "There never was much of that. Only no real wheat. Did you get enough?"

"You'd never believe it. We got a carload of odd-looking stuff, and it was *foot powder*. For infantry feet, you know. Not worth a good goddamn for biscuits or hot cakes, like Field Service Regulations prescribe when the quartermaster cannot supply baked bread."

"And you knew what son of a bitch pulled that one, but you couldn't risk shooting him for sabotage, or they'd do worse."

"Rod, let us swap jobs. You begin to understand. That is what made the presidency a farce finally, and ditto for parliamentary democracy, and fatal for the Empire. But you were speaking of government. Well, scraps survive or are coming back.

"As I said, with people working again, in some places for sane wages, there is gold and silver beginning to back the pazor before it becomes secondhand skivvy paper. The iridium, palladium, and really rare strategics they used to buy from Marxist satellites are coming from Mars and the Asteroid. Our stockpile of them is better than double the mass of gold."

"Government *coining* money?"

"Not yet, not until we can back our paper with actual precious metal money or bullion on demand; a few honest pazors going into circulation would start a panic, nation-wide repudiation of skivvy paper pazors. Fact is, if the news got out and enough people believed it, a rumor could start the collapse."

Kerwin paused. There was silence until Garvin finally spoke in a low voice. "Everything these days, this century, has to be democracy or nobody buys it. Give it the name and they'll buy anything. The magic boob tube. But it will take martial law to give it the first nudge."

"Sound off, Rod, sound off."

"Egalitarianism is the problem. What we need is a *limited* democracy. Restrict the franchise to the taxpayers who finance the system. Restore the poll tax so politicians have to buy votes out of their own pockets. No tax receipts, no vote.

"Do not rob the rich. They cannot possibly spend all their income drinking and whoring around. Instead of punitive taxation, leave them surplus money to invest, make jobs, productive work. I'd say, if you pay tax on a million pazors, you get votes to accord, like at stock-holders' meetings. One share, one vote. A thousand shares, a thousand votes. Quit crucifying the people who built this country and made it what it once was.

"General, what do you say?"

"*Fix bayonets!* But it is worth trying if maybe not as simple as it sounds. I'll bust my tail trying. It may start civil war, but I'll risk it."

"You mean that?"

"If I did not believe we have a chance, I'd head for the Pacific Ocean, walk in chin deep, and swim till I was too far to go back."

Kerwin poured stirrup cups. Neither man looked as weary as he had earlier.

"Rod, I'm drinking to Alexander and limited democracy."

"Bottoms up, Denny!" They drank. "Got a date with a girl."

Chapter 34

WHEN THE DETACHMENT halted about fifty kilometers from the east coast and made camp, Garvin took leave of uniform and personal flag. He put on a homespun jacket and pants and a government-issue shirt without collar ornaments. His heavy-duty shoes were custom cobbled. The 11.2-millimeter revolver with an eight-pound or more trigger pull was no longer a handicap; he had survived long enough to become accustomed to it.

At the outermost reach of the guard fire's glow, he halted and handed Captain Wilson, the escort commander, an envelope.

"Give this to General Kerwin. Your orders and your quittance, your 'well done.' I have mentioned your instructions to the guard at Jump Off, Post Number Three. I compliment you and Private Emberg. Confucius said that the right man using the wrong method succeeds, whereas the wrong man with the right method always fails. Emberg should be promoted to private first class. I suggested a boost for you."

Garvin thrust out his right hand. "I am going undercover. For Christ's sake, do not salute! You don't know what bastard may be looking."

Following a wagon track skirting a stream that wandered among scrub oak put Garvin into familiar territory.

At times voices, wood smoke, and the smell of cookery told him of settlements lurking in the darkness. The aliveness of the woods, the stirring of night prowlers, raccoon and possum, and the chirping of crickets called to mind his drive with Mona from Nameless Island to Four Seasons Palace.

Something like eight years, but it seemed a lifetime ago.

A couple of hours of easy hoofing got him to the parting of stream and road. Although alive with night creatures, this was uncultivated woodland. Presently he came to a pond, a black opal that mirrored starlight. Well away from where he and Mona had parked, he found the windblown oak near which they had unrolled their sleeping bags. Even in those long-ago days, it had been wiser to sleep in separate blankets, with a handgun under your head.

The sound of an approaching vehicle woke him from a light sleep. The moon had risen over the trees to silver the pond. A good siesta. The visitor was probably Mona, but still he pretended sleep, the 11.2 magnum no longer serving as a pillow.

It was Mona who pounced from the wheel and caught him with both arms before he had fairly gotten to his feet. "Have a good sleep?"

"Uh...um..." He patted her fanny. "Won't bother asking how you feel after that drive."

"As if you've not just now found out by Braille, you lecherous old bastard! So you didn't seduce any female Stompers at the camp meeting?"

"Too busy thinking of you, Madame Broadtail."

"I got absinthe frappés frozen solid and melted back about right during the drive."

Garvin followed her up the tailgate steps and into darkness that ended when she touched light to a pair of alcohol-fired lanterns. From a hot vacuum jug she took broiled flounders, rice, and hollandaise sauce, all fuming and savory. From the other jug, a double king-size ration of absinthe frappé.

"Here's the bottle—we'll drink the rest of it straight."

"Doc Brandon's disciple, bless you! But I have a feeling that we are in dangerous country wherever I go. I'll settle for porter or stout—well, after these frappés."

He sketched out the Maritania situation, the cruise, and what had happened when Private Emberg walked Post Three. "As I said to General Kerwin," he concluded, "sometimes I wonder who is infiltrating into North America, we or the Liberators."

The stout, black as coffee, foamed when she opened it. "I forgot the corn muffins in the hot jug."

"Save 'em for breakfast. Where is Lani?"

"Idiot! You don't suppose I'd bring her in that trailer, do you? We are going to her retreat, and *I* am driving. No dangerous speeding, not in those mountains.

"Kidding aside, I've kept this crate in a garage maybe twenty kilometers up the coast from the island. Burmese shell raced me up the coast by night. We are going directly to the coed nunnery-monastery."

"After we see her, we might come back this way. I have been wanting to study some of Doc Brandon's files."

"I brought files that I knew would interest you. Maybe for your mad scientists on Mars. If I skipped any, we can take care of that later." She paused and seemed to turn inward a moment. "Once I was well into the woods, it began to get stuffy in the cab. If there ever was insulation between engine and cab, it's fallen apart.

"Last one in the pond's a dirty name!"

"You're half undressed already," he countered, and drew the 11.2 magnum. I'll stand guard while you're mud-crawling. Soon as your hands are dry enough for trigger pulling, you take over."

"Are you kidding?"

"The son of a bitch Private Emberg blinded with coffee

has been giving me morbid and paranoid notions, and so did the cruiser we shot down in flames. You've got a gun?"

She shook her head. "Dizzy as usual. You know where my mind has been, ever since you phoned and I asked how you were feeling, and you said 'weeth the hands' in that Greek accent you love."

She snatched the revolver.

"It's got an awful heavy trigger pull," he told her. "Point that damn thing out the door."

She did so. The muzzle blast shook the camper compartment. Mona blinked. "I thought you said it had a heavy trigger pull."

"Wonder girl! You have a miraculous trigger finger."

"A real Simianoid could have done that with her toes," she declared, whimsically mocking, and resumed undressing.

Mona, peeling down, whether for bed or for a swim, was always a combination of elegance and quickness without hurry. Now she was simply graceful.

Peeled down to bra and panties, she wriggled her bare feet into driving shoes. Glancing over her shoulder, she noted that he was still fondling the blued steel and walnut butt of the magnum.

"You really weren't kidding!"

"How'd you get that idea, and so suddenly?"

"You're not your usual self tonight."

"Ever since Lani's brat son got away from his baby-sitter and she found him and another brat being interviewed by the girls in a combination dance hall-whorehouse, I have been morbidly suspicious, and Eileen's death and thereafter has been building it up." It was true and self-evident—plausible.

Mona laughed. "We'll both be dirty names!"

"Being born that way makes it simple for both!"

Stretching legs, extending arms, Mona soared into

shadow and moonlight. Taking the tailgate steps deliberately, Garvin followed.

He hoped that his quest was not putting Lani into danger. Although he had mentioned her to no one until just before the stirrup cup in General Kerwin's office, he developed qualms; something more than general wariness lurked behind him.

When, with a slinky twist, Mona flipped bra and bikini to a stump, along with her loafers, she waded breast-deep into untested water instead of diving. Once stretched out, her mud scrawling, as Garvin had whimsically called it, was twinkling, as sinuous as the antics of a seal in an exhibitionistic mood. Despite differences in structure, she reminded him of Lani in a swimming pool.

Lurking in darkness, Garvin got his mind back on guard duty.

After a circuit of the pond, Mona came ashore.

"Taking a dip?"

"Soon as you are dry, shoes on, gun in hand, yes."

Garvin fell short of an Olympic fifty-meter dash, but he did very well. Mona's question, as the door of the camper closed behind them, confirmed his hunch. "How long ago did you meet Lani, I mean, the very first time?"

"Maybe sixteen years, allowing for land duty. I don't smell Martian Madness or Passion on the Nile, but you are making this a Lani evening."

"Remember, at Four Seasons Palace, you and I had separate compartments, but neither of us was ever caught slipping into the other's rooms?"

Garvin shrugged. "I figured that was Lani's orders."

"Until a lady-in-waiting came to your door and asked if you had any urgent appointments?"

"And so?"

"Next time I saw you, the genuine Lani and I were watching the broadcast of you aboard the *Garuda Bird*, with Eileen introducing you to her staff and so forth officers."

"The lady-in-waiting took me to Lani's private apartment to meet the look-alike, to see how much difference I could notice."

"Just imagine you undressed Lani—how would she have looked compared with your best recollection of the girl who went to Mars with you?"

"While you were undressing for a swim, and while you were sort of dressing after you dried off, you made like the inventor of the female body, modeling the first and finest ever produced. Lani all over."

Mona nodded contentedly. "I was not making like Lani, but she and I did compare our ways and histories. She is one of Doc Brandon's genetic experiments. Like me, an infant adopted by a childless couple. A Simianoid wired up for polyandry. She dumped her home environment and became a deluxe hooker. All she got out of it was being Imperatrix. I got my degree from six years with Doc. I was the lucky one."

"Uh—um—"

"Lover, quit trying to be a formal gentleman. I am not asking you what it is like with an empress. Probably pretty much like it's always been with me."

"Madame, end of third degree?"

"Just beginning. How much have I aged, how and where, since our first time alone?"

"Mmmm . . . you've skipped the silly stuff, burning your hide to cordovan leather, getting suntanned. Your throat and chin line and skin texture look as fine as the day she and I met."

"I looked through Doc's files. She is a dozen years older than I am. Since she had taken off nothing but her 'flirtation' veil when you kissed her good-bye, you still had a fair glimpse—" Mona gestured. "—well, about this far. And she looked like me as far as skin texture is concerned."

"Correct."

Mona picked her silicon chip computer watch from the ledge and set the alarm. She doused the ethanol lanterns.

"Without hurrying anything, we can catch three, four hours of sleep and still have darkness for making our reconnaissance camp."

"Reconnaissance?"

"There is a shelf maybe fifteen hundred meters above the valley floor. We can spy out Lani's retreat from there and see if it is okay to barge in. I've got the darlingest binoculars."

Since racing in gloom was hazardous, neither was a dirty name.

Chapter 35

THE SECONDARY HIGHWAY was better than Garvin had anticipated. "There isn't enough traffic here to beat it up," Mona explained, "but when we get into the narrow valley, we'll meet stretches that never were any good, especially trying to pick up the wagon trail up to the old distillery. That's even worse than the left turn to the retreat."

They were still some distance from the ravine when Garvin glanced at his side mirror. "Someone behind us driving a comet—those headlights—"

As he spoke, Mona was easing off the throttle and taking to the shoulder. She jabbed the emergency blinker button.

"When that clown hits the upgrade narrow curves, he'll block the whole ravine with flying junk."

The overtaking vehicle slacked off, swung clear, and passed them.

"Be damned! A Benson."

"Limousine, though I couldn't be sure," Mona contributed.

"No mistake about the Megapolitan Motor Club emblem on the license plate frame," Garvin said.

Mona cut the emergency blinkers.

"Odd business. Nobody drives those gas-guzzling bitches except the official crowd blowing government money."

The taillights winked out. The winding nasty stretch was at hand.

"Jumping Jehovah!" Garvin exclaimed. "Headlights blown. Got fuses?"

"Sorry. I went on infrared."

Garvin did not like that a bit. He knew she was not fatigue-shaky. Not Mona! That black limousine, then. He yawned and then quipped, "You sound like Operator 009."

"One of Doc's whimsies. He had a lot of fun with gadgets." She paused. "The less we see of anything official, the better. When the curves slow those characters down to winding road speed, slower than we'd go, I don't want them to see our headlights. It's a long way past the climb to the Retreat before you get to any sizable town. I am trying to sneak to our observation post, maybe for a couple of days. I don't want the Retreat people to know we are here, not until we're ready."

That made Garvin feel better. "I get it." He chuckled. "I'm not used to people thinking so far ahead. With nobody ever coming to this corner of nowhere, we do not want to be noticed by other people who know nobody ever comes this way."

"Rod, you've said it!"

Moving slowly in darkness, it seemed to Garvin that they were taking a long time to arrive nowhere. Time and distance, however, became irrelevant when, as they rounded a sharp curve, he exclaimed, "That fellow's barely creeping!"

Mona was already braking to a crawl. The IR screen showed her the rear end of a broad-beamed car with a Megapolitan Motor Club emblem. Throttling finally to ten kilometers an hour, Mona played follow the leader. Garvin began to wonder when he would be reaching for his gun. Mona's mood was contagious, or had she read his? Neither spoke. Each was extremely awake. Ahead, brakelights blinked and then went out. The crawl was resumed.

Somebody has been hunting me, Garvin mused, *ever since I promised Eileen I'd pray for her and bury the remains beside Alexander's. First chance I get at doing some hunting, someone is going to lose his passion for stalking game.*

The other driver was interested in the left lane of the narrow road.

The camper's engine barely whispered. Garvin noticed an odd sound—*whump...chump...wup...clump*—though the intervals were so long that he did not realize for a while that there was a rhythm.

There was something familiar about the sound, but it left him groping for identification.

The car ahead was stealthily creeping. *Thump-clunk* became louder as Mona closed the gap. She whispered, "What's that odd noise?"

He explained in a low voice.

Four hundred meters farther, the car ahead halted. The dome light blossomed for a minute and then went out. The car moved on, picking up speed.

"As a guess—" Garvin raised his voice. "—they finally decided to look at a map and find out which way was up."

He could still hear *thump-whump* when Mona plied the spotlight to the extreme right, crawled along for a moment, and then swung into blackness. Gears whined. The engine revved up as the camper tackled switchbacks, zigzagging on a rutted road that went up an ascent far steeper than any vehicle could have made in a straight pull.

"That *whump-thump* must have been a landmark you can hear in the dark," Garvin said finally.

At last Mona swung the camper onto a spacious shelf and snapped on the parking lights to guide her to the rubbish-littered concrete slab of a shed that was ready to fall apart.

"Madame, you were magnificent, and I feel years younger. I was too twitchy to ask if this was necessary to keep revenue people from taxing liquor."

"This was legal. One of Doc's colleagues discovered a synthetic you mix with whiskey hot from the still, and it tasted like real sour mash, filtered through maple charcoal five meters deep and aged ten years."

"TV will sell anything."

Mona flashed her light into a limestone cave. A pool of water mirrored the beams until it touched a shelf on one side, perhaps three meters wide.

"I'll move the sleeping bags to the cave," Garvin said. "Leave a night-light in the camper."

The idea interested Mona. "While I hustle up some leftover whiskey-filtering charcoal, you get the sleeping gear and the chow."

He came back with some home-canned Creole shrimp jambalaya. "With all the rice in it, why fool with sourdough biscuits?"

Nice thing about porter or stout; they didn't have to be so cold that you could not taste them.

Mona got the charcoal going and pumped the bellows.

He poured snorts of brandy and took the bellows. "After that drive, don't slave in the galley."

"No wonder your three wives adore you."

"Remembering that drive will keep me awake. You catch up sleep while I stand watch."

"Rod Garvin, you are a selfish son of a bitch!"

That left him blinking.

Mona explained. "Lights in the camper to bait and kill prowlers, lawfully—and you won't let me watch. It'll all be over before I wake up."

"Before the *prowlers* wake up! You really do need sleep."

She feigned looking sulky.

He drew the massive magnum and offered it to her. "That trigger pull was nothing to your pale hands with the grip of a bear trap. Goddamn it, you stand guard, then."

"I want to watch and learn something. How you survived meeting so many nasty people."

"Honey, nobody but a bureaucrat would drive a car like that into country like this. You are as twitchy as I am. You need rest."

Mona's eyes narrowed. The charcoal glow did odd things to her eyes, and despite the ruddy light, they seemed greenish.

"You are going to kill a bureaucrat and won't let me watch. Paranoia, that's what it is, all those suspicions about some lost strangers."

"You feel crapped on, persecuted," he retorted. "Now shut up!"

The chill of elevation drove them to their sleeping bags.

When her breathing sounded right, he slipped out of his bag and sat on the hot limestone under the dead ashes until, at last, the light in the camper merged with dawn.

"Wake up, dreaming girl! Greet the rising sun!"

She slipped out of her bag, knelt at the edge of the shelf, and splashed her face with icy water.

"I faked sleep. Now we are taking a walk before breakfast."

These iron women! Garvin followed his guide. Although it was murky at cave level, the sun was putting a halo about the topmost peak some five or six hundred meters up a nasty trail. Glancing about him, he saw that nothing remained of the distillery that was worth hauling away.

Before bending into the climb, Mona handed him a thermos. "You take this." She pointed. "We're heading for the top. There is a ledge right below the Geodetic

Survey benchmark. From there we can spy out the promised land."

Long before he reached the goal, Garvin learned that he was not yet used to Terrestrian gravity.

The benchmark read six thousand four hundred eighty-seven and twenty-two one-hundredths feet. By the time she had taken the thermos, poured coffee, and laced it with brandy, Garvin managed to gasp, "Martian g does play hell! I once climbed Mount Whitney on the Pacific coast, three times this pimple's elevation, and no problem."

Once restored, Garvin took the binoculars and looked west.

"That, sir," Mona said, "is the promised land. If you're looking at the right plateau, you see some green acres and some fallow ground."

"I'll be damned! Monks, nuns, novices, hitched to plows."

"They play they are mules and rest at the plow handles."

"No tractors, not a working animal on the farm?"

"It's a vegetarian colony. Not even animals for eating. Now, lower right, peeping out from trees. Buildings, squared masonry, tile roofs."

"Got it. And smaller things, way off, left. Among trees."

"Shacks for real recluses."

"*Real* recluses." He lowered the binoculars. "Aside from one empress and other *really* spiritual people, how many political refugees might be there hiding from the Warlords?"

"You're hinting that Liberators get into cult spots like this to bide their day of better luck?"

"Never occurred to me," Garvin confessed, "until just now."

"Nor me, either! I'm so accustomed to my family-style

island, where strangers just naturally are screened."

"And sometimes beheaded," Garvin reminded her.
"Quicker we get her out of here, the better."

Mona resumed the tour by remote control: "... refectory ... original complex of cells for devotees and novices
... administration building ... infirmary ... chapel."

"Where's the standpipe, water tower, power line, or
windmill?"

"Never occurred to me," Mona admitted. "Been here
only twice after I brought her. All I know is it's self-
sustaining."

Garvin handed her the glasses. "Farther left border of
the farm. A sister bending on the plow handles. Four
monks pulling."

"I've got it."

"I need landmarks. Way to the left. A cornerstone,
reddish rock. A conifer, lightning-blasted. Windblown oak
nearby."

"I've got it. You must be psychic! Bisect the corner
angle and you'll see a trail. The only one except for forks
and branches once you're in the woods. Keep far left and
you get to Lani's cell—actually a tiny cabin. Eats at the
refectory when she feels like it."

Garvin took the glasses and surveyed the area again.
"Sit down. I just got a revelation. That peculiar sound
while that strange car had us bugged. That was a hydraulic
ram, ramming away happily. But the answer didn't come
to me until you said the Retreat is self-sustaining.

"There must be a spring, pretty well up the grade, and
down nearer the road, quite a piece down, the water picks
up speed like crazy. MV squared builds up lots of energy
from a little mass. One valve slams shut. Sudden checking
of the flow makes the water take an escape hatch, another
valve, and up she goes, into a big iron bulb. That com-
presses the air in the bulb, and back pressure shuts that
valve, and expanding air forces some of the water all the

way up to the plateau and cistern we can't see from here.

"Meanwhile, the exhaust valve has opened, and a lot of water races downhill while air pressure pumps a bit uphill."

"I can't picture it, those valves."

"Neither can I!" He never could figure how those valves were activated. "But you said there was electricity. So I am betting there is a pipsqueak turbine driven by waste-water moving fast enough to build up enough MV squared to spin a power generator, a little one to charge the batteries all day.

"So this is what we are going to do. This evening, around dusk, we'll wait in that blind curve down from the distillery till it is time for me to climb up the crazy steep slope, pulling myself up as I follow the pipeline. Give me an hour, and then you drive up to headquarters. That way, I'll brief Lani, and if there is any hassle, I'll pop up, ready to quell the riot."

"You can't! Not up that horrible grade!"

"Madame! Garvinizing is the way to solve the insoluble, mutate the immutable, and screw the inscrutable. Silence, please."

Mona sighed. "Hence the pyramids?"

"Hence the pyramids!"

"Just in case of minor foul-ups," she said, "like the abbot or Brother Desmond wanting to trot along with me to Lani's cabin, you want to stay undercover."

"Sure I do."

"All right. She and I were sisterizing at Four Seasons Palace while she was supposed to be aboard the *Garuda Bird* going to Mars. Hiding out was dull business, and I used to kill time singing some of Doc Brandon's favorite old-time songs."

"She never went for dirty songs, not in my—uh, our day. Mmm . . . If I could borrow a habit and impersonate a monk—suppose she'd have a spare?"

"It'd smell of Martian Passion, and they'd think you were a fruit."

"All right! I won't snoop, and you do the brain work. Now hear this—"

"Admiral, don't forget to say, 'this is no drill.'"

"Speaking of little bitches—"

"Next to Lani and your three wives, I'm the nicest one you ever met. You were saying?"

"We eat a square meal, get a long sleep, and no swimming in the whiskey water pool. I'll take first watch, you second, I'll take third, and you last."

Chapter 36

AS THE SUN sank, monastery, plateau, and wind break of conifers were silhouetted, each with a golden aura. Mona, however, still stood near the edge of the distillery shelf, an arm about a sapling to steady herself while she looked through high-magnification binoculars.

Garvin finally broke the long silence. "What is so fascinating way up the road?"

"So far, nothing."

"Benson limousine ghost still haunting you?"

"Every time you woke me to take my turn on guard, or I woke you, I was saying the same things over again. What eats at me, it simply is not the car that ought to be in this corner of nowhere. You never see one in Savannah, and where else would that one come from?"

"You're the girl who always lets me do the worrying."

"Don't tell me you just *happened* to notice that motor club dingus. You were on edge before I met you at the pond. You had to stand watch with that magnum while I took a swim."

"Goddammit, all right! Racing up after us with halogen headlights, then overtaking and dawdling along—honey, what you and I have been doing is trying to tell each other we are not the only ones looking for Lani. We are tied to

247

logic. Unless our reason tells us something is rational, we have to dismiss it."

"You have to downgrade intuition because it is feminine. If you couldn't mind read situations without logic, you'd have been dead years ago."

"If feminine intuition were worth a hoot in a hailstorm," Garvin retorted, "why do so many bright women marry such stupid slobs?"

That left Mona without much rebuttal power.

Finally she found her chance.

"Lover, take a look, quick! The darlingest black Benson limousine. Now don't you wish you were dead!"

"Score one for intuition. What's the Benson doing now?"

"Lost elevation, and it's out of sight." After a moment she added, "This shows you Zen doctrine really works. 'When in doubt, relax, and move like a dog or an idiot.'"

"Explain that one, please."

"This morning, around sunrise, you looked and knew you had to sneak up and go directly to Lani's cabin. With you as the idiot and me as the bitch, we are working beautifully. If there is a Benson parked there when I pull up at Administration, I'll have a word with Brother Desmond and find out about the important visitor. Won't have to explain who you are. Let's get going."

They talked their way down to the blind curve just short of the so-called highway.

"Nobody would be interested in my coming to see Sister Zenia. That's her retreat name. If someone has to be polite and walk with me, I'll sing a song, and she'll sneak you out the back door before she let's me and company in."

"We were talking about political refugees hiding out with cults? Too bad you didn't bring a gun."

She dipped into her jacket and produced a tiny chrome-plated syringe in a safety case, spring-loaded so that a thrust would drive the needle beyond its guard.

"Hooker's friend. She gave me this when I was leaving Four Seasons Palace."

"I can make it in half an hour," Garvin said, and set out downgrade. Presently, as the hydraulic ram's *chunk-thump* became louder, he came to the exhaust water rippling along the road.

Now that he was well out of her sight, Mona glanced at her watch at thirty-second intervals.

Not even the grandfather of all Simianoids could make that climb in half an hour, she thought. *That* clump-chunk—whop-slop *will drive me up the wall faster than he can climb. In twenty-eight minutes, levitation will get me to the top.*

In twenty-nine minutes she booted the camper from cover and, a hundred meters upgrade, barreled into the climb. Instead of the marked thirty-five kilometers an hour, she revved up to sixty-five and, nearing a hairpin, downshifted and booted the gas. That broke the hind end loose and put the front head-on into the straight stretch, just right and precise to the millimeter.

She enjoyed the challenging drive, but when she came to the plateau's edge, wrists and forearms knew that they had taken a beating, and it was good to come out of lower dusk and into the ruddy glow.

Out in the fields, monks, nuns, and novices were at work. The sun had not yet set.

There was no parking problem.

To Mona's right were Administration, refectory, and chapel, all of squared limestone. Dinky whitewashed cabins lurked among the second-growth conifers that girdled the plateau. These were in addition to the original monastic living quarters, which she whimsically misnamed "cell block."

Working in the fields was good therapy—anyone with spiritual problems or emotional grapplings would have no insomnia after a day of playing plow mule. The altitude offered something that Nameless Island lacked.

A black Benson limousine was parked near the arched entrance. Although Mona was not surprised, the sight ruined her view. A few strides brought her close enough to the visiting car's exhalation to recognize good fuel, fragrant in comparison with the stuff burned in rural areas. As a guess, the travelers had reached their destination, attended to their business up north, and were seeking lodging instead of going all the way back to Savannah.

The retreat did accept guests at times. However, the situation was less than ideal for Mona. Life at a monastery was sufficiently different to make guests curious and questioning. She had to corner Brother Desmond as soon as possible and give him answers as to why she was not wearing the retreat habit.

Brother Desmond was a sort of chief clerk, a lay brother who had no fine scruples against unharmful falsehoods.

Mental gears clicking, Mona made for the massive door. When she was three or four meters short of the oaken planks and wrought-iron hinges, she stopped short.

The man who stepped out was long-faced and dark. He towered well over two meters, and an ankle-length black robe made him seem taller. He was somewhat stooped, and until he smiled, his face could have been called saturnine. The deep-set eyes lighted with recognition; he was amiable, a good guy, quite in keeping with the Retreat.

"Brother Desmond! What a nice reception committee!" Mona exclaimed.

Stretching long legs, he extended his hand. "I heard gears screaming all the way up, and you kept the tires screeching. Nice seeing you."

She caught the long, muscular hand. "Remember me? I was Sister Wendy last time I was here."

Brother Desmond frowned and then chuckled. "If you

were not, now is a good time to start."

She had made a good guess. He remembered her, but he'd forgotten things and was groping. Mona played up her advantage.

"When one of the lay folk leave the reservation, on errands, for instance, they usually don't wear habits. And that'd explain me, wouldn't it? Well, I'm here to see Sister Zenia, and she might have a spare habit in her laundry bag. I mean, so when we go to the refectory, I'd not be so conspicuous."

"Since your last visit, Sister Zenia has been eating in her cell. The one you called a cabin."

"Cell sounds a lot more retreatish. Looks as if the abbot has important visitors. Probably I won't be able to pay my respects." She dipped into her jacket. "Suppose you take charge of my contribution for hospitality and good-will. I'll be leaving at a gruesomely late hour, so much to gabble about! Is it all right if I stay parked right where I am?"

"By all means."

"There's only a narrow footpath to Sister Zenia's cell . . ."

"It's gotten no wider since your last time."

A bell tolled.

"I bet that's the Angelus! What am I supposed to do now?"

"Keep on with what you're doing. We're quite non-sectarian. No prayer until washup and everyone is in the refectory."

"Be sure and tell the abbot—"

The massive door opened. Brother Desmond and Mona turned at the metallic sound of the latch. The abbot stood aside to give precedence to a tall man who wore layman's clothing, austere but elegantly tailored. The honored one, presumably the owner of the limousine, gestured to decline the compliment.

"You are our guest," the abbot insisted. "Our Moslem

brethren say that each guest is sent by Allah."

Hearing that one gave Sister Wendy a flash: *If the Stompers ever got an earful of that, they'd forget about the Harlot of Rome.*

Harry Offendorf, whether or not known as such, had come to the mini-Shangri La. The first time Mona had seen this impressive specimen was at Four Seasons Palace the day after he and Garvin had wrangled about the obliteration shelling—or bombing—of Calabasas Cay in the Caribbean. All that Garvin had told her of Offendorf, Minister of Something or Other, came back. She was glad that she and the minister had never met.

What made the Honorable Harry Offendorf dangerous was his total sincerity, she recalled. He towered fullfleshed, radiant as a harvest moon, yet not flabby; genuine kindness and unfeigned humility made him impressive and convincing.

Turning from Mona, Brother Desmond faced his honored guest and the abbot. "Sir, I am the Right Reverend Abbot's chief clerk. Sister Wendy here is by no means too tired to guide you to Sister Zenia's cell. The Right Reverend Abbot has not yet recuperated from some days of overexertion." He bowed to the abbot. "Sorry I was not at hand to take over."

The swirl of long black robe was followed by the click of the door closing behind the abbot.

Brother Desmond turned back to Harry Offendorf. "Fortunately," he explained, "I heard the familiar gear whine and engine noise and knew Sister Wendy was on her way. Otherwise, the abbot would have insisted on walking you to Sister Zenia's cell."

"Ah . . . Brother Desmond, my apologies to the abbot. I didn't realize I was imposing."

"Sir, he would never let you suspect. So dedicated, you know."

Offendorf turned to Mona. "Sister Wendy, evidently you have had a long drive."

"We are here to serve. We are never tired. Not until we're the abbot's age."

Then came an interruption. On the driver's side, the door latch clicked. Gravel crunched.

"What's the problem?" the driver asked.

"Meet your native guide," Mona said.

Mr. Offendorf took over. "Sister Wendy, this is my assistant, Mr. Wolf. George Wolf."

That Mona was half a head taller than the chauffeur did not give her delusions of grandeur or any sense of security.

Better looking by a kilometer than Garvin, even if you fitted Rod with a Sunday face. Not slick enough for a pimp . . . Rod would rate him as a bad egg, no good, and a shit-eater, senior grade . . . Mona rarely spoke Garvinese, but thinking in that language was easy and natural.

"Just a moment, I'll get my flashlight," she said. "Likely to be dark before we leave Sister Zenia."

Chapter 37

ALTHOUGH THE CLIMB was nasty going, the pipeline did help him claw his way through brush, thorns, and weeds. The *thump-whump-chunk* booted him; it finally had him clenching his teeth and shrinking, flinching from anticipation of the next relentless impact. By the time Garvin reached the level of the reservoir, he was twitchy and was cursing all the hydraulic rams ever built. When he let go of the vibrating pipeline and stretched out on the ground, he had just about had it.

However, his time was better than he had expected. Sunset thrust long red lances only a little way into the dusk of the pines. Guided by the reservoir and assisted by a cornerstone, Garvin oriented himself and maintained his general course. Sighting shots with a mapping compass helped. Since Lani lived near the rim of the plateau, he had only to avoid the five- or six-hundred-meter drop to the nearest outcropping of rocks.

He blundered through thickening gloom.

At last he saw a light.

Sometimes she doesn't eat at the refectory.

But just in case she was at the refectory—he advanced as though stalking dangerous game.

He saw a little clothesline holding underthings, including a slip, quite short, the kind an Amazon would wear. He tapped at the window, using the barrel end of the magnum. A chair scraped, and then there was silence. He edged from the window. She might be armed and twitchy.

Garvin sounded off in the language of the Asteroid. "If those are picnic panties on the line, someone is going to lose some of his original equipment."

"Rod, darling!"

The door opened. Lani was outlined by taper light. She grabbed Garvin with both arms. He stumbled over a rock and nearly took a pratfall, but a grip on Lani restored his balance. Together they staggered into the cell, neither letting go of the other lest they wake from an opium dream.

"Mona told you?"

"She drove me here. I climbed up from the hydraulic ram, the pipeline, and she's following, going to headquarters."

"What's going on? We don't have TV."

"Eileen died. I promised I'd bury her beside Alex. Did so."

Garvin sketched the cruise, the doings at the Stompers' camp meeting near Jump Off, and the black limousine. "There have been too many leaks," he concluded. "We've caught spies in Maritania and killed them very quickly, but we don't know how many we have not caught. Same for the pacified areas of North America and for the areas we're holding by martial law.

"There's too much gossip about your maybe not having gone to Mars. Some think you died. Others think you're away from Mars and recuperating from sickness. But someone knows that a cruiser that was supposed to stop and search the vessel that was carrying Eileen's body to the graveyard did not halt us, and the thing vanished without a distress call.

"Someone lost a cruiser and all hands. Didn't even

have time to sound general quarters. That is a dead giveaway. You have to get the hell out of here. Hightail it to my cruiser and head for Mars. With our armament, we can shoot down a fleet if they want to turn out in force."

"It's wonderful, your being here. But I can't."

"We are arming Mars against an attack. Dangerous attempt now, it'd be suicide later. Finally, we'll counterattack and obliterate the bastards till no one could believe they ever existed.

"Remember our phone talk, ages ago, on my way to the Palace?" he asked.

She nodded. "And now you're offering me a bigger empire than ever." Lani blinked tears against his shirtfront. "I can't."

"Can't run out on Alex?"

"You do understand! You know why I can't."

"Loyalty, yes. But to the Marxists you are a menace as long as you are even suspected of being alive. You are the glamour figure the Warlords need. I wish you'd tuned in on my talk with General Kerwin. When he retires— he is getting good and damned tired—the younger ones will carry on.

"For limited democracy. The unlimited kind became a tyranny as bad as any unlimited monarchy. You'd be more than a glamour girl. You'd represent Alexander, the first ruler in modern times who got off his fat prat and led troops in battle."

Garvin caught her by the shoulders. "Damn it, woman, so did you. Come out of cover and tell them so, from Mars. Do not insult your luck by hiding. Give North America the lift it needs. Decontaminate the country— hunt and kill! No other way."

Whether by a trick of taper light or Garvin's imagination, Lani's eyes were changing. Their longish, almond-shaped Egyptian darkness became half tawny, half greenish, as Mona's had changed when the fourth head had dropped at the sweep of a *parang*.

Garvin paused for breath. One more blast and she'd be a stand-up Imperatrix, inspiring the nation to get a fresh start, to become a freeman's land again.

Silence. He was weary. So was she.

Then from outside, they heard a woman chanting:

> The minstrel sings of an English king
> A thousand years ago.
> He ruled the land with an iron hand,
> But his mind was weak and low.

"Mona," Garvin said. "Bringing trouble. Where's the escape hatch?"

Lani pounced for the curtain and peeked out. Then she gestured. "That way! Get out and stand by."

Then, raising her voice, she sang:

> The monarch's only garment was a leather undershirt,
> It hid quite well the royal hide—

Garvin heard the remainder through the door that closed behind him. And then Lani called to the approaching visitors:

"Wait a second till I get dressed."

Garvin gave the magnum a hitch just in case he had to do some pistol whipping. There must not be gunfire, not with witnesses.

Lani yanked the door open. "Darling, what a lovely surprise! Come in, come in. And friends! If you'd not sung that dizzy old song, I'd have died of shock."

Under the guise of happy sorority, each fixed the other with eyes like lance heads. Then, as though snapping out of a dream, Mona blinked.

"Oh, I'm sorry, Mr. Secretary! And you, Mr. Wolf. Sister Zenia, the Honorable Harry Offendorf, Secretary of International Spatial Relations. Is it de facto or de jure?"

Offendorf chuckled. "Sometimes I think it varies from day to day."

"Let's imagine it is both," Lani said.

And Mona: "His traveling companion, who knows the country." Mona nodded toward George Wolf. "Sister Zenia, make your bow."

"Please be seated," Lani resumed. "There are only two chairs. Sister Wendy and I, we'll sit on the cot. This is an austere place. Nothing but herb tea. Wendy, darling, would you mind serving? I'm quite too fluttery. Where have you been?"

"Making a survey of other retreats. The abbot dreams of amalgamating some of them."

Sister Wendy pumped the bellows and got the charcoal glowing.

"Unusual folk song, Sister Wendy," Harry Offendorf said.

Mona laughed. "I didn't want Sister Zenia to have a heart attack. I've been gone quite some while."

Barley cakes, berry jelly, and pine nuts were served.

Lani led off. "Mr. Secretary, I do not deserve this distinction. You must have some purpose far more important than I could possibly serve."

Getting to his feet, Offendorf bowed. "Imperial Majesty, Imperatrix Lani, I invite you to make a public appearance in Megapolis Alpha to end this coast-to-coast anarchy."

"Lani blinked and then gulped. "This is a mistake. People have said, well, some years ago, that I did look like the Imperatrix."

"Madame, I am aware that your life has been in danger because of such statements. It is in danger even here. Our agents in Maritania learned that the look-alike empress died. Dedicated fanatics consider you a menace. We moderates take a different view."

"I don't want to hear another word! Even hearing what you say is putting me in danger."

"Ignoring what I say is the actual danger. We want you to help us restore the Democratic Imperium. Stabilize the nation. Bring your son from hiding on the Asteroid. You would be regent."

"Can't I convince you that I am not, never was—"

"We have tapes of your talks with Alexander in his mobile headquarters. In facing death, he prevailed as he did not during his life."

Although his audience was two women and a chauffeur, Harry Offendorf had the voice and presence of an Old Testament prophet. Rivals declared that when he talked to himself, his rehearsal convinced him that he spoke eternal truth.

"... even the most idealistic finally realized that we Liberals had been duped by extremists, that radicals had made a deal with the enemy. It is not too late to restore the Empire. During the minority of Alexander's adopted son, you will be regent, Dowager Imperatrix, with Maritania the capital of North America, Mars, and the Asteroid."

Garvin broke out in a sweat. What Lani believed was immaterial. However much of this proposition was top secret, there was a group in North America and a group in Slivovitz Land—the two in Lani's cabin were only the field men. Once Lani and her son were baited out of hiding, there would be their assassination—public, spectacular, a magnificent production.

Offendorf had to be extinguished before he awoke from his idealistic opium dream. Nor should George Wolf carry the story to headquarters. Whatever Offendorf had told the abbot was of ordinary prudence a falsehood. This kept things simple.

The surge and thunder, the vox humana stop, the eccle-

siastical drone, the clarion voice of liberty—all but the
blare of trumpets. Then there was cathedral silence. Wind
stirred conifers to a soft murmuring. This was the dangerous moment.

Lani spoke. Her voice was level and low, yet it carried.

"Mr. Secretary, I have been stupid. *Empress Dowager*
. . . my son's future."

The plateau was consecrated to meditation and con-
templation. Respect for privacy took the place of locks.
Garvin fingernailed the edge of the door, working it out-
ward until, fingers closing tight, he yanked it open.

The Supreme Idealist had enchanted himself into a
vision world midway between trance and awareness.
George Wolf, the little dark man, had not been hypnotized. In an instant, a simple situation became complex,
especially for him.

Chapter 38

NORMALLY, MR. WOLF'S reaching for his shoulder holster would have terminated in a simplicity: two magnum slugs dropping him before his gun was full drawn. But this was not normal. Mona's pouncing was more leopardlike than human; Garvin held his fire. Too much risk of drilling Wolf through and through and thus wounding Mona.

Her hand motion was a blur. Out of his chair, Wolf was knocked slantwise. His 9-millimeter automatic came free of its holster and skated across the rammed-earth floor. Startled, Harry Offendorf had not yet moved.

Clawing the floor, Wolf twitched and shuddered. His breathing was harsh, then wheezing, and in a few seconds, inaudible. By then Mona had regained her feet. She slipped a small syringe into her jacket pocket.

"The hooker's friend," she remarked casually.

Lani was not as bemused as she had sounded. She pounced for Wolf's handgun.

"He won't ever move," Mona said. "He got the full charge."

Although Offendorf still did not understand, he was alarmed by Garvin's abstracted fingering of that 11.2-millimeter gun.

"Sit down, Mr. Secretary," Garvin said amiably. "Your

man shouldn't have gone for a gun. Such a move startles people, and they act impulsively."

The golden voice of idealism recovered rapidly. "That was daring, your saving this fellow's life," he said to Mona. Then he turned to Garvin. "What's all this mean? You seem quite too well known to Her Majesty and Sister Wendy."

"Mr. Secretary, I did have the privilege of paying my respects to Her Majesty a number of years ago."

"Most amazing tackle. Sister Wendy, was that one of those karate tricks? Amazon business, no doubt."

"There still seems to be confusion," Garvin cut in. "I doubt that your man will ever move again. Under his own power."

"Crippled? Paralyzed? Outrageous. There should be a law to prohibit karate."

"Life is strange," Garvin said. "If Wendy had not tackled him, I would have blown two holes through him before he got his gun out of the holster. She saved his life, but he must have had a heart condition or something. I'm sure he is dead."

Garvin knelt, took the wrist, released it, shook his head, and got up. "No pulse. No breathing. Next incarnation, he won't pull a gun on a harmless stranger."

"I do not think much of your levity. You seem to know who I am."

"I ought to. I listened in on your dreams of empire."

"My assistant's death bears looking into. It seems to me I have seen you before somewhere."

"We wrangled about who leveled Calabasas Cay—an Asteroidian bomber or a North American battleship."

"Now I remember. You're the war criminal whose atrocity won the battle of Kashgar."

"And you are the idealist who is putting Sister Zenia in a fatal position by declaring that she is the widow of the late Imperator, Alexander Heflin. That helps me make up my mind. Each has a strong cause against the other."

Garvin kept his handgun at his hip. "You and I are on opposite sides of a high fence. There is only one way we can settle our differences. Zenia, get me that hearth brush, please."

Lani did so; he hefted it with his left hand.

"That will do. Mr. Offendorf, you are not familiar with weapons, so I do not ask you whether you wish to use my revolver or the late Mr. Wolf's automatic pistol."

"Does your challenge allow me the choice of weapons?" Offendorf's color had changed, but his voice was steady and flavored with contempt. The man was game all the way through. Garvin regretted the necessity that the situation had imposed.

"Sir, this is not the conventional challenge. I have used guns since I was the length of a rifle. So I'll hand you this revolver. My weapon will be the hearth broom."

"This is no occasion for mockery!"

"I am not mocking you." Garvin turned to Lani. "Your Majesty and Sister Wendy, in case there are not enough wraps to keep you both from shivering when you go out and let me and your enemy settle this matter decently in private, take this." He twisted out of his jacket and tossed it. "Now, please get out!"

"Rod!" Lani cried.

"Madame, let me and our enemy decide which dies in peace and which leaves in peace."

"But you can't! A broom against a gun!"

"One of us has not long to live. Please leave us."

When the women had left, Offendorf demanded, "What do you mean saying you'll hand me your gun and face me with a broom?"

"I am sorry you do not believe me. This is the only way I can level the odds. When I explain, you'll know that the risk I am taking is not as great as you imagine it is.

"I have done this with swords but never with broom versus gun. Even so, I'll level the odds a bit more. In your favor, of course. I'll put my left hand on my chest, thus."

Garvin placed his palm.

"Observe how I hold this brush," he continued. "The way a fencing master would hold a dueling sword, except that I have the fiber of the brush instead of the point of an épée touching the floor. Instead of saluting an opponent, he proposed to parry. So do I."

Offendorf was now quite irritated.

"What does this nonsense have to do with pistol versus brush?"

"Instead of pistol, the master of the sword invited me to extend my blade until the blunted point was against the back of the hand he held against his chest. The game was this: When he dropped his hand, I was to lunge. He would parry my thrust before it could travel the thickness of an old man's hand."

"No game! The fencing swords were blunted."

"He knew that I'd not have the guts to run a sharp épée through him if he failed. He knew the risk would cramp me, freeze me. Anyway, he parried my thrust, and with time to spare. He could have done as well if I had been an enemy with a live blade.

"You and I are not friends. I must not let you live. You see me as a war criminal who should have been put to death. Here is your chance. Live up to your ideal."

"You mean that I am to jam this revolver against the back of your hand, and when you lower that hand, I am to pull the trigger?"

"Yes. But I'll bring brush from floor and knock your wrist aside so your shot won't touch me. I forgot to tell you, this is a double-action revolver. A continuous trigger pull cocks the weapon and then fires."

He lowered his left hand. "While you are making up

your mind, I must rest my arm and hand. They should not be cramped."

"Goddammit, I can't blast an unarmed man that way. What do you think I am?"

"I have a light brush broom. Would you feel better if I took the six-gun and gave you the hearth sweeper?"

There was silence.

"You'll be acting for the nation and for humanity. Here, take the gun."

Offendorf accepted the weapon. The way he hefted the revolver, he looked as much at home with a gun as any man would be at home squatting on a French girl's bidet.

Again the brush fibers touched the floor. Garvin put his hand back, palm against chest. "Harry, nothing personal in this. Simply my duty and yours. Put the muzzle against the back of my hand. Lightly. I must have free motion."

Garvin drew a deep breath. No matter how awkward a gunner might be or appear—he inhaled again, exhaled. Not enough to establish a rhythm yet—

Left hand flashed down. The brush came up, striking Offendorf's wrist.

The revolver dropped, unfired. An instant of kung fu did things to the extended right arm and to the man's balance. The big man made a loop. He tumbled, and thumped to the floor. Garvin went with him. There was a crisp snap.

Garvin got to his feet and went to the door. "Come in. Mission accomplished."

Lani led the return, with Mona at her heels.

"You idiot!" the Imperatrix cried. "Risking all that!"

"Someday I'm going to lose. This was not the time."

"You gave him—that gun—was it really—loaded?"

Garvin unlatched and swung the cylinder out. "Take a look."

Lani nearly folded. Mona edged her to the cot. "It was

not quite what it seemed. The poor son of a bitch didn't have a chance."

"Don't feed me that crap!" Mona flared. "I was getting pretty sick myself."

"I could do with a couple of snorts of Demerara rum," Garvin admitted. "But there was no gunfire. Even so, no time for hysteria and postmortem. We've got to get these two stiffs out and over the rim rock, first stop nearly a kilometer down."

He grabbed Lani by the shoulders. "On your feet, Amazon!" Then he turned to Mona. "Get your camper out and down to the road. Wait for us in that S-curve where we waited for dusk. You can talk your way clear if need be. Tell the abbot or whoever you might see at Administration that Mr. Offendorf and Mr. Wolf are conferring with Sister Zenia and ran you out, confidential stuff.

"Soon as Lani and I do a bit of mopping up, we'll follow the pipeline down and head for where you're parked. You have Mr. Wolf's gun?"

"Trying to take it away would be suicide!"

"Lani and I are going to that hideout, that Egypt spot. I don't think you'll have trouble waiting, but if you have to shoot yourself clear, don't wait for us. Get going, and we'll walk."

When darkness took charge of Mona, Garvin turned to Lani. "Anything but novice work clothes or your refectory robe?"

"I kept my Amazon things. Sentiment. Last days with Alex. My shoes are okay, and I'll wear my field clothes for meat wagon duty."

Not being heavy enough for weight-lifting contests, Garvin was glad to have Lani's help. After taking car keys, papers, and wallets and cutting identification from the garments of the evening's casualties, they stripped the bodies and dragged them to the rim.

"Whether or not we are concealing identities, each scrap of paper is worth Security's looking over. When and if I get to General Kerwin's headquarters, he gets the loot."

"What's this business about my going to Egypt?"

"Let's get the enemies over the side."

It was a long, long drop. They did not hear the thump.

On their way back to the cabin, Garvin said, "While we are cleaning up and making sure we are not leaving anything that enemy security would find helpful, I'll brief you. Correct me when I am wrong."

"Count on me!"

"I'm assuming that the abbot would not believe anything that his deceased guests told him about Sister Zenia. Also that no matter what he thought the facts were, he would play dumb and innocent, thereby keeping his nose clean. You know him a lot better than Mona could."

"You said something about Egypt."

"That's another settlement—"

"I know about it," Lani interrupted. "Mona and I talked about Egypt. I should have gone there in the first place. The Brandon Foundation paid my way from the start. The man who runs Egypt is not a psycho who thinks he is the reincarnation of Sir Something or Other. The colonists, or call them cultists, dye themselves for protection against skin cancer. And to look like ancient Egyptians, redheads, blondes, the whole pack dye their hair black so they look like the people in papyrus scrolls. They wear clothes like the natives in temple paintings. Happy farmers, they look all alike—the way blacks or Chinese look all alike to white Anglo-Saxon Protestants. Good people, no crazier than Mennonites or Amish. Just different. If they were Bible thumpers, Stompers or Testifiers wouldn't hate them."

"Anyway, it's another cult hideout. People usually come from all over to spots of that sort."

She nodded. "That's how it is here."

"Meaning everyone is a self-displaced person, everyone is out of place, and almost any story would get by. Take the other extreme, those Stomper colonies in mint julep land; each is a clan, and a stranger is as conspicuous as a carnival parade in a graveyard. Everyone thinking Egypt is crazy, that is an advantage. But the way things turned out tonight, it's clear you are hot as a firecracker. This is wilderness country, unsettled. In these war years, people have gotten used to vultures circling about. Feud killings and martial law keep things up. People are inclined to mind thier own business, especially people like the abbot.

"But whatever Offendorf's true story is, whether he was picking you out for assassination or really intended to use you as a political figurehead, he has managed to stay clean on the surface, and whatever he's been up to undercover, there is going to be hell to pay.

"We can head for my cruiser. It's berthed in the turpentine belt near Pensacola. Warlord Number One has troops in the area, and the ship's crew I left there are a grim set of veterans. You can be aboard and heading for Mars before the news about Offendorf circulates. I'd been thinking Egypt so much that I misspoke myself. And I heard enough to know you wanted no more of Offendorf's deal than you wanted a spot in a snake pit."

Lani laid a hand on his arm. "You've been the most loyal, ever since our idiot start years ago. And as a point of honor, you've been figuring on getting me one boost higher than Imperatrix." She sighed and shook her head. "Lover, I can't. I simply cannot."

"Oh, for Christ's sweet sake!" He slumped, dejected. "Well, all right. I was half afraid of that. Tell me and get it over."

"You already know. When Neville Ingerman nearly cost us that battle and the Slivovitz slobs used tactical nukes against our only friends, the Canadians, Alex did what he had to do.

"He was badly shot up and feeling no pain when he grabbed my hand and said, 'Now we're decontaminating the country! Get away while you can. Hide out wherever you can and wait for the day!'"

"That's just what I'm asking you to do!"

"Alex used to say, 'Space be damned, when people don't even know how to live on Earth.' He was thinking of North America and the neighbors, the only ones that stood by and with us when the last chip was on the line. All his life, he fought mediocracy, idiocracy, socialism, and egalitarian fool's bait! Rod, Alex is gone. I can hide out in that spot, but here is where I belong. I cannot abdicate."

She paused for a moment. "Remember the time you blew your own ship to a puff of flame to keep news of that Asteroid from getting to North America and ruining the little planet you'd discovered? You never expected to see Flora again, nor Azadeh, nor this country of ours."

Garvin sighed. "That does show I am as crazy as you are! So I'll go back to Mars, herd the scientists around, and make the defenses of North America foolproof. Azadeh's son will marry Alexander's daughter, and there's an imperial dynasty."

Lani blinked away her tears and gave him a thank-you kiss. "Before you and Mona hustle me away to become an Isis worshipper, you have to tell me how you dared that idiotic trick, hearth brush versus a loaded revolver."

"So simple, he never suspected he could not win. I knew when I would bring that long handle whisking from the floor. He did not know. He did not know when my left hand would drop and my right one move. I had that gun knocked out of line before he could pull the trigger. Reaction time, you know."

Lani shivered a little, and not from the evening chill. "So you had it all figured and smooth talked him!"

"Offendorf was an assassin at heart, however much he talked up his sense of fair play."

"Oh? Well, you *are* a mind reader."

"No, Madame Imperatrix. He did not ask me what we would do to settle our problem, just supposing I did knock the gun from his hand. Mona had the nine-millimeter automatic we would have needed then for a decisive duel. He was sure he would win. Isn't it grand to quit while you are winning?"

There was a long silence. Lani had met the ultimate in Garvinizing. Although she and Mona were genetic-experiment sisters, Doc Brandon's creations, Madame Broadtail would have needed scarcely a split second to digest the planned and executed death sentence. Her response would have been spontaneous applause. Garvin sensed that for Lani there was emotional damage that had to be repaired. Instead of explaining and making matters worse, he changed the subject.

"Let's keep Mona waiting another couple of minutes. With that nine-millimeter handgun, she could stampede anything up to a platoon! A three-cornered debate is sure disaster, and we have some decisions to make. Every damn one of us. Whether you sound general quarters or punch the damage control button, it's got to be right, and let's not waste time."

Lani's expression changed; she sensed concern for her welfare and she recalled that she herself had once done a very neat instant execution—so why the emotional puking at instant planning? Mona's needle jab had given Wolf silent death. And Garvin's inexorable computer had devised silent doom for Offendorf.

Now her response was a blend of sadness and affection for a friend and playmate with whom she had shared critical experiences.

"Rod, you do want me to go to Mars." She caught him with both arms. "I know you're still hoping to get me out of danger. But I can't leave. No more than you could have left Alex. That took my trickery. I never loved you more than when I had you between my legs and gave you that needle jab."

"You win."

"No one has beaten you. It's more than me, more than Alexander."

"Understanding does not make me dance from joy! Doing it with an empress was different. But you still win. Only there is one thing you have to do! Goddammit, yes. I said you have to!"

"Tell me! The only time you've ever been wrong was when you bitched up the black box and got us shanghaied to Mars instead of honeymooning in Katmandu."

"Imperial Highness, if I had not done exactly that, you would never have become Imperatrix of North America. Now for Christ's sweet sake, *listen to me!*"

She listened.

"Mona has to dump you in Egypt and stay away for keeps. I mean for keeps. Offendorf watched Mona and found you. She is the Brandon Foundation. She has to find a new fiscal agent to get your expense money to Sir or Mister What's-His-Name. The late Harry Offendorf whose carcass is a thousand or so meters in the ravine was a Marxist stooge. The country is full of them, and you are in danger till the last one is hunted down and killed."

"You tell her. She'd listen to you."

He shook his head. "Doc Brandon was the only man who could tell Mona anything. She's fond of me; she worshipped him. I'll ride with you two as far as the outskirts of the first town that has an airport or bus station. I am an exile. I have been newsreel filmed too much. There is a reward of a hundred thousand pazors on Neville

Ingerman's head. His crowd offers a bounty for my scalp."

Garvin caught the imperial hand. "I'll tromp the thorns and stuff. You follow and keep a good grip on the pipeline down that nasty grade. Goddammit, if you can't do what I tell you, imagine it is Alexander telling you how to operate."

Epilogue

_____

LONG RETURNED TO Mars, Admiral the Governor-General of that planet and no longer a war criminal, Rod Garvin remained an exile because of duty's compulsion. Until Limited Democracy was firmly established in North America, he had to carry on. As the years accumulated he wondered ever more, when he thought of Lani at all, whether the bonds of destiny that had linked him and the Imperatrix had finally fallen apart. Otherwise, his advance to the post of Governor-General should have been accompanied by Lani's emerging from seclusion and peril to be Imperatrix of North America, Mars, and the Asteroid: First Lady of the Solar System.

That Garvin's fate and Lani's seemed no longer interlocked left him at once liberated and lonely. But it was not as simple as all that. Every evening that he sat in his private observatory to wait for his native Earth to rise suggested that Lani wonderings were only one of the faces of homesickness. Earthrise had become more important by far than the ascension of Mars—which, during his early years, had baited him into spacefaring—had ever been.

Every evening before he exceeded his ration of emotional wallowing, lovely Azadeh came in wheeling the absinthe wagon. Whatever the hour, it was time for cocktails and first sight of his Number Two Wife when Terra gleamed bluish-green on the horizon.

Number One Wife, Flora, once intercontinentally famous because of her Sudzo TV show, was still in France. Aljai, the Asteroidian sleeping dictionary who became his third wife, had not returned from visiting relatives in her native planetoid. Fascinated by the North American customs she had observed during her brief sojourn in the Parliamentary Republic during the war that had made it an empire, she had gotten a California divorce by remote control, on grounds of desertion; after all, Garvin had not accompanied her on her visit home and had thereby embarrassed her.

All in all, Garvin was enjoying single blessedness in his home with but one wife.

The Governor-General's palace was an architectural mess that featured a dome, of all things, in an agricultural-industrial complex that retained its atmosphere only because of interlocking bulbs. Not to be outwitted by a bureaucrat, Garvin had elevated the dome, laid circular track, installed gear to keep a 400-millimeter refracting telescope trained on celestial bodies, and charged the cost to a study of asteroids whose orbits intersected that of Mars or Terra.

The Warlords who had almost decontaminated North America to establish Limited Democracy were now elder statesmen. The imbalance between agriculture and technology was being corrected. Meanwhile, the Martian consortium of elite scientists had created a network of satellites that made attack on either Mars or Terra a simple mode of suicide.

During all this progress, Marxist idealists knew well what too many bemuddled democracies ignored: that with effective subversion, the most heavily armed nations can be taken over. The rights guaranteed by democracy gave the subversive termites every advantage. Limited Democracy planted so many booby traps that the enemy, disguised as protectors of civil rights, were kept screaming themselves hoarse protesting. To cope with this problem, Garvin had devised solutions, few of them approved, yet managed so well that there was rarely a protest.

It was the advance of spacefaring that complicated matters for the Governor-General and the security people. Travel from Terra to Moon, to Mars, and to the Asteroid and, bit by bit, traffic to space stations multiplied the space tramps, who had been quite scarce until a dozen years before. Garvin was getting a continued education with never a diploma in sight.

Thanks to well-meaning Americans, Mars was going to hell. Some of the Aborigines stuck to their traditional ways. Others missed the good and bogged down in the worst of an alien culture. These, along with space tramps, were becoming a subculture.

Terrestrian parasites, frustrated by the bankruptcy and abolition of unrealistic social programs, shocked by learning that lives prolonged by science became drab and dreary, with corrosion on delivery instead of the Golden Age, took to space. There they found neither fortune nor glamour. Old letdowns wore new masks. Science and schools, having promised paradise for the stupid, the indolent, the bungler, and the chiseler, produced no antidote to the horrors of having to pay one's own way.

This subelite included the talented no-account who had every qualification except solid character, the kind who had to be "happy" twenty-five hours per diem. Some of these earned, borrowed, or embezzled transportation to the Fourth World's Lunar projects and of course did not like what they found. As paying or stowaway passengers, they made for high-tech Mars and sought work or rented gear and ventured into the red deserts and among tremendous peaks that were not peppered with iridium, platinum, or rare isotopes. Once North America became sufficiently tough to make its parasites become space tramps, to become an annoyance and then a pest, enemy agents and other subversives had begun to impersonate them. Many were political idealists. Others were purely industrial operators, out to steal high tech.

Garvin published no orders. There were no threats. But immigrants disappeared. Established and accredited residents did not. Rumor exaggerated the relentless methods of Martian security. The final resort of the dissillusioned was planned crime, such as bungled attempts at industrial espionage or running amok. In these doings, the tramps differed from the happy Simianoids and the Gooks, the former having the common sense and sturdiness of the chimpanzee, the latter the savoir faire of an ancient race. These made the despair of coddled Earthlings even darker.

"Shot while resisting arrest."

These occasional revelations gave meaning to mere vanishings.

And a few mavericks were good copy for the *Maritania Gazette*.

There was one who had sought the Utopia of America's New Egypt where the reincarnation of Sir E. A. Wallis Budge was preparing his followers for the Avatar of Isis and the resurrection of Osiris, after which the Ever-Virgin Goddess would give birth to Horus, the Rising Sun. Journalists found this fellow to be literate and, like a proper intellectual, sufficiently gullible to have been expecting so much more than reality ever offered.

"Most outrageous. A damned slave pen. Nothing but farmers. In our spare time—" The victim laughed bitterly. "—we were driven to building a snotty little temple, and there was talk of pyramids."

With the smooth irony of the newspaperman who has seen all and at its worst, the interviewer said seriously,

"Well, you could strike or appeal to the Labor Board, of course."

"No work, no food," the disillusioned one retorted. "And when we did eat, all we got was loathesome *dhurra* bread and that awful *dhurra* beer."

"You or any of your fellow slaves get to bed with the real or imitation avatars of Isis? Or did the boss monopolize the glamour girl?"

"Couldn't imagine any male creature able to impersonate Osiris well enough to get one of those hags pregnant."

"No attractive *dhurra*-fed girls recruited?"

The disillusioned one sighed. "Some say an actual beauty has been glimpsed. I had my doubts, so I quit while I had a few pazors."

With minimum persuasion, he portrayed the avatar. "Like an Egyptian temple painting. Or in *Going Forth by Day*, the papyrus that illiterates call *The Book of the Dead*."

By the time the Governor-General heard of the girl with Egyptian eyes, all information had boiled down to a peace officer's report: "Your Excellency, when those fellows get a wild look in their eyes, they are likely to be dangerous. We took him to the infirmary, but he was dead on arrival."

"Anyone else hurt?"

"No, indeed not, sir. The regulations forbid us to take needless chances."

Garvin almost smiled. "I wrote that page myself. But next time you see one who's escaped from the Land of Egypt, I want to talk to him before he runs amok."

Several years passed, during which Garvin still waited. At times he wondered whether the scarcely glimpsed girl could be Lani. He did not doubt Mona's report on her friend's confidential history. But remaining youthful in figure and face did not mean that a resurrected Osiris or

anyone else could get her pregnant. If not, the self-styled
Sir Ernest Alfred Wallis Budge was in serious trouble.
The hormone that the consortium of scientists had pro-
duced had indeed done things for Flora, who was not a
Simianoid.

Life was far from dull.

There was the time when the Marxist-dominated Fourth
World Coalition of Nations invited Garvin to appear, with
the coalition's safe conduct, for a meeting in neutral territory as the first step toward international harmony, evidence of North America's sincerely peaceful intentions.

Garvin and the North American Warlords had been
systematically feeding selected spies convincing and totally
false information regarding Martian armament systems.
A repetition of the invitation to a Peace in Space conference moved Garvin to take the only step that could result
in peace:

The Governor-General's reply was in formal and elegant Americanese, an expression of profound regret that
his duties did not at the present permit acceptance of the
coalition's invitation. At the same time, Martian security
was broadcasting translations, in Arabic, Urdu, Pukhtu,
Chinese, Uighur, and some really exotic languages, of the
Governor-General's expressions of deepest regret.

Then, as if someone had failed to cut the transmission
circuit at the end of the broadcast, Garvin sighed gustily,
cleared his throat, and sounded off. "If those pigs had the
guts and the gear, they'd come and get me! Not having
either, the silly slobs thought they could sweet-talk me
into a nest of assassins! They must be nuts and fruits!"

All this was faithfully rendered into the languages of
friends, of resentful satellites, and of bitter enemies of the
Slivovitz Empire and its puppet coalition of nations.

Having lost face globally, they called his hand. The
satellite network warned Garvin, with an hour to spare.
He gave Azadeh the news. "There'll be a traffic jam when

the alert goes out. Shall I drive you to the bombproof?"

"What are you going to do?"

"I'll bust my tail to get back to the scope and watch the show as soon as it's visible."

"I'll bring the wagon, and we'll imagine it's the second Earthrise for the day. And if you don't let me at that scope, I'll hate you for at least three minutes."

When the purple pilot light winked and the hotline phone from headquarters rang, Garvin got the coordinates from Colonel Drummond.

"So," Garvin said, "this is no drill." He paused. "Phil, they are not really as dumb as they seem. Between having to save face and being bogged down in a bureaucracy even worse than we have back home, they had to call our hand. But they didn't and don't know what they've bitten off. Take charge and get command experience. I'm awfully busy right now. Call me when you get to the mopping-up phase."

The attack was an hour overdue when the show began.

There were far-off blobs of incandescence, and great splashes of red when rockets from space stations homed in on invaders not visible until destruction turned them into blazing junk that cooled and went into orbit. Later, choice specimens were towed to point of origin and dropped for the enemy to inspect at leisure—a dare to improve their design.

A few bombers got through the screen and were shot down, to land in the Martian wastes. Rescue parties saved many of these crews, who were shipped home to tell what had happened.

The Sane Scientists of Mars were awarded distinguished service citations.

Colonel Drummond got two stars.

The Coalition of Nations began to suspect that if Mars was such a tough bite, Terra would be a nastier morsel.

All but idealists saw the merits of modern armament.

Only a few pacifists still held out for unilateral disarmament.

And then, with fond memories dismissed, Garvin would have gotten back to his telescope had not Azadeh returned with a radiogram from Bayonne, France.

"I *knew* I was forgetting something!" she exclaimed, handing him the message.

Garvin read it aloud.

> MELISSA CAMILLE ENTERED SORBONNE. FELIX COMPLETED MILITARY SERVICE AND QUALIFIED FOR LYCÉE MARACQ. BIARRITZ IS IN AGAIN. GET FURLOUGH BRING AZADEH AND TOGHRUL BEK AND ALJAI AND CHILDREN IF ANY. HAVE FAMILY REUNION. LOVE FLORA.

A long, long look passed from Azadeh to Garvin. Each saw how the radiogram had moved the other. Garvin almost spoke; he swallowed words but not the flood of thoughts and memories. When Azadeh found words, there was in her voice a note he had not heard for a long time.

"We're both awfully homesick," she said, "the way Flora was when she went to France. We are exiles, you and I, the way your Amerindians are. I want to be with my own people for a while. I'll be seeing our son while you're getting acquainted with Felix and that water and tree world of yours."

"We'll soon get good and fed up with our kinfolk and our home worlds. Madam, you've been wonderful, staying all these years, watching Mars going to hell!"

"Don't blame Flora for going to France! And I might as well admit I've met a few congenial North Americans right here in what's left of my old home."

"You'll be back?"

"Yes, and if you're not here, I'll hunt you up and down North America, or France, or wherever you are."

"If you're not here, I'll tow the whole damned Asteroid to Mars and hunt you in my spare time!"

"You sound as if Mars had become your second home."

"You've never nagged me to retire the way so many North American wives do. I still have a lot of chores ahead of me. And you and I may live to see the domes lifted and the air turned loose to spread, and Mars will be red and green and beautiful, the way it was when your starfaring people found it. And if Felix gets a taste of Mars, he may amount to something."

Azadeh turned to the absinthe wagon. "Let's drink to that."

ABOUT THE AUTHOR

E. HOFFMANN PRICE (1898–present) soldiered in the Philippines and France during World War I. At war's end he was appointed to the United States Military Academy, where he entered intercollegiate pistol and fencing competition. He was graduated in 1923 and commissioned in the Coast Artillery Corps. His first fiction sale was March 1924, to *Droll Stories*. By 1932, he was writing full time—fantasy, adventure, westerns, detective. When the pulps folded, he earned grog, gasoline, and groceries by holding two jobs and by filming weddings and practicing astrology in his spare time. Thanks to his incessant motoring, he met and made enduring friendships with Farnsworth Wright, Hugh Rankin, Otis Adelbert Kline, Lovecraft, Howard, W. K. Mashburn, Clark Ashton Smith, Edmond Hamilton, Seabury Quinn, Jack Williamson, Robert Spencer Carr, Leigh Brackett, C. L. Moore, and a comparable number in the nonfantasy fields.

Since 1964, Price has been known in San Francisco's Chinatown as Tao Fa, the *dharma* name conferred by Venerable Yen Pei of Singapore, and he is mentioned in prayers every new moon and full moon in two Taoist-Buddhist temples. As a gourmet, he cooks shark fin soup, sautées *bêche-de-mer* with black mushrooms, and steams "tea-smoked" duck. He declares that in addition to silk, gunpowder, and the magnetic compass, beautiful women were invented in China. Doubters are invited to meet him at dawn, on horse or afoot, with sword or pistol.